GEODE

THE INSIDE STORY OF A SMALL TOWN

CORLISS CORAZZA

Black Rose Writing | Texas

ISBN: 978-1-68513-591-1
PUBLISHED BY BLACK ROSE WRITING
www.blackrosewriting.com

Printed in the United States of America
Suggested Retail Price (SRP) $20.95

Geode is printed in Garamond Premier Pro

*As a planet-friendly publisher, Black Rose Writing does its best to eliminate unnecessary waste to reduce paper usage and energy costs, while never compromising the reading experience. As a result, the final word count vs. page count may not meet common expectations.

PRAISE FOR
GEODE

"Stepping into Corliss Corazza's novel, *Geode*, is like stepping onto three fresh perspectives, all with wise eyes observing their world in very different ways. History is presented in a manner that is compassionate, but brutal, but also intensely understandable. The three main characters of this novel, Olivia, Anna, and Emmaline, will step into your life as they allow you to step into theirs. The book is rich and layered with multiple storylines that will not let you go until the last page. And then . . .you'll return to the first page to have the experience all over again."
 –Kathie Georgio, author of *Hope Always Rises* and *Don't Let Me Keep You*

"A cozy novel of friendship and healing set in an inviting third space."
 –*Kirkus Review*

"A historical novel explores with skill and grace several different topics from U.S. History that are closely related to our current national dissonance."
 –Shirley Miller Kamada, author of *No Quiet Water*

I dedicate this novel to all the lost souls over time who suffered from the
effects of greed, prejudice, and hate.
May they rest in peace.

GEODE

1
TUESDAY IN THE WOODS

The woods were quiet except for the occasional bird squawk or trill. Wind ruffled the tops of the conifers, the sound of their footsteps muted by the deep matting of pine needles. Emmaline no sooner noticed the feeling of being watched than Hershey alerted toward the same direction that Charlie also turned to look. Now Hershey's ears were up, and he sniffed at the air. Charlie was stopped mid-trail. She knelt to look at his face.

"What it is, Charlie?"

"Mama, why is he so sad?"

"Who is sad?"

"The boy on the horse."

"Where, Honey? What boy on a horse?"

"Mama, he is right there." Charlie pointed away from the trail and up the hill a short distance. "He is on a horse, that brown horse. Can't you see him? He's looking right at us, but he won't talk because he's crying. He looks like he has a suntan, and he isn't wearing hardly any clothes. He's too small and the horse is gigantic. He can't get off. Help him, Mom. You always help me when I cry."

Charlie's big, blue eyes filled with tears, and Emmaline pulled him in for a hug. "I can't see what you see, Charlie. Can you describe the horse and the boy for me?" Emmaline wondered if he was getting tired or just what was going on. Still, she was determined to show support.

"I believe you can see this boy, but I truly cannot. I don't know what to do, honey. Of course, I would love to help him. Could you get him to talk to you and tell us how we can help?"

Using his sleeve, Charlie wiped his tears and looked up the hill. "I like your horse. He's pretty and brown. You're brave to ride without a saddle. How do you hold on? Don't be afraid of my mama. She helps people."

"I want to help you, boy. Where do you live?" Emmaline felt silly trying to continue a conversation with the invisible horseman as Charlie walked ahead, shoulders slumped.

"He's gone, Mama. He didn't talk."

2
BESTIES

The door slamming against the wall alerted Anna to the arrival of someone in a hurry. She was filling bowls with kibbles and replenishing water crocks for the current homeless furries in residence. Quickly, she wiped her hands on a clean fluffy white towel as she headed to the front of the store.

A desperate looking fortyish dad with two frantic children strode toward her, his long legs making short work of the distance. He was carrying a large cardboard box as though it were about to explode. The children were animated, talking at once: "Please, can you help us? We found her. She is hurt." The boy looked to be about ten years old and his sister maybe six. Anna appreciated him for trying to be brave and taking charge while his little sister caved in and was sobbing.

"The kitty is bleeding," the little girl stammered, not bothering to wipe away her tears.

"I found her by the tracks and brought her here," the boy boasted, trying to sound like a tough guy savior as he worked to hide his feelings.

Trying to be the hero, Anna thought. *A seedling man.*

The dad had gone silent. When Anna looked up, he was staring at her while trying to give a comforting pat to each kid—distractedly and without result.

"Put the box on this counter and let's hush a minute." Anna addressed the children while opening the unnaturally quiet box. "A mama and four kittens."

She swung to her right and raced to gather her tiniest bottles, syringes, liquid kitten food mix, flipping towels and damp facecloths into the warming drawer as she hustled past. Running back to the box, she began belting orders, "Wash your hands, all of you, with that soap." She pointed out the orange-colored, antibacterial soap at the sink. "Use paper towels to dry your hands, then each of you grab a towel from the warming drawer."

The dad was standing mouth agape at the sudden whirlwind of activity.

"Go!" Anna said. "Are your feet glued down?"

As he hustled back to her, drying his hands, Anna handed him a kitten she had been working on. Using a suction bulb, she checked for a mucous block, pulled its tongue to the front of its mouth, and while gently holding the mouth closed, gave two light, short puffs of air into the nostrils. "Hold the kitty upright, with your fingers around the body just behind his elbows. Massage the sides gently; that's where you'll find the little guy's heart. We need that heart to start beating and to get him breathing. Keep feeling for a heartbeat. Once you feel a heartbeat, start massaging him. Massage him more strongly than you think you should. I mean vigorously. We need to stimulate these tiny hearts."

She talked as she kept working on the kittens. Kitten number two was next for a heart massage. Using her best no-nonsense voice, although she didn't feel too confident about saving the kittens, Anna said, "Dad, hold him like I showed you, and do what I do."

The man began gently massaging the tiny body of a black and white tuxedo who lay completely limp in his large hands. Anna leaned over and gave the kitten a puff of air.

"Heartbeat?"

Dad nodded.

"Now start rubbing his fur in soft stokes—against the grain. They are brand new. The mama hasn't even cleaned them up yet. Her licking would get their hearts in rhythm and breathing started, so rub like a mama cat would lick." She talked as she moved, massaging the second baby, another tuxedo. This one had a wide white blaze between his eyes. She felt a fluttery heartbeat. Knowing the urgency of the situation, she picked up the third kitty, whose heart was already beating. One in each hand, she massaged them both with her thumbs.

"Okay, this guy is breathing. Boy, take him and grab a damp facecloth in the warming drawer, wipe him clean, not wet. Then get a warm towel, wrap him up and keep him warm. Keep your hand under the towel to make sure his heart is beating, and he is breathing. Keep up the massage. Stay right here. I want to be able to see you." Speaking to the mama cat, Anna looked down at her. "One of them is going to make it, Mama. You just hold on, and I'll get to you soon." Picking up the fourth kitten in her one free hand, she said, "Your turn, baby. Stay with me."

Just then, the first little tuxedo squeaked, and Dad gave a whoop. "He's breathing! I did it! I saved him. This is amazing, a miracle. Would you look at this guy?"

"Yeah, you are now officially a human mama cat." Anna rolled her eyes. But when she glanced up, he looked wounded. "I'm sorry, always a sarcastic witch when I'm trying to save lives. You did a great job, amazing for a first time. It is your first time, isn't it?"

"I've never done this before, never had a pet, never thought I wanted one."

The third kitten, a little calico, was showing some life. A little pull in of breath and then a squirm. "Okay, girl, take this baby, wipe her down, then wrap her up like your brother did. She needs to stay warm."

"How do you know she is a girl?" asked the sister.

"She is calico colored. Only females are destined to be calico. She is going to be a beauty." Anna turned her attention to the last kitten, thinking to herself how lucky she was to have dodged the anatomy lesson of male vs female. If this girl wanted more information, she could Google it.

Anna began to vigorously rub the last kitten. Tiny, mostly black, with four white feet and a white chin, looking like it had had a play date with a paint can. Then, a last resort, mouth to mouth resuscitation, suction bulb first. She breathed short, soft breaths into the sweet little face. One every four or five seconds. After too long, she stopped, wrapped her in a soft cloth and laid her aside. She needed to stabilize the mama cat and get the babies to feed from a bottle. The crying had to wait until later. Mama cat was in no condition to nurse them.

"Now flip the babies onto their backs. Make sure you hold them securely. I'll check each one while you hold still."

"Should you listen to their noses?" the girl asked.

"If their tongues and inside lips are Pepto Bismol pink, they have oxygen."

A mere seventeen minutes had passed since this family had blown in. Anna poured liquid kitten food into one of the sterilized glass jars she kept on hand and started the electric warmer. She gave herself about ten minutes tops to assess Mama before she started the bottle-feeding lessons.

"While I look her over, tell me quickly as possible how you found them and what you think happened to her." Anna thought she might have barked too hard at the man as he stood massaging the little tuxedo. He looked at her as she talked, and she was stricken by his stark eyes. His irises were very pale, like a wolf. As he told his story, she began her careful search for broken bones and lacerations on the mama cat.

"First, I'm Jack, and I am sorry to have barged in on you. But obviously we came to the right place, or person. We were on our bikes, on the trail that parallels the railroad tracks, and my daughter heard a cat crying out in the bushes. We didn't see that she had stopped, and we were about fifty yards ahead when she screamed at us to come back. Here was this cat. She couldn't get up. There was some blood, and she was all bloated. By the time we looked at her and tried to decide what to do, my daughter was frantic. It was awful. The cat kept crying out, and it looked like she was having seizures. My son jumped on his bike, yelling over his shoulder that he would be right back. He managed to find this cardboard box. I tried to be careful as I picked her up and slid her into the box. She was doing this weird hysterical purr and wretched meow at the same time. My daughter was distraught. I don't know what happened to the cat, why she couldn't get up, but we could see blood underneath her and one leg looked wrong. The whole thing was horrifying. My son used his bungee cords to secure the box to his bike and hollered as he took off that he was going to Besties and that the lady there would know what to do. He was afraid she wouldn't make it all the way to the vet hospital. Hell, I wouldn't make it. My legs ache and my butt's sore from just riding here."

"Thanks. That's what I need to know. For starters, you are out of shape. It is not a long bike ride from the tracks to here." Anna smiled. She felt a little evil pointing that out, but she could tell he was curious about her, and she wanted to squash that curiosity. "Also, what you have here is a new mother cat with a cracked bone in her leg, hopefully not completely broken, and an open wound from whatever bit her and shook her around. The seizures and odd sounds were her giving birth, and you might have noticed that she is no longer bloated. These babies were born in that box as you three bumped along on those bikes. This furry girl is a little warrior. I'll give her a sedative and painkiller while I clean, disinfect the wound, and stitch it up. I'll bandage her leg with a splint. You need to take her to the doc for an x-ray on that leg but let her rest until Friday before you do. Meanwhile, she can't nurse her babies for at least forty-eight hours. Let's get her onto some clean bedding, bag up that bloody cardboard box." She looked up at Jack. His face was flushed, and his eyes shined with unshed tears. Nope. She was not going to let herself like him. She'd already decided, and that was that.

The bottles were ready, the liquid kitten food warmed just enough, Mama cat sedated and sleeping. Now to begin the kitten feeding lesson. "We need to see if we can get these babies to swallow. Who is going to take care of these kittens after today?" Anna took the tuxedo from Jack and looked sternly from him to his kids.

"They are ours! We will feed them," cried the girl as her brother nodded.

"Let's see if you still feel that way after I show you how much work this will be. If you change your mind, I have two friends who are excellent fosters."

"What is a foster?" asked the boy, his little sister paying rapt attention.

Anna hesitated with her answer as she hoped this family would keep the cat family. "Fosters are wonderful people who take in homeless animals and care for them until a permanent home is found. Let's not think about that until we get these kitties fed. I have much to teach you and I need to do it quickly."

"Who are you, anyway?" said Jack, his face questioning. "I thought this was a pet supply store. Are you a veterinarian?"

"I could be, have chosen not to." Anna hated to explain. "I graduated from the University of California, Davis, and have my license to practice. "I can explain later. Now kittens need food."

The little calico squeaked, bringing smiles and relieving the room of its tension.

"I have filled these bottles with a kitten formula. If you decide to keep them, you can come in and get more from Besties. The formula must be room temperature. Not too hot or too cold. In a twenty-four-hour period, one kitten will need only thirty-three cc's. About two tablespoons. They need to be fed every two hours and only a few drops each time. Now picture a kitten nursing from its mom. It will be belly to the floor and head up. This is the way I want you to hold them. It's belly to your wrist so you can hold their head up with one finger under their chin and your pointer finger guiding the tip of the nipple. Even as little as they are, they will back off when they have had enough." Anna was praying the babies would take to the nipple and be able to swallow. "Just a few drops to start. Let them get the idea. Newborn kittens will latch on to a nipple, wrapping their little tongues around it, within minutes of beginning to breathe. They have no gag reflex yet, so you must be careful they are swallowing and not choking."

She moved carefully around feeders and kittens, repositioning hands, and checking liquid levels in the bottles. From the warmer she pulled three wash cloths and dampened them with warm water. "When they have taken at least a few drops, give them a break and wipe them down with these cloths. Their little faces and mouths need to be wiped clean. That's what mamas do. We don't want bacteria build up." She wasn't looking forward to explaining to the kids about the kitten's genitals needing to be wiped down after each meal to stimulate the elimination process.

Two hours later, the kittens were ready for a second feeding. The kids were keeping them warm, holding on like they never wanted to let go. Mama cat was coming out of sedation with a bandage on her stitched wound and a splint on her leg with a cracked but not an obviously broken bone. They had cleaned up all four of them. Mama was nestled in a crate with warm towels.

Anna and Jack solemnly walked in through the back door together, having buried without talking the one baby who didn't make it.

Anna went directly to mama cat, looked into her eyes, "Oh, you didn't lose your babies. You have three beautiful kittens being cared for by this great family who found you." A soft purr rumbled, then stopped as the mama cat slid back into a deep sleep.

"What was that?" Jack whispered as he stepped beside Anna. "She seemed to understand you."

Looking down and thinking, *well hell, I am too worn out to explain this*, Anna said, "I have a gift that allows me to communicate with animals." There it was out. Let Mr. Jack think what he wants. "Let's talk about that later. We need to decide who is really going to take care of these babies and their mother."

"We will do it!" A trio of voices in perfect harmony.

With a huge smile, Anna said," This makes me happy! Let's talk about logistics. You can borrow the crate for as long as you need. I'll send you home with five days of kitten food and prescription food for the mama that has supplemental nutrients. We were lucky that her wound from the bite won't affect her being able to nurse. Be sure you have clean cloths and towels. You might have to coax the mama to eat. The drugs should be out of her system in two days, and then you can put the babies in the crate with her to see if they will latch."

"What's that mean?" Little sister was ready to take in all the information and make this work.

"Oh, well, that's when the baby finds the nipple and figures out how to suck and get milk." Anna noticed the blushes and thought, *what wonderful lessons come from having pets.*

She organized a feeding schedule with them, and after a few last-minute questions and answers, and hearty handshakes all around, the newly expanded family and their latest additions bumped out the door. "Oh, here is my card. You might have a question or two and don't forget about getting her x-rayed. That splint is only temporary." Anna followed them out.

Leaning against the counter, she took a few seconds to process the last few hours. The door opened, and two new customers came in, then three more and a single. Interesting that no customers had come in while the mama cat family was there.

3
GEODE CAFÉ AND BOOKSHOP

Even through the lashing rain and surprising gusts of wind, Olivia took her time getting to Geode from home. She needed the time and space to think. Main Street, Umbra River, where the sidewalks were broad and the streets narrow, was lined with ornamental pear trees in full bloom. Every year, the blossoms blew off and collected on the ground in snowy drifts. Genetically altered never to bear fruit, their value was in their ability to soften the landscape, provide shade for mammals, and homes for birds.

For Olivia, Geode had been her dream since her grandmother took her for Saturday outings as a child. First stop was to a bookstore where she chose any book she liked. Then lunch, where she was allowed to order whatever she wanted from the menu. While enjoying lunch, she and Nana planned her dream café, making drawings, and noting ideas. Once home, they carefully placed those plans in a special oak box carved with planets, stars, and clouds, which featured a hasp, but no lock.

The carved oak box stayed on a shelf in her dorm room, then in her subsequent apartments, and now in her snug craftsman bungalow, built in 1938, the same year her parents were married. This date felt significant when she signed the escrow instructions, an omen, a validation. Thirty-five years of teaching English at the same school, in the same town, had been a gratifying means to live her life, raise her daughter, and value herself. The time had come to live her dream. Jennifer was about to graduate college and start a life of her own. Retirement and a pension were within reach.

On the day she completed her retirement details, a former coffee shop on Main Street came on the market, as well as the vacant retail space next door. She jumped on it and within fifteen hours of the listing having been posted, she put down earnest money and signed the agreement to purchase it.

The building had lived many lifetimes, its history partially preserved by a lineage of former owners who, with implicit agreement, did not replace the doweled, eight-inch plank oak floors. Its beauty, like the smile lines in the face of a beloved ancestor, showed in the scratches, divots, and wear gathered from myriad years as a saloon. A rowdy gathering place, catering to gold miners, gunslingers, and thieves. Stories had been passed down, and a few tintypes were left hanging on the walls by previous owners, depicting the large room at the back where several bathtubs once stood. Men paid two dollars to use a towel and to soap and soak while their filthy clothes were sent to the Jian Ling laundry two doors down. Jian Ling charged the going rate: fifty cents per piece. According to the stories, it was not unusual to see a man wrapped in a towel sitting at the bar, waiting for his clothes to dry. A scar on the bathroom floor marked the spot where a barber chair once stood. Haircuts were a dollar-fifty and shaves a dollar. Up the well-worn oak treads on the twelve-step staircase, a brothel once did business. Several small rooms still existed, mostly empty but otherwise unchanged. Two of the rooms sported antique iron bedsteads to stir the imagination of those interested in the "soiled doves" of the Goldrush days.

The original bar dated to 1849, the date carved center front in its scrollwork. Olivia had sanded and refinished the top, then painted the spool-back barstools in a variegation of the same soft forest green. She found the old cash register under rubble in the storage room, which matched the one in one of the tintypes. She tried to put it back into action but had no luck. In the end, she positioned it in its original place of honor at the end of the bar. There it remained, useless except for its nod to history. She polished and repaired the ornate back bar with its carvings and molding. The original mirror had long ago broken—something about a rowdy crowd and a shootout. When entering through the front French doors, the back bar stood on the left toward the far end of the room. On the same wall, toward the front of the room, the wide entrance to the bookshop invited readers to browse. Rather than replacing the backbar mirror, workers cut open the wall and framed where it had hung, adding glass shelves across. She heard Lucy, her irreplaceable dining room manager, regularly complain about how much she disliked those dust catchers. But Olivia appreciated the fact that the openness allowed a view into the bookshop. Adding to the eclectic vibe, she installed modern pastry and deli cases. Temperature controlled, their glass doors and shelves displayed pre-made salads and side dishes, deli meats, imported cheeses, and bakery goods from Sweet Things, the pastry shop across the street. Behind the case, along the back wall, stretched the workstation. The crown jewel was the glass and chrome counter, which housed an espresso machine, bean grinder, stove top, microwave, and sandwich press. The bar added seating and nostalgia, but the workstation was the business end of Geode Café and Bookshop.

Directly across the room from the historic bar, sat an antique player piano. A local family had donated it to Olivia. They swore it originally came from the saloon but offered no proof. Pumping the foot pedals activated the bellows that made the cylinder holding the paper rolls turn. These rolls contained tiny holes that corresponded to the keys on the piano and generated music. Adults and children claimed they felt like real piano players after pumping through a few tunes.

To the side of the piano, a five by ten-foot wood framed whiteboard ran horizontally along the wall, inviting customers to post their notices and encouragements. Magnets that constituted a collection of travel destinations donated by customers held notes in place. Every spring, Olivia marked off a graduation section where high school seniors posted their photos, plans, and capabilities. Often these opened doors for summer job offers.

Olivia's favorite bit of the building's history had to do with several writers of the Goldrush era who spent time at the saloon gathering stories, descriptions, behaviors, and personality traits for their next books. She began a search for the books, hoping to display a collection in the planned Geode Bookshop.

"Geode Café and Bookshop: See What's Inside." The name she planned years ago when she envisioned customers coming in merely looking for lunch but finding a comfortable place for conversation, connecting, learning, and relaxing. She planned for it to be not a grab and run sandwich shop, but a destination serving delicious sustenance for the body, with the opportunity to find great reads for the soul. She hoped patrons might find the bookstore side as inviting as the food-ordering counter.

Lucy—being Lucy—was ever on the alert when a customer walked in then balked in indecision about which way to go first. She quickly called out, "Aye, bookstore to the left, food right here. Just nip in first one, then the other." Added to that, students were welcome to come in after school with their parents or tutors to work on their schoolwork at the tables along one side of the bookshop. Olivia wanted a bubbling cauldron of young to old minds exchanging ideas and information along with refreshment. And this was exactly what she had created.

Lucy turned out to be the perfect addition. A favorite part of Olivia's workday involved working alongside Lucy in the mornings, preparing food for the day. Young moms came in with their little ones after dropping off the older siblings at school. Olivia and Lucy both kept one ear to the book side, listening to stories being read and the questions and giggles they spawned.

Geode's forest green and bright white striped awning came into view as Olivia passed Chapman's Cocktail Lounge. Chapmans was not yet open, but she heard the hum of a vacuum cleaner inside. Lucy had opened Geode this morning. Olivia heard the loud ribbing and laughter from three happily retired gents who took a table on the outside deck almost every day, rain or shine. She kept the big sun umbrellas up even in rainy weather, just for them.

"For God's sake, Albert, that ugly hat makes your butt look fat!" followed by guffaws and more snide remarks. They already were having a great time.

Before the Geode grand opening, Olivia had installed a redwood deck that spanned the forty-foot frontage of the shop and extended fifteen feet from the building toward the sidewalk. Built up on four-by-fours that sat braced onto concrete created a slight step that a low ramp mitigated. The deck covered unsightly aged cement work and provided outside ambiance. She added eight tables with two, four, or six chairs each, which were usually filled by ten in the morning on sunny days, in particular, and on most afternoons, regardless of the weather. The colorful awning covered about half of the deck. As soon as this storm passed, Olivia planned to put up an assortment of blue, forest green, and white umbrellas over the tables not otherwise covered. She felt a blush of pride as she neared Geode. It looked festive.

Just as Olivia stepped onto the deck, the door flew open and out came Lucy, carrying a tray of coffee and pastries, apparently oblivious to the fact that it was still drizzling rain. Her hair was a wild fluff of bottled red, matching her lipstick. Bright green denim overalls and sneakers rounded out the picture of "the little Irish elf," as Mike, one of the retired regulars, liked to call her. Olivia was reminded of what a jewel she had found when one man at the table asked Lucy why she didn't have an Irish name. She replied, "Och, came here to immigrate, right enough, not to give away where I came from—the arse end of nowhere, so it is. I'm American now, d'ye hear? Albert there, want a wee bit of cream?" Turning on her heel before he answered, she swooped back through the door with the empty tray followed by good-natured laughter.

"Hey Liv!" Emmaline arrived from the opposite direction. "Did you walk to work too? Needed some time to think, huh? Me too."

"Yes, exactly, Em. Looks like you have writing on your mind. I'll see you inside."

After greeting the deck crew, and other customers sitting outside, Olivia pushed through the door to find Lucy sliding a pan full of croissants into the top oven while she chatted with a customer waiting for milk to steam. A woman had walked in after Olivia, a question on her face. Lucy quickly understood the woman's request and pointed to the shelf where she had stored her lost cell phone for safekeeping.

"Lucy, when you have a minute, I need some of your ideas," Olivia said.

"Och, a wee minute. I've got a full oven and batter mixing. Aww shite, I forgot Albert's cream." She ran out and back before Olivia could blink twice.

"I'm going to rough out a floor plan of the kitchen area. It might be time to make some improvements or adjustments." Olivia grabbed her sketchbook and pencil.

"Go on then, have a pew. I'll need twenty minutes, won't I? Don't forget to use a pencil with an eraser," laughed Lucy, as she waved her croissant flipper in the air.

"You know, Lucy, the oven isn't big enough, and we need one more dishwasher. Counter space is at a premium, and it might be good to plan a dining counter with comfortable stools."

"Aye, twenty minutes and I'm all yours."

"No rush. Emmaline is outside. I spoke with her for a minute. I'll see what she has in mind. She is outside talking with Albert and the guys. I didn't expect you to have such a crowd this morning."

Olivia had her hand on the door when a rush of emotion washed over her. Life was good. Jennifer was about to graduate college, the café was doing well, and she loved her friends. If only the migraine headaches would leave her alone.

4
EMMALINE

At times, life felt like a quagmire, so Emmaline often turned to her reliably soft place to land: putting words on paper. Even if she explained herself only to herself, she found contentment in the practice.

With Charlie stashed securely in preschool for the workday, she cleared her head by walking to work. "Come on, Hershey, let's have an adventure," she said, and her chocolate lab jumped for his leash and beat her to the door. He loved taking walks as much as she did. When he hesitated and watched birds fly over or stopped dead in his tracks at a rustling sound in the underbrush, he reliably looked back at her as if to say, "Hear that?" She often felt Hershey was her twin in animal form. They even looked a little alike, both with deep brown hair and eyes. Once they were through the wooded area bordering their neighborhood, they headed for the half mile path into town. Umbra River was a walkable town with friendly people and interesting shops. Emmaline loved living here now that she was free.

Her creativity had stalled lately, though, and she searched for a way out of the slump. Insecurities turned into roadblocks with each idea, every creative curve in her road. *There must be something missing, something I can't see that holds me back. Maybe I'm not good as a writer.*

Out of the woods and onto the sidewalk, Hershey's anticipation appeared to ebb until Emmaline mentioned Geode. As much as they both loved and needed those walks in the outdoors, she and he loved Geode and Olivia even more.

"Oh Hersh, I love this town," Emmaline whispered. Hershey looked up at her and wagged in agreement. She had lived in Umbra River most of her life. Every inch held a memory. They rounded the bend onto Main Street, and she sighed and said to Hershey and herself, "I can't imagine a more welcoming sight, Hersh. Even the white blossoms on the ornamental pear trees invite us in. It looks like popcorn, doesn't it?" Hersh knew the word popcorn and jumped up on his hind legs. She occasionally gave him a few plain pieces.

The entire four blocks of downtown were visible from where they stood. Main St. was narrow, as it was when buckboards carried people and supplies. Each building projected its own personality. The first corner on the left housed Ernie's Spirits. The original horse hitching posts stood in front of the ornate, red brick, two-story building with a saloon on the first floor and apartments on top. Down the street, storefronts with facades in different styles and colors stood like dressed up dancehall ladies in complementary array.

Umbra River was named after the wide, rolling river about a half mile to the west that once put forth fortunes in gold. But the name also spoke to the area's shadowy past. Emmaline often thought, *if Umbra River talked, what stories it could tell.* For close to ten years, the area hummed with miners panning and digging all day. They supported the businesses in town at night until they stumbled back to their riverside tents to sleep. The historical museum featured an exhibit about the many criminals that had filtered through at that time, asserting that there was as much criminality as there were humanitarians. A hand-painted quotation over the display of daguerreotypes, crumbling wanted posters, and old pistols read, "They swarmed over the mountains by the thousands, with varied nationalities, every sort of character from low-down, thieving, conniving scallywags to prim, proper upstanding citizens." An interesting mix.

Emmaline passed Sally's Gifts with its dramatic Doric columns and broad, shallow stairs spilling down to the sidewalk. She thought it looked like a library. Sally did a great job of dressing it up, with deep purple and red geraniums spilling over the window boxes. Three dormer windows on the second floor sparkled and showcased colorful glassware and crystal.

After Sally's came the saloons, two on each side of the street, all of which were named for their male proprietors: John Barleycorn's, Chapman's Cocktail Lounge, and Paul's Hideaway Club—where they always answered the phone with, "Paul's Hideaway, nope he's not here." At the far end on the right was Jerome's Pool and Brew. Jerome had opened his beer pub in the former National Bank building. A lovely balcony with an ornate balustrade spanned the upper story veranda. A pair of classic Greek columns standing on the street level entryway held up the balcony. Shallow marble steps spilled out from the matching marble-floored foyer, appropriate for a bank more so than a saloon, but nonetheless stunning. When she stopped to think about it, Jerome's did move a lot of cash, as it drew a hip, higher-end crowd, mostly out-of-towners.

Turning to Hershey, Emmaline whispered, "I'd feel like I would have to dress up and mind my manners to grab a beer in there, let alone shoot pool. What do you think, Hersh?" Hershey gave her a slow wag and turned toward Geode.

Emmaline, always on the lookout for material for her writing, observed the details. Umbra River's architecture was interesting not only in its diversity but in its tendency to emulate wealth and success. Each roofline had its own personality. Either the eves had cornices, the roof was gabled or hipped or, her favorite, a finial on top—the ultimate pigeon perch.

Hershey pulled at his leash. Emmaline took the clue and continued on their walk. Sweet Things, the pastry shop, featured a bow window with gingerbread trim and was adorable. The addition of lace doilies and crystal plates full of colorful, tempting delights turned it into a scene from a fairytale. A temptation for the little girl in her, but also sold in quantities. She was about to be the most popular person with the morning crowd at Geode. Emmaline told Hershey to sit and stay, while she went inside for a pink box of treats.

Swinging the pink box by its navy-blue ribbon, she took Hershey by the leash again and strolled past the antique dealer. The brick entryway was made more obvious by a three-foot-high wrought-iron fence and a gate featuring a large TWT in ironwork filigree. Time Will Tell sold junk and garage-sale quality goods but also precious antiques.

"Hey Anna!" Emmaline stopped as she passed her friend hosing down her front stoop. "What happened?"

With a roll of her eyes, Anna smiled and said, "A little too much excitement for the newest rescue pup. She lost her lunch and then piddled all the way to the door." Striking a thinking pose, with hand to chin, Anna said, "So, Hershey, wouldn't you be in the market for a little sister? She is adorable, a mixed breed, but looks mostly Brittany spaniel."

"NO, NO, NO, one dog is plenty," laughed Emmaline, as she pulled Hershey away from the aromas of the pet supply shop. "I'll see you in a bit. I'll save you a pastry. Want me to bring lunch?"

"No on the pastry, but thanks. Come on, Emmaline, think about how cute this puppy would look next to big brother Hershey,"

Shaking her head, Emmaline moved on. Anna, her absolute best friend and now her part-time employer, knew her weakness for animals in need of a home or any kind of care.

She felt proud to be Anna's friend, even though Anna made her feel like the little sister at times. That was the difference between being a mom in her twenties and being fortyish and single with no children. Anna was a veterinarian by education, and she had a license, but she refused to hang up a shingle that said so. Emmaline and Olivia were constantly telling her that Umbra River needed a vet, but Anna argued that there were plenty of vets in nearby towns, and that she didn't want to run a vet office. Instead, she owned Besties, the only pet supply and rescue store in town. The only place to grab supplies, get advice about feeding and training, bring in a stray, or find a new four-legged love to take home. Anna might be fooling herself that she was not a vet, but Emmaline and everyone else knew she was treating pets in secret and not charging a dime.

Everyone also knew that Anna had a gift for communicating with animals and understanding them better than most people understand their fellow humans. In fact, she had the same gift with people, often shocking them with the things she could tell them about themselves. She insisted that she was just good at reading people, but Emmaline had personally experienced Anna not intuiting but *knowing* her most personal details and blowing her away with her perceptiveness. Anna was always right. That was Emmaline's bottom line. She'd seen it often enough.

Besties storefront windows were stocked with merchandise and a photo board of animals, ready for adoption. Over the window was a big hand-carved sign showing a black and white Bernese Mountain dog sheltering a tiny calico kitten between his huge front feet. The sign read, "BESTIES Pet Supplies." The store, painted medium grey/brown with creamy white trim around the casement windows, could be entered through a Dutch door dotted with Dalmatian polka dots. Anna left the top half open on warm days. She kept a bowl of fresh water on the stoop and a blue bucket of dog cookies in assorted flavors hanging on a nail just inside the door. People could do worse than emulating Anna's small acts of compassion.

Emmaline looked up to see Olivia walking toward her. Another check in the plus column for Umbra River was Olivia. Olivia owned Geode. Geode was the center of the universe.

Next door to Besties was Geode. Another custom sign, this one with books and coffee mugs framing the words "GEODE CAFÉ and BOOKSHOP—See What's Inside" hung center stage over the entryway. "Liv, you have truly gussied up this deck! It looks so inviting."

"Thanks, Em. Amazing what a little cleaning and petunia potting can do for a space. I thought you were working at Besties today."

"I am, the afternoon shift, but I came to town early to enjoy the sunshine. Well, to be honest, I want to duck into my cozy writing niche and polish up the last few lines of my latest poem. But before I go next door, I'll order a couple of lunches to take over for Anna and me. Oh, and have a pastry."

"I'll pass on the pastry. Set them on the counter, though, and someone will eat them. Say, boy, you look stunning in that new purple collar. Come here for your hug." Olivia's voice trailed off as they went inside. Geode and Olivia were Hershey's second home.

Olivia is the stunning one, Emmaline thought. Lean and lively, she moved with the grace of a Friesian horse, simultaneously energetic and gentle. She filled the surrounding space with her presence. Her pretty smile attracting attention while her hands constantly moved to pick up used dishes, serve new orders, and refill water glasses. Emmaline tried not to feel clunky and slow next to her and often felt intimidated by her efficiency and confidence. Although Olivia did feel like an aunt or mother rather than just a friend.

Emmaline looked up at the rich green window boxes trailing with pink and yellow verbena, underscoring the gleaming pair of mullioned picture windows flanking Geode's streetside French doors. Glass-topped tables, each held a small milk bucket bursting with impatiens, begonias, and soft coleus in an explosion of purple, pink, green, and peach. Those tables with more sun exposure held buckets planted in pink cosmos, purple petunias, and bright yellow super bells. No doubt, the buckets had been purchased at Time Will Tell.

Geode's old plank floors gave Emmaline the feeling of being pulled into Geode's warm, calmly lit space, and if the appearance didn't do it, the aroma of dough baking and fresh coffee did. Geode was a magnet for just about everybody in Umbra River. Little happened in Umbra River and the world that did not get sliced and diced at Geode. Also, the food was fantastic.

Emmaline rushed to catch up with Olivia and Hershey. The dog was completely uninterested in her arrival as he was having his ears rubbed and being plied with dog cookies. "Bring him back when you finish spoiling him," she said to Olivia, and headed to her nook, excited to have some writing time. Settling into her chair, she recognized that this was where she felt she had power. Outside of that space, she mostly felt like she was bumbling along with no direction in mind.

***

Emmaline walked through the door from Geode to Besties and spotted Anna sitting on a stool at the counter, mindlessly staring out the window. She stopped swinging her foot. "Hi Em, you're late."

"Hi Anna. I'm sorry, I was so immersed in my writing zone, I lost track of time. Please don't be mad. I am ready to work and make it up to you." Before Anna could reply, Emmaline continued without taking a breath,

"Hershey and I walked this morning. Could you give us a ride home? And pick up Charlie?"

"Ordinarily I would say yes, you know that, but I bet you won't believe this."

Emmaline felt her heart quicken. Shoot. She would have to walk the entire morning's journey in reverse, and she was for some reason feeling tired.

"Well? Aren't you going to ask? No, don't ask. I'll just tell you. I was invited to dinner by a handsome customer and his kids! You know that family I mentioned that came in four days ago with the injured cat and four non-breathing kittens? I haven't had a date in I don't know when. I haven't had a desire for a date. But this guy. I don't know."

Emmaline felt flabbergasted. "You're going on a date? Olivia didn't say a word! Wait! Wait! Let me run to the bathroom."

Anna followed, talking as if breathless. Emmaline had rarely, if ever, heard her like this.

Anna continued to talk after Emmaline closed the door to the toilet stall. "Jack called this morning and said he and his kids want to take me out for pizza since I helped them with their kitties. Then he said he chose the pizza place so while the kids play in the arcade, we can get to know each other! You know, I never encouraged him. This was a surprise."

Emmaline couldn't speak. She found it humiliating to speak to someone while she was using the bathroom. Besides, she was in shock. Anna, dating? It seemed impossible. Anna hated men. She only pretended to tolerate her male customers and steered clear of anyone who dared to look at her with misty eyes. As much as Anna had a reputation for compassion when it came to animals and being basically psychic, she also had a reputation for having a chip on her shoulder when it came to the opposite sex. No one really knew why, but it was a point of discussion among some people, this Emmaline knew for truth, as she had overheard people, especially the older men who congregated on Geode's front deck in the mornings. "That one's got an icicle stabbed through her heart," she once heard Albert say.

Emmaline came out of the stall and washed her hands, stifling a laugh and trying to sound supportive, instead of sounding like she wanted to run out into the street and share the news, which she did was dying to do. "Of course, I believe this! It is about time, and he sounds like a good guy. I might say the right guy, but you might run from the room like your hair is on fire." Emmaline smiled.

"Oh no, you don't. Let's not make too much of this. It has been a long time since I have been out with a gentleman, however. He said the kittens and their mama are doing great. I'll be eager to hear more."

"Hershey and I walked. Can you give us a ride home, but first pick up Charlie?"

"You already asked me that. I said no, but I can make time if you will do a few extra things. The kennels need cleaning, and I started inventory, so try to get that finished. You need to handle the front for about an hour while I run to Stitches to grab something to wear tonight. Stop with the big smile. It is because the only clothes I have are shot. No other reason." Practically bouncing out the door, Anna said over her shoulder, "And yes, I will pick up Charlie on my way back and then take you all home. But only if you stop smiling and don't tell a soul. Let me have this all to myself."

Emmaline started with the kennels. She put one dog or cat in the corral, cleaned and disinfected the crate, let it dry, then put the animal back in and grabbed the next. A familiar routine. Hershey stayed in the corral to supervise the kennel dwellers and entertain them. As much as Besties was a pet supply shop and an off-record vet's office, it was also a halfway house for animals needing a home. Anna maintained eight kennels, and they were frequently occupied.

When Emmaline worked the morning shift, she looked forward to spending the afternoon in the writing space Olivia had set up for her in the back of Geode. Now that her morning had started late, she wouldn't have as much time as usual to do the only thing she took seriously other than Charlie: playing with language. Kennel cleaning, done on automatic pilot, allowed her creative mind to work on poetic phrases, imagery, rhythm, and bursts of inspiration. She had to stop every few minutes to jot something down. *Write it or lose it.*

Olivia had taught English at Umbra River High. She had been Emmaline's favorite teacher. During class, Emmaline felt like Olivia was talking directly to her, teaching what she hungered for. The students in her writing group felt the same way. Emmaline wasn't sure she had the aptitude for teaching, but Olivia had ignited a fire in her, and she at times thought she'd like to be able to do that for another person. Olivia recognized that fire and knew how hard it might be to sustain creative momentum in a house with a small child and no mate to share the responsibility. So, Olivia presented a proposal. She offered Emmaline a former storage room, too small for her own needs but perfect as a small office. It needed only a desk and a chair, which quickly appeared from Time After Time. Olivia offered the space to Emmaline in exchange for a few hours a month, organizing and cataloging the Geode Bookshop. A win for both.

Emmaline agreed enthusiastically to follow Olivia's vision for Geode's Bookshop. The plan was to entice browsers furnishing it with overstuffed chairs begging to be sunk into, flanked by tables perfect for holding something to sip, and a read-by lamp on each. The cozy reading area, surrounded by organized and polished oak bookshelves, called to her. Emmaline's task included keeping the books in genre and author order by alphabet. Though she was tempted to group them by the color of the spines or by her personal favorites. Also, she looked forward to meeting local authors and to searching for and ordering newly published books. She did not look forward to the sad job of culling out the ones left too long on the shelves. Such things were part of running a bookstore, Olivia assured her.

The children's area was better than a playground for those little folks with a sense of wonder and a craving for stories. Framed, blown-up pictures of favorite book covers danced around the walls. Shel Silverstein's *Where the Sidewalk Ends* hung beside Sandra Boynton's *Let's Dance Little Pookie*. EB White's *Charlotte's Web*, to the left along with one of Emmaline's favorites, *Fly Away Home* by Eve Bunting—a way of understanding homelessness. Then of course the great imagination teaser by Maurice Sendak, *Where the Wild Things Are*. All in their glorious colors, framed in colors as well. Several more frames with easy access fronts dotted the remaining wall space and kept for the swapping of covers of exciting new books. Copies of these books lined shelves at just the right child height.

The adult side of the bookstore was also adorned with book covers, set up to rekindle memories of well-loved stories, as well as showcase up-and-comers. The bookstore side of Geode was another of Emmaline's safe places to land. Whenever life overwhelmed her, Geode pulled her in and smoothed out her feathers. On her first day as a writer with an office, Emmaline arrived at Geode to find the large east-facing window cleaned to a sparkle. The morning sun softly bathed a potted orchid with white blooms already celebrating the space. Even though she'd been there a thousand times, that morning she felt the building was specifically welcoming her and her intention to write.

As much as Emmaline loved handling books and keeping the bookshop in order, she treasured most the fat rollers on the chair legs. Those rollers made the chairs easy to move. The evenings when she and Anna and Olivia merged the chairs into a conversation configuration to share their thoughts and intentions were golden. In the beginning, they tried to call it a book club but couldn't keep a straight face. They settled on ladies' night out. After locking up Geode and pulling down the shades, the three friends uncorked a bottle or two, along with their hearts.

The last kennel sanitized and ready, she sat back on her heels, realizing she had daydreamed the entire time. Inventory needed her attention and musing needed to end. Taking her checklists, she headed for the storage area first. The organized shelves made for fast tally work. In fact, the entire store was set up for easy shopping and merchandizing.

An hour later, Anna swooshed in with a handful of shopping bags and a huge smile. "There were so many choices! I haven't bought clothes in such a long time. I bought one of each! Em, the place smells great and the kennels are spotless. We need some new boarders."

"I'm sure you won't have to wait long. It's almost kitten season around here. I brought the inventory up to date. I only need to add in the linens, but they're in the dryer. They were disgusting. Oh, and I made a list of pet food and supplies you are low on. It's on the counter."

"Look at you. What an asset you turned out to be! Now, if you would just take that course on dog training, I might retire."

Emmaline couldn't help but smile. "I'm going to walk Hershey, and when we get back, I want the details on your date tonight!"

When Anna protested, Emmaline held up her hand in stop position, "Don't even go there, it is too a date."

A teenaged customer coming through the door stepped back and held it open for Emmaline and Hershey, who gave him a slow wag. During the day, business lagged but late afternoon always picked up. Folks retrieved their kids from school, stopped at Besties for pet supplies, then headed next door to Geode for snacks and books and sometimes for kids to do homework. Olivia made it convenient for students to come to Geode after school for tutoring and study groups by adding tables between the children's and adult sections.

Emmaline stopped short, throwing herself back first inside the store and said, "First, where is Charlie? Don't tell me you forgot to pick him up. And I keep forgetting it, but I have something for you in my car's trunk. Next time you see me driving it, please remind me. Now, where is Charlie?"

Olivia threw her keys at Emmaline. "Umm, well, obviously I forgot him. I have to stay here and keep the store open, so take my car and go get him! Remember, I still have the car seat set up for him."

***

The return drive to Besties was short, but as Charlie was already snoozing in his car seat, Emmaline decided to quickly drive over to her place to look through her car for the item she wanted to take to Anna. Charlie continued to nap in Anna's car while she rummaged through her car's trunk. "AHA! Here it is!" She held up a dented fishing tackle box spray painted hot pink.

When she arrived back at Besties, Anna came out of the back room, wearing a new dress. "What do you think, Em? Where's Charlie?"

"He's asleep in your car. I was hoping maybe you'd be ready, so I left him in the car seat. I parked right out front. I can see him from here." Emmaline sat the pink tackle box on the counter.

"What is going on today? First, I forget Charlie, then here I am in the first dress I've worn in a decade but not glamourous enough to garner the slightest notice from one of my dearest friends. Instead, I get a fishing tackle box. A hot pink fishing tackle box that looks like someone bashed it on the rocks. But I am not going fishing—for evidently female fish, so what on earth gives?"

"Wait until I show you what is inside before you make any snarky remarks," Emmaline said, scooping out a small package. "And yes, the dress is great, of course I love it, but now I'm stressed because I'm in a hurry and because Charlie is sleeping in your car instead of having his naptime at home. But this," she said, waving the package around, "Anna, I have something very much like a magic potion. Are you with me? Men can't resist a woman with well-fitted false lashes! True story."

"NOOO," Anna said, but stopped cold as she looked inside the tackle box. She looked up at Emmaline as though she didn't know her. "Emmaline. Makeup, mascara, eyeshadow, face cream, rouge, and . . . a half-dozen packages of false eyelashes? What does this mean?"

"Oh, yes." Emmaline said, "I think this probably does need an explanation. No time for it now. Let's get me home and you get ready for your date. We'll talk later, and I want to hear everything about this night, just as much as you want to hear everything from me. We'll just sort of hold each other hostage." She scooped up Hershey and dashed out of the door to sit with Charlie, leaving Anna to lock up, and the hot pink tackle box on the counter.

5
LUCY'S FRIGHT

A piercing scream reached the retired coffee group on the deck just as Anna was approaching Geode. Albert and Mike, at a table with two newcomers, shoved back their chairs and turned toward the sound. Barreling toward them through the swinging doors in the back of the café came Lucy, clearly spooked.

Not until later in the day did Lucy calm down enough to explain what happened. Olivia sent her home to rest. Anna heard enough of Lucy's story to know she was going to be needed. She put a sign on the door to Besties asking customers to find her on Geode's deck. The retired gentlemen were back at their table. All had gone home after seeing that Lucy was in good hands, but Mike and Albert couldn't stay away long. They returned to check on Lucy.

Anna asked Albert to repeat everything Lucy said. "She heard some noises from the second floor. It sounded like footsteps and something heavy being dragged across the floor. A door slammed shut. You know Lucy, she wasn't about to put up with any "shenanigans" up there. There were no customers but us, so she scooted around the bar and headed for the stairs. She got as far as the landing, where there was a terrible smell. She thought some dog had left its 'calling card' but she saw nothing. The stair treads were clear. The smell lessened as she reached the second floor. She had a funny feeling that someone was watching. She peeked in the doors. All but one stood open. She scanned the mostly vacant rooms quickly and saved the closed door for last. As she walked toward it, those stories we have all heard about lost souls and hauntings were going through her thoughts. The upstairs was for the dance hall girls, you know."

Albert's fluffy white mustache puffed slightly when he spoke. Anna couldn't help but be mesmerized by it. The mustache was that big. "When our little Lucy tried to open the door, it felt like someone was holding it closed from the other side. She tried again and heard an unearthly wail from inside just as the door gave way. The room was almost empty, and the old high boy dresser was partially scooted across the floor. It was obvious the window was still locked. There was no one there. Lucy turned to come back downstairs, when a soft voice close to her shoulder said, 'help me.' That's when she screamed and flew down the stairs. She was shuddering like a poorly timed motor. I'll be damned if she didn't run straight to Mike and throw her arms around him like he'd save her."

Mike smiled slowly and said, "Of course she did, Albert. You know why."

"I don't know why. You look skinny and worn out to me. Just because you're retired police doesn't mean you still save people."

"Evidently I still do."

Anna stood to leave. "Where are you going?" Albert asked.

"Going to see Lucy."

Geode customers often hugged Lucy as they left. Anna felt the same fondness, along with a sense of responsibility to help her friend understand spiritual energy and not to be afraid. Fear like Lucy's, which Anna felt obviously was based on her Irish family traditions around elves and leprechauns, ran deep. Anna wanted her to understand the difference between spirits and Spirit, but Lucy's superstition was a bit of a brick wall in that regard. Anna couldn't get it through to her that resident spirits aside, Spirit with a capital S was about the belief in something larger and more knowing than we are, not something to fear but to be embraced. If she could get ahold of the idea of Spirit with a capital S, she might understand that Geode's resident ghosts were merely lost and looking for guidance. There was no need to run around screaming every time she ran into one. Goodness knows Umbra River had its share of unsettled souls.

Anna went back to Besties, which she had locked up without notice, removed the handwritten sign that said, "BE RIGHT BACK," flipped the closed sign, and locked the door. She wouldn't be gone long. Sparky, the newest lodger, would be fine. Lucy lived in a cottage at the southern edge of town. An easy walk. Lucy's side yard, filled with sun on most days, helped her grow vegetables in abundance. Most of which made their way into Geode recipes, adding a special freshness to the menu choices.

On Lucy's front door, hung lush wreath in variegated greens, greys, and soft pastels. Fresh herbs and flowers, all from Lucy's garden. The fragrance made Anna's stomach growl.

She knocked, but there was no sound inside. She knocked again, then called out, "Lucy, it's Anna." Just as she was turning to leave, the lock snapped open.

"I thought it was Albert." There stood a disheveled Lucy. Her face puffy, her eyes still held the shock. She had pulled on a robe over her work clothes. Her feet were clad in pink fuzzy slippers. Anna had never seen Lucy so untethered.

"Och, Anna. It's you then. Please come in. You must be thinking I'm thick as a short plank the way I reacted this morning. Sit, won't you? I'll get tea."

Anna looked around the tidy living room. The profusion of flowers on the chintz curtains. A framed Irish Prayer, "May the road come up to meet you. . ." and no surprise, a pair of pillows with subtle shamrocks woven through the fabric. Directly across from the front door, a stone finished fireplace topped by a carved wood mantle. A gaslit fire softly glowing gave off more heat than the outside temperature warranted. Anna stood for a closer look at the glass front case chock full of Irish Belleek Porcelain plates, vases, and figurines. *Oh, my goodness, a complete tea set of it.* The almost translucent delicate pieces showed faint pastels. Some had a border of tiny shamrocks. *Gorgeous. A sweet room.*

"Here we are, then. How about a cuppa?" Lucy entered the room with a tray.

"Thank you, Lucy. I'm here to help you through the shock of today and maybe help you understand what happened. But why do you have the fire going?"

"It was a wee bit of a shock, chilled me to the bone, but I'll be right as rain, so. At first, I thought a joke it is. One of the gents outside having some fun. But then ..." her voice trailed off.

"Lucy, no one pulled one off on you, but you also weren't meant to be harmed. You know I have been blessed with second sight or being psychic. I've never wanted to put in the work to train to give readings, but I do get thoughts and images. I think we're all one big sphere of energetic vibration. What you saw or heard today is as much a part of me as I am of you. To me, it's a gift to be able to connect with the Universe or Truth, the Collective Consciousness, God. There are several ways to name it. I kind of like calling it the Uni–short and sweet. Do I make any sense? I'm trying to soothe you."

Lucy trilled out a laugh. "Ah, Anna, right enough. I'm soothed, all right."

"While I was setting up Besties, Olivia let me use one room upstairs at Geode to set out and organize my supplies. I spent many evenings up there sorting, pricing, and packing boxes to go downstairs. Several times I felt the presence of someone near, though I couldn't see anyone. Often I'd have an overnighter cat or dog in a portable crate who would alert to a sound I didn't hear. Whichever it was would send out a low warning growl, then stand up and stare in the direction of whatever our visitor was."

"Jesus, Mary and Joseph, what is it you're saying?"

"I'll tell you just a little more and then I'll leave you to sort it out. I know it is confusing and you'll have questions. You know that collection of books Olivia has displayed at Geode? The ones written by authors who visited during the Gold Rush when it was a saloon. I have read them all and many of the stories refer to inexplicable happenings in the building. One writer talks about noticing two ghosts who frequented the upstairs. One was a young boy whose mother was one of the in-house prostitutes. Dance Hall girls, whatever. He was born in one of the upstairs rooms, a product of one of his mother's customers. The piano player from the bar had been teaching him to play but stopped when he couldn't stand the smell of the child. I had the impression that up until his illness, he was a sort of mascot for the business. His cause of death, which we now recognize as cancer, was likely colon cancer and occurred at a young age. He knows he still reeks from the terrible gas it caused. That is what you smelled on the stairs. The landing is his favorite place to stay. He means no harm and time has no meaning for him."

Lucy sat, never taking her eyes off Anna. "What is the boy's name?"

Anna felt Lucy was beginning to understand. "His name is O'Connor."

Lucy put her hand to her chin. "Ah. That would be the case. Back in history, the Irish gave their newborn boys surnames, taken from the first names of relative. With an O' in front. O'Connor, you see. He was an Irish boy, so it is. And the lass?"

"I don't know her name, but I read that a young woman, only about eighteen years old, was being held upstairs against her will. The writer didn't know the reason, but she escaped by breaking the window and jumping out. She hobbled on a broken ankle to the river, where someone helped her board a raft, and then she disappeared. The writer didn't disguise his admiration for the woman's looks. All the while, the townsfolk were up in arms that such an undesirable could go free. And might still be in their midst. You'll see the article that was in the newspaper at the time. The author included it in his book. I've always wondered if there was a connection between the author and the woman's escape. Somehow, he knew she wound up in San Francisco and was murdered in a street crime only a year or two after her escape. It is interesting that she returned here as a tortured soul."

"This is enough to throw at you for now, Lucy. I'll grab that book I mentioned and bring it by. Please know I am here for you. We can talk more anytime you are ready."

As she walked to the door, Anna noticed Lucy was looking brighter. Lucy called after her, "Aye, right enough. Put that book on the bar. I'll nip into work early."

6
THINGS DON'T CHANGE, PERSPECTIVE DOES

Customers dwindled down to one lady who picked up an order for her morning scones. "Lucy, it's Friday. Ladies' Night. I can't believe how last week zoomed by so fast," Olivia said. "Are you sure you won't join us?"

"Och, no. I'll help with the tables, but I'm not quite up to scratch, going to my easy chair. Feet up, head back, I'll be right as rain in the morning."

"Okay, let's leave the table polishing to tomorrow, but one of these Fridays, we hope you will join. It's fun."

"I'll just nip out, then. You ladies have a good earwigging now."

Lucy flipped the open sign to closed as she left and secured the door behind her.

Olivia walked toward the back of the building to dig through the shelves in the secondary storage closet. This had become the repository for anything she couldn't fit in her home. "Ah, here it is!" she shouted, holding up her forty-five-year-old high school yearbook. The plan for the evening included sharing their yearbooks. All part of the quest to get know everything about themselves and each other. Olivia couldn't remember what started it. Probably Emmaline. She was always full of ideas for nurturing their friendship. Somewhere along the line they had made it a goal to be the best friends possible, as if they were still in junior high, age differences aside, and even if Olivia was everyone's former teacher.

Anna arrived next, talking fast, describing her afternoon to Olivia: She had scooted home to change clothes, throw in a load of laundry, and take a shower. As she locked up Besties, a familiar customer had come in with her new puppy. She needed supplies and wanted Anna to meet the little guy. The very minute Anna picked up the puppy and held him up to look in his eyes, he projectile vomited the entire contents of his stomach down the front of her shirt.

"The woman was clearly horrified," Anna said, "But I thought it was funny. I told the woman I was excited about meeting him too! She never laughed."

Anna arranged chairs in the bookshop side. Meanwhile, Emmaline came in from the adjoining door to Besties. "Hi, Ann! Hi, Olivia! Hey, I left Hershey home tonight because Charlie's sitter loves him. But that means Sparky is all alone next door. Can I bring him in? By the way, have you thought about keeping Sparky?"

Emmaline tossed her yearbook down on the table with Olivia's and Anna's. Anna didn't answer in the time it had taken her to set out wine glasses and two bottles of Merlot, at which point Emmaline spun back toward Besties and soon enough came back with Sparky. Takeout menus from the best of the local dining options were at the ready, and Sparky slept happily on his sky-blue corduroy bed.

Emmaline said, "Before you fill your glasses, check the bottom."

"What is the number for?" asked Olivia.

"That's the order we talk about our yearbooks. It seems too disorganized to just grab and jabber, so I organized it." Emmaline smiled.

"That's the teacher in you, Em," Olivia said. "If the writing thing doesn't work out . . ."

Olivia watched with interest as Emmaline belted down more than a half glass of wine before she or Anna took their first sip. Olivia and Anna had just decided on pizza when Emmaline began talking without taking the time to agree. She acted like it was Christmas morning and she was a kid wild to open presents.

"Come on, Ann! Don't make us wait any longer. It's now been an entire week! How about the date with Jack? What do you think of him?"

"Honestly, Emmaline, what are you? Thirteen? I've been busy. You've been busy. It's been a busy week." Anna rolled her eyes. "Well, and to be honest, sometimes you just want to keep things to yourself for a while. Okay, but I'm serious. I don't want to be hounded about this. I hope you hear me."

"I hear you!" Emmaline said, topping off her wine glass.

Olivia watched Anna toying with a cocktail napkin, trying but failing to act nonchalant. Despite her protests, the woman they all thought they knew so well was nearly shimmering with excitement.

"Perfect gentleman, I guess, opened every door, pulled out my chair at the restaurant—so awkward and unexpected I nearly fell—and told me to order whatever I wanted as dinner was on him. The kids were excited, not about me being there, but about the arcade games and foosball. Once they reported the progress of the mama cat and kittens, who are recovering just fine, by the way, not that *anyone* has asked. Jack sent boy and girl galloping off into the room of doom, as I like to call it, into the cacophony of mechanized blips and bleeps and blasting strobe lights, and that's not even hyperbole. I don't know how anyone stands the noise or the lights without having a stroke."

"Hmmm, doesn't this all sound titillating, Emmaline? Aren't you glad you asked?" Olivia said.

"Oh, so good to hear all felines are healthy and getting into trouble," Anna said. "The good trouble that curiosity brings on. Jack brought Mama cat in about a week ago. Her break is almost healed, and her coat looks shiny and sleek. The album of photos the kids had compiled is adorable, and I can tell they take good care of these cats. Already the dialogue has begun about keeping rather than adopting out the kittens. I told Jack, 'Good luck. These kids are saviors now, and it's like pulling a thorn out of a lion's paw. They'll be connected for life.'"

"What did he say to that?" asked Emmaline.

"He laughed and said they may find homes for every kitty except the little tuxedo he saved. So, Jack is just as dialed in as the kids are."

"Enough about kids and cats, Anna. What else did you talk about? Who is he?"

"Evidently, he is a lawyer. A disbarred lawyer. He must have done something awful because disbarment doesn't happen easily. When I pried, he changed the subject and admitted he works as a consultant. He's intrigued that I am not using my vet license."

"You two are doing the same thing, working around a license. Key to his character is to find out what disbarred him."

"I'm not that interested, Liv. We had a good time. He is good company and wants to go out again. I'm just not sure. What's the point? I am not looking for any kind of relationship, and I'm too busy to adopt a man-sized pet." Anna said, glancing at Sparky.

"Oh, for God's sake, Anna. Just have a good time. You don't have to marry him!" sputtered Emmaline.

"I know you miss Trevor, Em. It must be so hard raising Charlie without him. But I fear you are projecting your own desires on me. You would love to have another good relationship with a good man, but I don't. I want nothing to tie me down. I regret that I'll never have children of my own sometimes, sure. But I have hundreds of furry babies that I have saved and sent to suitable homes. My goal in this lifetime is to run Besties and take care of animals. I want to enjoy my time on my own terms."

"What about adopting a child, then keeping Jack as a loving companion?" Emmaline wouldn't give up.

"Emmaline, please stop! You know I was adopted. You know the pitfalls. The wondering who my birth parents were, why they gave me up, what is in their medical backgrounds. No, I lucked out and had fabulous adoptive parents, but I didn't look like the woman who was raising me. Never did anyone say, 'Oh, you have your mother's smile.' My adopters gave me everything else—truly everything. They were the kindest, most loving parents I ever could have wanted. I called them Mom and Dad from as far back as my first words. But that blood connection was missing. It just was. Even if they didn't feel it, I did."

Olivia watched Anna fold a little further into herself, move deeper into the seat. She tried to remember herself in Anna's place, at midlife, and with big midlife decisions to make. Stay or go. All midlife decisions come down to that.

"One of my favorite memories is when my mom, big sister, and I, were walking through a department store and a woman stopped us," Anna continued. "Evidently, my mom knew her from church. The woman said something about what beautiful daughters my mom had and then added, 'Now, which one did you adopt?' Remember, my sister is their natural child and was a carbon copy of our mom. Calm as could be, Mom pretended to ponder, looking from one of us to the other, and then said, 'You know, I can't remember.' I felt so loved at that moment. But I hated seeing her put in that position to play act. So, no I won't adopt. I won't give birth, and I will never ever marry."

Anna stopped and looked at Emmaline first, then Olivia, with what Olivia had long ago tagged her "back the hell off" look.

For a moment, no one spoke.

Olivia stood and said, "I'm going to pour more wine! Emmaline, please call in the pizza order, assuming you're okay with that, and then we want to hear about your writing. Tell us how it's going."

"I'm sorry everybody," Anna said. "I'm irritated about having to explain this to my best friends, because I don't understand it myself. I am getting thoughts and psychic hits about Jack that I can't decipher. This happens when I am uncomfortable about a person. Jack is hiding something, and I can feel it."

"Anna," Olivia said. "You know you don't have to apologize."

"Let's change the subject! I know I drew number three, but can I go next?" Emmaline said, breathless, and not waiting for an answer, her voice slightly shaky.

"I haven't been honest with you about Trevor," she said. "Anna, that's what I was trying to tell you when I brought the pink tackle box in. Many memories tumbled out looking at my yearbook earlier, reminders that I am a fraud. The yearbooks, plus Jack coming into our lives, and Olivia, your talk about my needing to find another man as good as Trevor. For Charlie's sake. You only know the fairy tale side of my relationship, and I can't hold it in anymore." Her chin quivered as tears dropped down her cheeks.

Anna reached over and hugged Emmaline's shoulder while Olivia offered a tissue. "Pink tackle box?" Olivia said. "Do tell!"

"You two know that my parents were totally against my relationship with Trevor. But we were a couple since middle school. The cutest guy in seventh grade had his sights on me. I fell so hard for him, but now it embarrasses me. Maybe that's why I seem like I'm still in junior high. Maybe he stunted me. I did his homework, prepped him for exams and gave up my friends. He didn't like them to be around and always said he wanted us to be alone. We went to dances and proms, but always just the two of us. Never with a group, sharing a limo or joining a pre- or post-party. If I wanted to do something that wasn't his idea, he put it down as stupid. If I forced anything, he made sure his attitude made the occasion miserable. Then, in our junior year of high school, he distanced me from my family. The worst part is I allowed it. I thought that's what love was all about. All-consuming. I thought he loved me so much he wanted me all to himself. Now I know he didn't adore me. He controlled me. Other people got in the way of that. He didn't want to be found out. At one point, my dad likened him to a bad habit. Dad nailed it. Trevor ignored holidays with my family. We always had to be with his. I was so furious with my folks. I never understood why they didn't see me as the lucky one, that I was chosen, I was the one that Trevor had chosen. Isn't that what Cinderella and all those other stories tell us? What matters is that we are chosen? It took me becoming a mother to make me see how deeply I broke my parents' hearts."

"Oh, Em!" Olivia and Anna spoke at once.

"I'm not done. Not even close. When we graduated from high school, my parents planned a party for me. They invited him and his family, grudgingly. His browbeaten, lackluster mother came and acted more pleased than she should have been to be attending a party. Like she never got to go out or something. Trevor showed up late and left early, ruining the entire experience for me. I drummed up an excuse for him, sold it to myself first, then everyone else. I don't know what I said now. Probably that he had to work or had car trouble. Soon after, Trevor suggested we get married. He gave me a ring, and we eloped, and that *really* broke my parents' hearts. They retired and moved out of state. We completely lost touch. Because of my absurd confusion fueled by insecurity, immaturity, and misunderstanding, I lost my family and my friends, like they all disowned me, but I know it was me who vanished. Trevor made sure of that. They have never even met Charlie, and they don't know Trevor died."

Olivia started to interject, and Emmaline held up her hand. "Wait, there is so much more. We had fun while we were expecting Charlie. We worked on our house, and I decorated the baby's room. But Charlie was only a few months old when the shine came off the prize for Trevor. He began emotionally disengaging from us. He acted jealous of the baby. I thought maybe I was imagining it, but his interest in our little family waned. The older Charlie got, the more jealous Trevor became of him. I tried being the best wife in the universe. Loneliness was an everyday experience, except for Charlie. There were no girlfriends or family to turn to for advice. When I overheard Trevor on the phone one night, my personal light bulb finally flashed on. The call ended with sweet talk and a promise to get together the next night. A night he claimed to be working a shift for a buddy. He was working, all right. Working *it*." Emmaline paused. "You know, in literature they call that a coming-of-age moment. My innocence shattered that night. I saw Trevor for what he was."

Olivia said, "I remember Trevor from when I was teaching. He gave me the impression of a young man trying out personas. A boy who walked like someone important with all the ego and none of the grace. A classic Narcissist, Em. You could never fix that, no matter how clean your house was and how great your casseroles. He had a personality disorder. He needed drugs and medical attention. God, I am so sorry you went through this. How do we not know about this? Is that why you planned this yearbook thing? You didn't have to go to such trouble. You could talk to either of us any time. You should know that, Emmaline."

"Now, I have a horrible confession to make," added Emmaline. "When the sheriff came to my door to give me the news Trevor died, I collapsed. Not from grief, but relief. The thought of being forced to share Charlie for the rest of my life terrified me."

Anna's phone chimed. "Dinner's ready," she said. "Back in a few."

"You know, Em," Olivia said, while Anna was gone, "a confused man, ill with a personality disorder, might have known very little about sustaining relationships. But it doesn't mean he didn't love you and Charlie. It sounds like he didn't know how."

"Trevor told me the worst part of any relationship is dealing with someone else's insecurities. I thought he meant him having to deal with my lack of confidence. Around him, I always felt insecure. Now, I wonder if he showed me a brief insight into himself, wittingly or not. I don't want to harbor hate for Charlie's father. It will ooze out and affect him. I have read there is a connection between narcissism and projection. He projected, taking his personal ugly emotions and perspectives, and painting them onto me. I took it all in because of my insecurity. But he was the source of my insecurity. It was like he walked around with a scalpel, shaving off one tiny piece of me at a time, so slight I didn't even notice until after he was gone. He did one good thing for Charlie and me, though. I was shocked to find a life insurance policy in his desk. For hundreds of thousands. The weird thing was that he'd taken it out only six months before. That is what makes me think he wasn't evil. He knew. He knew something was coming. That money saved us. It's given me the time to figure out what I'm going to do next."

"Look at you, Em. One Friday Ladies' Night and you have changed your entire perspective. You know things don't change, and people don't change unless they have to, but the way we see and understand them does. It's you and Charlie now. And Hershey. I am proud of you, my friend," Olivia said as Anna walked through the doors with a stack of pizzas, bringing their herb and onion smell with her.

"This is a good time for you to get some professional counseling to be sure you understand what you and Trevor were to each other, Em. Then, maybe you could reach out and grab those grandparents for Charlie Boy."

Anna looked at Olivia as if to inquire further, but Olivia waived her off.

After eating the pizzas and tidying up the place, neither Olivia nor Anna mentioned their yearbooks. Emmaline hugged and thanked them for letting her talk and listening without judgment. Olivia grabbed Anna's hand as they stood watching Emmaline walk out into a magnificent full moon, highlighting the town like a floodlight.

7
LIKE A GEODE, SEE WHAT'S INSIDE

"Emmaline! Where are you Em? You are going to like—no—love my news!" Anna walked through the common door into Geode with two frosty drinks in her hands.

"Out here, Anna. I'm glad you're back. I am not cut out for customer service. One customer dithered endlessly over two brands of dog food, then finally chose neither. All I want to do is get to my writing. I just . . . Oh wait, what? Your face is glowing. Did you say you had news?"

"Well, you little romantic, I have another date. As I walked out of the laundry, Jack was going in. He said he was on his way here and saw me there and asked if I had a minute to hear his idea. We are going on a hike to a beautiful spot he loves, and he is bringing a picnic dinner. We will be on the river, secluded and surrounded by boulders and huge timber. He said to bring a swimsuit because there is a perfect swimming hole."

"What fun! You work so hard, Anna. You deserve a break. You'll have a wonderful time. I love this news. Remember, Sparky is always welcome to stay with us. I am so excited. This guy is amazing. What do you think? Maybe he is the one?" Emmaline was talking fast. Her words tumbling from her mouth. "By the way, I can tell Sparky is part of the family now."

"Let me think. Yes, fun, I don't work that hard, thanks for the help with Sparky. I agree, he's become a permanent part of things. Jack seems like a nice guy, but I'm not ready to call him amazing or The One. Now I have work to do." One clap of her hands, a warm smile for Em, and Anna retreated to her back room.

"You aren't fooling me, Anna. You are excited and I can see the sparkle in your eyes. This guy must be special. Wait! When is it?"

"Thursday afternoon. I'm closing Besties early for 'inventory' or something. Tell you all about it Friday night at Geode."

Anna headed to the back of the store, but not before she did a little shimmy dance that made Emmaline laugh out loud.

***

Jack took the picnic cooler and blanket from the back seat and, with this other hand, took Anna's, leading her into the forest and out to the river. Although she felt strange in her gut, she decided to think of it as a sweet gesture. The trail was wide enough for two people to walk silently side by side carrying their dinner and swim tote. Giant, billowing evergreens swayed above them, hosting a raucous group of crows. Beyond the birds, the forest grew quiet. Secret-holding quiet. They walked along the path carpeted with pine needles, feet making hardly a sound. Much like Anna imagined stealthy tribal deer hunters had done many years ago.

As they rounded a bend, Anna let out a gasp. Up ahead, the path snaked through a forest of giant redwoods . Redwoods to her represented power, strength, and wisdom. She felt their presence, and her ears buzzed from the silence. She wanted to stay still and take in the magnificent sight. The moment felt spiritual, holy, a time and place to stand in reverence. Jack pulled at her hand, urging her to keep going. "Don't tell me you're a tree hugger," he said.

The path descended slightly, and a new sound overtook the silence. The river was one solid roar. As they walked, she noticed the increasing dampness in the air. The satisfying scents of pines and redwoods gave way to that of fresh, roiling water. The Umbra River.

Still holding hands, they cleared the woods. Ahead, giant boulders sat hunkered, like protective spirits, or as if they were sheltering hidden sprites—they felt that alive. Gushing water played leapfrog between and over the rocks, then plunged down, flipping and whirling, then pounding the deep pool below with a rapid *plonk!* Over and over again, one barely finishing before the next one arrived. Along the side of the river, swirling eddies housed minnows darting in and out of crevices in the rocks.

Anna felt rooted in place. Her senses buzzed at the edge of understanding something crucial about this place. Although she had lived in the town of Umbra River for many years, this magical spot had remained elusive. *How do I not know about this place?* She let out her breath with a whispered wow. Jack loosened his grip on her hand. He climbed down the bank to her left. Rocks and sand from centuries of granite grinding and erosion carpeted a flat spot, perfect for lounging and a picnic. Anna no sooner had the thought that Jack must have been feeling like a pack mule and eager to unload, than he dropped all he was carrying, declaring that he was not hungry yet and wanted to swim.

They both had worn their swimsuits under their clothes, but only Anna remembered to bring towels, one of which she now passed over to Jack. He thanked her, then shed his shoes, shorts, and shirt, stepped through the rocks, and smoothly shallow-dived in. He turned toward her like they were in a scene from a movie, standing waist deep with droplets hitting his shoulders. Anna felt woozy momentarily, like she had been drugged. He looked film-star handsome standing in the water, calling her in. She had shed her clothes down to her swimsuit and was trying out the water slowly. The rocks were slippery, and she wasn't interested in getting completely submerged. Jack waded back to her and held out his hand. She felt charmed. How thoughtful to help her through the rocks.

The water turned out to be above her knees and with a whip-snap-tug, he pulled her fully in. She wasn't ready. Water went up her nose, and she came up sputtering. Her first reaction was disbelief, then fury. She swam over to get her footing, but he was instantly beside her. Just as she was loading up to fire a cannon of rage, he wrapped his arms around her and kissed her not forcibly, but with more passion than any man in her history, what few there had been. Her mind kept going to movies. A Hollywood kiss. He did it two more times. She felt weak, her arms trembling. The vitriol that had been churning inside her dissipated like a wisp of fog.

Anna, still a little shocked and a lot confused, allowed him to pick her up and carry her to the beach spot. He put her down, grabbed a towel and wrapped her up, all the while telling her she was beautiful, a good sport, so much fun, etc. He was sorry to have shocked her, didn't realize it would. Thought he was being playful.

***

Friday night finally arrived, and Anna swept into Geode. Her friends were waiting with full glasses. Olivia poured a third and handed it without a word to Anna. Emmaline was almost hyperventilating with anticipation, reminding Anna of a retriever waiting for the ball to be thrown.

"You know," began Anna, "I was reading Geode's sign for the billionth time, and it occurred to me that it's quite the metaphor for taking the time to get to know someone. 'Geode, See What's Inside.' Isn't that exactly what we need to work on when it comes to people? And isn't that exactly what we do here on Friday nights? We get to know each other more every week. I love these evenings together. I discovered my two truly best friends here. Well, of course I include several furries in my best friend file. But you know what I mean. How insightful of you, Olivia, to come up with this name. I guess that's why we call you the smartest pug in the pack. Added to that, look at all the information coming from the books in Geode."

"JEEEESUS! Anna stop!!" Emmaline exploded. "We can go over this any time. What the hell happened on your hike, picnic, whatever you call it?"

"Oh, I'm sorry, Em. It was nice, really fun. We took a trail through a beautiful part of the forest. Breathtaking, really. Wow, I could hear the river before I saw it. It was a magnificent spot to wade with a deep swimming hole beyond. I brought you a rock, Olivia. It might be a geode. How do you know unless you crack it open?"

Clearly exasperated, Emmaline said, "Come on, Anna. Get to the point."

"Okay, Em, before you begin to orbit, I kissed him. He kissed me and said he had met no one like me. He has a good sense of humor and can tease with the best of 'em. We chatted for hours, and I told him I loved that he listened more than he talked. He said that was because I am more interesting than he is. Isn't that sweet?"

"Okay, now we are getting somewhere," said Emmaline as she scooted to the edge of her seat.

"What do you think about him as a person?" asked Olivia.

"Did I tell you already that his wife left him after the DUI? Which seems a little harsh. But she has been great about shared custody if he doesn't drink or drive. He swears he is clean and has an AA sponsor. He asked if I wanted his sponsor's contact information. Isn't that strange?' Anna looked over at Olivia, who nodded.

"I told him no. He is responsible for himself. Also, it sounds like he won't be getting his driver's license back anytime soon. He didn't elaborate. Now that I think about it, he wasn't highly informative about himself."

"Give him points for being a good dad and loving animals!" pleaded Emmaline.

"Em, you are more interested in my having a beau than the quality of said beau. It's way too early. I would of course refuse to commit to anything until he is well vetted. The alcohol issue is an enormous red flag. I do like his kids, so someone is doing a good job there. And he is good company, not to mention quite good looking."

"Well then, let's have question time. Where did you change into your bathing suits?" said Emmaline.

"Wore them under our clothes."

"Did he make the picnic? Was it good?"

"Delicious, made at Geode by Lucy."

"What a cop out. He should have made it himself. Were you out there after dark?"

"I know where you are going with this, Em, and I'm not tellin'."

With a harrumph, Emmaline said, "Those are all my questions."

"He asked many questions about spirituality and how it works to tele-connect with animals. So, I shared a funny story that I'm not sure he believed. But it really happened. Truly, it was fun to shock him. As I was trying to make ends meet during my college years, I worked as a notary in a real estate office. My boss scheduled a meeting for a Tuesday evening, in the most run-down area of a beaten-down city. Papers needed a signature with a thumbprint notarization, and then I planned a fast exit toward the interstate. My eighteen-year-old Ford pocketed along, and I kept thinking, *please don't conk out here* and *please nobody steal my car*. It was a trailer park, which is normally no big deal, but this was a *trailer* park. Sketchy vibe. Most of the front porches hosted at least three men on folding metal chairs, enjoying their beer and smokes. The occasional group of kids kicking a ball or digging in the dirt. I waved and smiled. They stared back."

"The numbers were getting closer, and just as dusk moved in, 151 appeared. No lights shining from inside. *I can do this,* I thought. *Bada-bing, bada-boom, and it'll be all done.*"

"I said 'Hello?' and heard a groan. Frozen, I said, 'Hello' again, and this time heard a thump. Just then, the sweep of light from a car illuminated an enormous dog with a heavy chain tying him to the porch. I sat right down on the top step next to him and said, 'Oh, sweetheart, how long have you been chained?' He was silver. A pit bull. He stretched and groaned and laid his pony-sized head on my lap. He had water and a roomy, padded bed. Even so, the chain was awful. Another arc of lights lit up the space as a car pulled in next to mine."

"A man in a security guard uniform stepped out of the car and clicked on a giant flashlight and said, 'Jesus, lady, what are you doing? He's dangerous! Did you walk up to him?'"

I said, "Obviously, I did. And we have become quite close."

"Jesus, Mikey, you can't let just anyone up these steps. What are you thinking?"

"Another stretch and groan from Mikey and I said, 'Mikey!! What kind of name is that? You could have at least called him Sniper or Brute. Of course, he is confused.'"

"The man said, 'Sorry I'm late. Are you the notary?'"

"I was still steaming mad. 'Yes, I'm Anna and why does he have to wear this horrible chain-link fence around his neck? Has he been out here all day? It's getting cold. He needs to be inside.' Mikey thumped his tail. Obviously, he agreed with me."

"Mikey was unchained, allowed to roam, then brought inside. Papers were explained, signed, and notarized while the big dog lounged on the couch ignoring T.V. news. As I packed my papers to leave, Mikey looked up. I felt the words rather than heard them: *Please keep our secret. I am supposed to be a guard dog.* I kneeled at Mikey's big old head and sent a telepathic message back: 'Goodbye sweet boy, I'll keep the secret. But be careful. People judge your breed before they even get to meet you.'"

"What did Jack say about this?"

"He listened to the story but didn't comment, Olivia. He rubbed his hand over his face and thought for a minute. Then, he wanted to know more about how I knew I was psychic and if I was ever wrong. I told him I realized I knew things other people didn't know, even about themselves. He looked stricken for a minute and asked if I could read minds. I assured him I could not, but I get impressions and sometimes dialogue. I felt silly and flattered, wondering if he was thinking about us together. But maybe not. However, I said that whether I am right or wrong, I don't share my thoughts often. It was a fun and romantic day in such a magnificent spot in the world that I'm sure I heard only what I wanted to hear. Doesn't matter. Plenty of time to discover Jack, and my eyes and ears are wide open."

The evening rolled into other topics. As they were cleaning up to leave, Olivia sidled up to Anna to say, "As you get to know Jack, there will be changes in your perspective. It is very much like upgrading the magnification of your make-up mirror—you see what you have missed."

Passing it off as a funny metaphor, Anna laughed as she went out to her car. How fortunate she felt to have these great friends and all that came with it. She pulled into Emmaline's driveway to pick up Sparky, who apparently had become her dog by default, when a thud of dread hit her midsection. *Changes in perspective.* All at once Olivia's words felt like a warning.

8
SOMETHING I'VE NEVER TOLD

Olivia hated painting, but she promised Anna. With shops and businesses closed for Sunday, Besties' back room was getting a fresh coat of paint in Tiffany blue/green.

"Liv, I am so pleased you and Em came in on your day off to help paint!" Anna said. "I think this color will look classy yet calming."

"It sounded like fun when we planned it. After moving this heavy furniture out of the way, I am not so sure! 'Tiffany blue/green' sounded a bit much but it works." Olivia pushed a curl off her forehead. She still wasn't sure about the vanilla blonde she let Anna and Emmaline talk her into, but it was only hair. It would grow out.

"Good thing it is just the back room. If we don't finish, it won't affect the front of the store. Holler uncle when you have had enough," Anna said.

"I was at uncle the moment you mentioned paint."

"Ha-ha," Anna said. "No one was forcing you, dear Olivia."

With a four-inch brush full of paint dribbling down her arm, Emmaline said, "Hey Anna, tell Olivia about your phone visit with Grandma Ming."

"Emmaline! You can't talk while gesturing when you have a full paintbrush in your hand. Oh my god, look at the front of your shirt." Anna snorted out a laugh.

"Gosh. Well, anyway, tell her about it."

"Do we ever gather just to enjoy some quiet time together? That would be an idea. All right. I confess. I'm a little worried about Grandma," said Anna. "She was having memory problems. Names, dates, and details were eluding her. I have never noticed that before."

"My mother would say that aging has a learning curve," Olivia said. "You might have had a fulfilling, demanding career, put your heart and soul into raising kids or whatever. Then you notice you can't immediately retrieve words, or you need help getting bills paid. Thank goodness for an online thesaurus. The worst is names. Particularly names you know very well. My mom said, 'Don't scramble to remember, call everyone, Honey!' About dates, you might remember a birthday or two but time swooshes by so fast, you forget to send a card. Mom kept a list ordered by date, hoping that would help. It didn't. But truly, how life changing can it be to send a timely greeting card? She thought sharing her wisdom at appropriate moments was more important. And wisdom that comes with age has a huge perk—you can spot bullshit a mile away. And she could. Boy, could she ever. Mom often wondered if this is part of the grand plan. Our younger years are for gathering and building, and our elder years for focusing deeply and reflectively. Do our bodies turn on us, no longer knuckling down to our commands because we need to dig deeper and pay better attention to spirituality rather than physicality?"

"Your mom sounds like someone I would have liked to know, Anna said, her head tipped and her eyes searching Olivia's. "I don't remember her. Did she live here in Umbra River?"

"In her later years, she lived with me. She was splendid company after Jennifer left for college."

"I'm getting some images," Anna said. "Did she have a little fluffy dog?"

"Yes, Rumsey was her constant companion. She would have taken to you, Anna. She was into the spiritual side of things. Just like you, there wasn't a dog she didn't fall in love with. She took in any stray that needed her." Olivia caught her mistake and laughed.

Anna, with a wry smile, said, "Are you implying Jack is a stray? I am going to assume you didn't mean that the way it came out."

Emmaline looked up from her entwined fingers. "Olivia, what happened to Jennifer's father? You never talk about him."

Eight or ten heartbeats later, Olivia pulled in a breath and answered, "Oh well, that's a long story. Maybe for another time."

"Oh, no you don't. We all share, and you are not getting off the hook," Emmaline added, palms up and paint dripping from the brush.

With a soft laugh, Olivia began, "I don't want to taint your expectations with my views on marriage, Em. You and Trevor may have had a troubled relationship, if short, but I wouldn't want to discourage you from trying again. You are young and have a boy who could use a father."

Emmaline waved her off. "This is about you, not me."

"I thought we were talking about Anna's visit to her grandmother! Emmaline, honestly. You need to respect people's boundaries a little better. But all right. Here goes. Clayton, Jennifer's father, and I never married. We worked at raising her together, even though we didn't live together. He attends holidays, birthdays, all important life events. His vacation times from work have always been with her. He loves her and works to make sure he is a part of her life. I'm happy he does. He is a good man, but he never married either. He made a few relentless attempts to get me to change my mind and marry him, but I wouldn't. Don't ask why. I am not sure I have the answer. There was no dearth of love, only my lack of confidence in it lasting. I felt I didn't deserve it, I guess. Having a baby out of wedlock in that day and time messed with your head. Made you feel less than. Best not to set myself up for further disappointment."

Anna stood up straight, mid brush stroke, "Olivia! My god that is exactly how I feel. My adoptive parents had a good marriage by appearances, but I never witnessed any I truly wanted to emulate. Once I read a list of steps to a good marriage that impressed me so much I tacked it on the fridge and committed it to memory: attraction, discovery, affection, growing respect, love, commitment, teamwork, then mutually supported individual growth. A few times, I made it to 'growing respect', then something would happen, the respect would quit growing, and I would bolt. Give up at the first sign of trouble. You see why I am pessimistic when you two ask me about Jack with such hopeful anticipation? I am *always* waiting for that moment when I am proven right. We can never really know another person and so lasting love is a fallacy. A fairy tale." Anna saw her friends' shocked faces, their eyes searching hers. "What? Too cynical?"

"My goodness, so skeptical. Who broke your heart and when?" A can of paint tilted precariously as Emmaline turned to talk.

"Emmaline! Look out!" Olivia shouted.

"I was given away!" Anna said. "Handed over! A baby! How can someone reject a tiny baby? Evidently, unlovable as a newborn translates into over-educated, opinionated, and happy to be independent. I don't need anyone and not a single human needs me. No reason in the world I need to attach myself permanently to anyone else. Surely you can understand and back me up on this. And for god's sake, Em, grab that can of paint before I have something else to be upset about."

"Enough, you two," Olivia said. "Anna, I'm sorry. You were not rejected as a baby. Excuse my language, but shit happens. Who knows what your birth mother went through. It was a different time. Look at Jennifer. Do you have any idea how people looked at me when I was pregnant with her? You would have thought I had leprosy. Completely snubbed by our loving local inhabitants. Now that we've all opened these cans of worms, I'll tell you something else I never shared before."

Anna and Emmaline both stopped and turned to Olivia. "Yes!" they said at once.

Emmaline came down off the ladder and sat on the lower rung. Anna turned an empty five-gallon bucket upside down and sat. "Okay, shoot."

Olivia took a deep breath. She couldn't understand why she suddenly felt the need to share this long-held story.

"This was a while ago. Ringing, ringing, ringing. I can still hear that sound. The phone wouldn't stop ringing. I was huge with Jennifer, and it was on the far side of the room. I had to move the table holding saltines and ginger ale out of the way even to push myself to a sitting position. That's how far along in my pregnancy I was. The next step was the toughest, hefting my bulbous self to standing. People talk about loving pregnancy. I did *not* love being pregnant. That familiar wave of nausea swallowed me, and I thought back to eight months before when the smug damned doctor told me nausea usually only lasts about three months and then I'd feel terrific. Well, I was certain there'd be no feeling terrific until I had my little miracle in my arms. Meanwhile, the phone stopped ringing before my swollen feet could shuffle my unbalanced body across the room. The ringing stopped and the answer machine flipped on."

"'Please pick up the phone, something terrible everyone help . . . call me . . .' the frantic voice cracked, then clatter, click, then silence."

"Within an hour, in a fog of discomfort and disbelief, I found myself in the sandwich assembly line hastily gathered to support searchers canvassing the woods, creek banks, outbuildings, garages, and homes, anywhere a little girl named Crystal might hide or have been hidden. The group, mostly women, was trying to push through their shock and fear with this minor act of support—while keeping their own children within their reach. Crystal's home was the epicenter. Police officers swarmed, detectives scoured and questioned. Eight women kept coffee perking and a sandwich assembly line moving. As they assembled food for the search team, the sobs and occasional screams from an inconsolable mom filled the rooms. Crystal's mother kept insisting on going out there to help search, but the female officers worked on convincing her to stay in the house and wait. I heard that at one point, the woman flung herself on the ground in the backyard sobbing into a Crystal's favorite doll. They had to call in extra officers to help get her back inside."

"Crystal was only six, hard of hearing, wore hearing aids. Someone grabbed her from her own front yard while she jumped rope on the sidewalk. She was out of her mother's sight less than ten minutes. The sandwich makers took small comfort by wondering aloud if the hearing aids had made her a target. Surely their children with perfect hearing must be safe. The neighborhood was usually strewn with bikes and skates. A working-class neighborhood where unleashed dogs and playmates filled the yards and sidewalks, then were escorted home as the sun began to set. Crystal disappeared mid-afternoon."

"Did you know these people? Dear God, it's horrifying, but I'm trying to understand why you are sharing this with us today," Anna said.

"I get that," Olivia said. "I will come to bear, I promise. In the following weeks, the newspaper reported what few bits of information various law enforcement agencies gathered. Article after article hinted at misplaced egoism between departments. So frustrating, and it wasn't helping find the lost girl. The picture of a distinctive van was on a newspaper front page. It was spotted near Crystal's neighborhood with a little girl inside, but the driver who saw her couldn't get to a pay phone fast enough to report it. This was years before cell phones. The authorities released the description of a man of interest. His face was forever etched in my memory. I would recognize him today. He had been seen visiting the grave of another murdered little girl. When authorities eventually found and searched his van, they found a display of photos of missing little girls, including Crystal, plastered all over the inside. They found all of this within a twenty-mile radius of each other and where I lived. He was weird, had no alibi, and yet slipped from the grasp of law enforcement."

"Three months later, summer had shifted into a cold, windy autumn. I had stuffed down the terror and felt contentment as I sang to my perfect tiny human swaddled and nursing. Being a mom was rigorous but joyful. I felt fulfilled as a stay-at-home mom while my leave from teaching lasted. I didn't want to be anywhere else. Crystal's story and her fate were still a mystery. The horror of what Crystal's family was living through had to take a back seat, because I refused to let it dilute the happiness in my home. The community's shroud of despair might have lifted inside my house, but my body knew the truth. I began to have headaches. Mild at first, but still, they kept tapping me on the shoulder."

"Months rolled by, and the more autonomy Jennifer acquired, the more fearful I became. I swore to myself I'd never let this child be out of my grasp or my sight. Although, I realized this wasn't possible and not what I wanted for her. Errand days became exhausting. Planned adventures had to be safe. I'd stop at the park, or the library for story time and then the ice cream shop just before the finale of grocery shopping. All the while keeping my Jennifer as attached to me as possible. Being terrified became a low growl in my gut. The upcoming weekend was the Labor Day holiday, and my grocery list was long. I had thrown some toys into my purse to keep my little shopping partner invested. After getting settled with a basket, I started toward the store when I noticed a van parked three cars down from ours. It looked just like the van featured in the news reports about Crystal's disappearance. Surely it couldn't be. My heart was racing, and I steered the cart close to it. There were three windows, a windshield, and one on each side door. The sun was glaring so I couldn't see inside without getting too close. But that familiar insignia—the one about a plumbing company and then the golden sun above the wording—oh my God. All I could think to do was jog the basket to get inside the store with the safety of other people. My stomach was clenching, but the baby was giggling, head thrown back, loving the motion and the speed. The doors whooshed, and I felt safer inside. I was working on calming my heart rate and breathing as I picked through some vegetables. A little dazed, I realized the squawks coming from the basket were from my fussy child who wanted me to go fast again. Instead, I quickly pulled out some toys to settle her before she drew attention. A prickly feeling in my upper back made me slowly look around. Five feet away, there he was. The man whose picture had been on the front page of the news, the man with the familiar van. I almost buckled. Had it not been for mom instincts, I think I might have."

"I gathered up every bit of strength I had and walked carefully to the next aisle. About half-way down the frozen food aisle, I turned and looked right into his eyes. Pits of pure evil. His gaze slid from my face to Jennifer. He was close enough to touch the shopping basket, and my scream must have echoed throughout the store. I grabbed my Jennifer out of the basket and ran—not stopping until we got to the car, jumped in, and locked the doors. I didn't take time to buckle either of us in. I drove off the main road into a neighborhood where I pulled over and panted through the anxiety before I had the brains to buckle us up. I drove fast but with intent, constantly checking the rearview mirror. Driving in circles, I took obscure turns and pulled into strange driveways, hoping if he were following, he'd be thrown off. I was terrified to the maximum. The sound of crying in the back seat seeped into my consciousness, making my hands shake. It took a minute for me to sort out Jennifer was crying for the toys that were left with the groceries."

"My innocence was destroyed by the fact that children can be taken and never seen again. I had to be Mama, chief protector, FBI, Secret Service, and first responder all in one. On high alert, our fun adventures now became even more exercises in security and surveillance."

Olivia stopped talking. A migraine was coming. First, the lights flashed into her eyes from the side. These always fooled her into thinking they were coming from an outside source, a firefly or small angel flitting by, if such things were possible. Her eyes watered, and she reached toward the light switch on the wall behind her out to turn down the lights. *Oh no*, she thought. *Here it comes.* Her head felt like an expanding balloon as the blood vessels in her brain dilated. The pain behind her left eye made her want to find a dark place before the nausea took over. Anna and Emmaline both appeared to see the change in Olivia and, at once and stood up, preparing to help. They had witnessed it before. Softly, Olivia said, "Please don't go. I haven't yet shared the worst. The root of the pervasive guilt that never goes away."

Emmaline tiptoed away and brought back a glass of water. Carefully setting the water in front of Olivia, lukewarm, no ice, she said, "It can wait. I'll walk you next door to your cot."

"No, please, let me go on. I need to."

Olivia hissed out between her clenched teeth as she closed her eyes and held the water glass to her temple. "I made one of the worst mistakes of my life. I didn't contact the police. The idea was too terrifying, and the what ifs overwhelming. He might find out it was me who called the police and, well, I can't even say it." Then, quietly, she added, "One of the two worst mistakes."

Emmaline broke in, "Don't beat yourself up over this, Olivia. It was years ago, and it might not have helped, anyway."

Anna's voice was so low Olivia could barely hear her, "I see. After that, three more little girls went missing, and you think you could have stopped him. I'm sorry Olivia, what a burden for you all these years."

Emmaline opened her mouth, but Anna shook her head no and took Olivia's hands. "Come on, let's head for your cot. This is enough for tonight."

The two women walked carefully to Geode's back room, where Olivia kept a cot, and the windows covered with blackout curtains. These headaches were familiar old enemies. She also knew Anna would see to it she had hot tea and her migraine medicine. Pain pulsated through her head like a jackhammer, and her watering eyes felt as though nails were being pounded through them from behind. Olivia slowly let her head touch the pillow. She wondered what made her think telling secrets was a good idea.

9
CHARLIE HEARD THE KITTEN'S FEAR

"Charlie boy, what's going on?" Anna said while shouldering a thirty-pound bag of dog food and dragging in a bucket of cat litter. She dropped them both and was straightening her back, stretching her torso. "Charlie, when you are a teenager, can I hire you to load up supplies for me? It's all getting to be too heavy."

"I'll be big enough soon. How much dollars will you give me?"

"Well Charlie, there is inflation to consider, the state of the economy in general, and the health of Besties which is good since there is no competition. Also, I'd have to consider my income and expense ratio." Anna couldn't help but smile at the earnest little boy trying to sort out her words.

"Sounds like a 'we'll see.' Mom says that all the time. Auntie Anna, Sparky has a sore in his mouth." Charlie said as he gently petted the little dog on his lap.

"Oh, maybe that why he wouldn't eat this morning? Let me see."

"Right there." Charlie pulled open the dog's jaw with both hands, leaned over and pointed with his nose to the angry red pustule on the inside of Sparky's lower gum. Sparky was relaxed, as he always was with Charlie. "He was acting weird this morning, didn't want his breakfast. I asked him, and he told me in my brain. He's hungry, but it hurts. Will you fix him?"

"I'll take care of it right now." Anna took Sparky and headed for the back room and her medical instruments. "Come on, Charlie. You can talk him through it while I concentrate on fixing. Watch what I'm doing and tell him exactly what is going on. He trusts you. Where is your mom, by the way?"

"Mom's in the bathroom."

"No, I'm not! I am in the storage closet straightening things up," Emmaline's muffled voice chimed in.

While working to clean out the infection, Anna thought about Charlie and his ability to communicate telepathically with animals. She felt full responsibility for helping him navigate his gift with all the snags he was bound to encounter. People didn't understand such gifts. More than a few people called her a witch behind her back. Thankfully, Emmaline understood what he was capable of. First, skepticism, next cautious realization, then awe. Emmaline had her shortcomings, but she was a good mother to Charlie.

As Anna worked on Sparky's mouth, she recalled an incident Em had shared a few months ago. Emmaline and Charlie had been walking through a neighborhood enjoying a beautiful, quiet summer morning when he dropped her hand and took off. He went scooting around a corner, running like his pants were on fire. He was almost three blocks ahead when Emmaline caught up, breathing heavily and not sure if she was more mad or terrified. Ahead, she saw a kitten with a string around its neck being terrorized by three boys with sticks. Four-year-old Charlie rammed the boy holding the string, the string dropped, and Charlie scooped up the kitten. He was on the run, little legs pumping, kitten held to his chest and three older boys in hot pursuit. Emmaline said she had flashed back to her high school track and field training, shifted her body into gear and sprinted top speed toward the perpetrators. When she nabbed the biggest one by the collar, all stopped mid-flight, and the verbal reprimand began. Imagining the exhibition, Anna laughed out loud.

"It's not funny Auntie Anna. Sparky hurts. Can you hurry?" Charlie's indignation was adorable.

"Oh, honey, I'm not laughing at Sparky. I was just remembering a funny story. The shot I gave him will make the pain go away. It should begin working now."

"Yeah, he is feeling better, but he is hungry. So, what's so funny?" Charlie asked, with his big blue eyes blinking up at Anna.

"I remembered the story about your mom running full throttle after those boys who were after her favorite guy. They didn't stand a chance."

Charlie laughed too. "She was fast. Then she took them all home to tell their moms. They were so scared."

"You heard that kitty's fear from two blocks away. It was a thought, not a sound, right?" asked Anna.

"Yep."

"Not everybody can hear those thoughts. Just those special people who can listen."

Anna pulled a nasty foxtail from Sparky's gum. Luckily, it came out whole. She medicated the site, and it didn't need stitches. Anna held him on the floor until he steadied himself. "Charlie, would you add water to Spark's food, make a kind of mush, and see if he wants to eat it?" Happy to help and obviously thrilled his friend felt better, Charlie hopped up and sprinted to the food bowl. He ran smack dab into his mom with her arms full of paper and plastic recyclables.

"Sorry, Mom. I'll pick 'em up, but I gotta feed Sparky first."

"That's okay, Buddy. I'll take care of it. But let's go home soon. I have a meeting tonight with the committee planning the festival parade." Emmaline said. "They are coming to our house."

"They're coming to your house?" Anna asked.

"Yes, I've been puzzling over the purpose of the meeting. I always volunteer for something, wanting to be a part of this annual festival. Maybe they want me to do more. It is becoming more difficult to find quiet time to work on my poetry. But the festival is short and the fact that it honors the history of Umbra River makes it worthwhile. I guess I can put my writing time on hold if I must."

"Maybe inspiration will grab you again. Remember last year when you saw those stunning Clydesdales in action? Your poem about them is amazing. This year's celebration will have a new twist. For the first time, the animal species who supported the forefathers are being honored as well. The parade will be chock full of horses, goats, oxen, and mules. Draft horses and mules will pull wagons full of dignitaries. A team of cowboys are planning a cattle drive down Main Street! Then a rodeo including a branding demonstration. It will be an enormous job for Sheriff Dobbs to keep everyone safe and the streets cleared of cow poop. It might inspire you. Take a notepad."

"Great idea. My tiny recorder would work too. Why are they making a bigger deal out of the festivities this year?"

"My guess is it's fiscal. The town needs money and money comes from growth and therefore taxes. This feels like a huge advertising campaign for Umbra River." Anna turned a thumb down.

"I hate to see Umbra River grow. It's perfect as it is. We have to get going, Charlie."

10
GENTLE HEARTS ON PARADE

Emmaline got through dinner and preparing refreshments for the festival committee meeting. Charlie asked to stay up a little later so he could join in. Although, she guessed his true intent was to partake of the lemon tarts, oatmeal cookies, and chocolates she had out for guests.

The doorbell announced their arrival, and it surprised her to see ten people on her porch. In they came with smiles and warm greetings. Emmaline quickly surveyed the seating, then set off to nab her four dining room chairs as fill in. After inviting her guests to help themselves to coffee or lemonade from the sideboard and sweets on the coffee table, she sat on the hearth, unwittingly putting herself center stage.

After everyone was seated and snacking, the president of the Chamber of Commerce stood and cleared his throat. Emmaline felt bewildered.

"Emmaline," the president began, "First, thank you for being a gracious hostess. I know we have sprung this evening on you."

Emmaline acknowledged his thanks with a smile and a nod.

"We are here to pay tribute to your writing talent by asking if we may use your poem, 'Gentle Hearts on Parade' on our posters and in the advertisements, to call attention to the Umbra River History Festival. Olivia alerted us to it after you posted it on her board at Geode. She made a copy and sent it over, thinking we might be interested, and she was right. It's a lovely poem and we think it's appropriate to showcase a local talent. In fact, would you do us the honor of reading it for us right now?"

Emmaline, shocked, could only smile and say, "Thank you, and yes, of course, let me just go get my copy."

"Oh, no bother. We have it right here. Here is the best part, Charlie. We invite you and your mom to ride in the wagon pulled by the same team of Clydesdales she wrote about."

With a loud, "Whoop!" Charlie raced the perimeter of the room to the delight of everyone present. Phones came out to record him, but Emmaline shook her head no. She stopped short of people photographing her child. People instead congratulated Emmaline with handshakes and hugs. One person asked her to sign a paper allowing a picture of her and the poem to be published.

Feeling strangely outside of her life's station, but also right at home, Emmaline could hardly control the shaking in her voice as she began. "First, let me say thank you so much. Charlie and I will never forget this."

<u>GENTLE HEARTS ON PARADE</u>

Necks bowed, ears tipped front.
Nostrils billow steam
Dinner plate hooves slick black
Plow snow aside, demanding.

Anxious for the driver's click.
These gorgeous titan twins.
Curried gloss caramelized butter
Slate harnesses offset their buckskin.

Soft eyes deep with wisdom
As they step out with pride.
Onlookers standing stunned,
Awed by the team of Clydes.

Giant heads toss with pleasure,
Trotting their course, haunches taut.
Sprays of snow puff from each thud of hoof
What delight their performance has brought.

With a shake of their regal heads,
A soft nicker for their handler
They stomp to an instant halt
At once, their manner demure.

11
FEAR CREATING PREJUDICE

Anna burst through the door between Besties and Geode Bookshop singing "Ladies' Night!"

At the exact time, Emmaline came in from her writing room behind Geode singing the same song. "Jinks, you owe me a Coke," she said.

"Not quite Kool and the Gang, are we?" Anna said.

Olivia stood waiting in the doorway. "I'm here ladies. Whose turn is it to order dinner?"

"My turn, I'll do it now," Emmaline said. "How about those delicious meatloaf sandwiches from the deli and fruit salad?"

"Sure," said Anna. "Lucy isn't coming again tonight. Her son is expected to call from Ireland, and she doesn't want to miss it. Let's get comfortable, I'll open the wine. It's a crisp Pinot Gris. Should fit well with our dinner."

"Guess what? We're having dinner delivered by a courier!" chirped Emmaline.

"I didn't know Umbra River had couriers. What, when, where?" Anna said.

"You know the new kid who makes sandwiches? Well, he proposed the idea to his boss, and she thought it was great. He is young, fast, and has a bicycle. I asked him to knock when he leaves it at the door."

"I think it is my turn to share a piece of my life and bore you all to death," Anna said.

"There are no bores here," said Olivia. "You were going to introduce your family on the Ming side. You never did finish telling us about your grandmother."

"Yes, and there is much to tell. My adoptive great-grandfather told stories about the poor treatment of the Chinese who worked the mines. No. Wait. He must have gotten the stories from my great-great-grandfather. Look at me. Practically an adopted native daughter!" She grinned, palms up." GG, we called him. It took years for it to dawn on me it stood for Great-Grandfather. He called it his duty to make sure I knew as much family history as he 'might muster up.' He passed down stories from his father and grandfather."

Olivia looked surprised. "My goodness! You know, I wrote a thesis on exactly that topic. I think I titled it something like 'The American Treatment of Immigrants in the Quest for Wealth.' Humans have treated each other horribly throughout history. Still do."

"See? We have even more in common than we knew!" Anna said, then continued, "GG would have been an excellent resource for your thesis. He worked in the mines in the late 1890s and hated the way the Chinese laborers were mistreated. He was a teenager. The story goes he took food with him to the Chinese as often as possible. When the weather turned cold, he brought blankets. He had to watch out because there were those who didn't want him to help these people. As if they were an enemy. Can you believe it? Years later, he carried a newspaper article with him. I'll see if I can find it in *The Chronicle* archives. It described him as a charming hero. Whenever trouble loomed with Great Grandma Ming, he brought out that article, to remind her what a charming hero she married. When they were young marrieds, workers followed him home for his wife's good cooking. She sent them back to camp with knitted sweaters and hats. She loved kids and if there were any babies, she put herself in high gear to make blankets, clothes, and little hats for them. Also, supposedly, GG had second sight. He was psychic, too!"

"Anna, you have never mentioned this relative of yours. What else do you know about him?" Emmaline, as always, interested in a good story. She drove Anna crazy with it. "Has anyone written about him, maybe like a diary or journal? If you'll give me his full name and anything else you know about him, I'll Google and see what I can find."

"Em, you remind me of Hershey waiting for a ball to be thrown. You are almost panting and wagging. I'll ask my grandma about his first name. This is her husband's side of the family, and I have never thought to ask her about their past. Thank you for the nudge. I'm due for a visit. Maybe I'll travel down there and ask in person."

"I have so many questions. Can I go with you to Grandma Ming's? Do you mind? Can I record what she says? Can I ask whatever I want? Oh, I'm forcing myself on your Gram, no, no, no, I'm sorry. You can tell me what she says." Emmaline's eyes blinked almost in time with her toe tapping.

"Of course, Em. Grandma Ming will love you. I remember one story Grandpa Ming heard from GG when he was a kid. One of his school friends descended from a Chinese immigrant who had worked in one of the hydraulic mines. In school, during a history lesson, they saw the parallel in their lives. Both had ancestors who had been gold miners in this area. And both had ancestors who stayed in the area, owned businesses, raised families. GG's school friend talked about his Chinese relative who brought his wife and son to America when only a few Chinese women and children lived here. He had to hide them. Many were abused or forced into prostitution. I think GG called it 'being with men.' I figured he meant playing cards or something. They had a young son, tall enough to seem older. The father passed him off as old enough to work the mines and took him along to do a man's work."

"I wonder if any supervisor cared about the boy's age, just as long as he worked his poor young body to death," Olivia added.

"I think most of the mine owners cared only about making money. The workers made low wages and took terrible chances with their lives. According to GG, the men worked all week while living in tents, eating mostly rice and fish. There was no way to keep food fresh, so they had to catch their fish either before work or after quitting time when they were exhausted. GG said they made net bags out of rope, put the fish in the bags and left them in the cold water until cooking time. Poor fish. "

Emmaline asked, "So, why on earth did they leave China to work under these conditions? It couldn't have been a step up."

"Because of high taxes after the Opium Wars and crop failures. They scattered all over the world, trying to make a living," Olivia said. "When gold was discovered in California, they streamed into the U.S. hoping to make money in the mines. Trouble started. People who lived in the U.S. before the gold rush complained about the influx of Chinese workers."

"I suppose they felt they were taking away jobs," Anna said, "although there were many jobs to be had. I think fear created prejudice."

"I've read that California imposed a Foreign Miners Tax on 'non-Americans.' Three dollars per month," Olivia said. "Eventually, the Chinese were barred from immigration. Chinese were beaten and murdered for the smallest infractions. Any law enforcement just looked away."

Anna noticed Emmaline tearing up.

"I will never understand how people can hate each other just because they are afraid of their differences," Emmaline said. "Native Americans were treated with similar meanness. This reminds me of a chicken coop. Put a new Rhode Island Red in with a Polish and all hell breaks loose." A knock at the door sent her rushing to bring in their dinners.

"I hope I somehow garnered some of GG's empathy," Anna said. "I loved him. When the topic of my being adopted came up, he liked to remind me they chose me because I was the missing piece of the family puzzle. I remember a conversation I overheard as a child. Grandma Ming said something about GG and I being so similar she wouldn't be surprised if we were related by blood. When she realized I heard her, she walked it back and made a joke. I had forgotten about that bit of information until just now."

"I'm trying to figure this out. Were your adoptive mom or dad related to the Mings?" asked Emmaline as she popped open food containers and passed them around.

"Yes, Grandma Ming is my adoptive dad's birth mom. She may be my adoptive grandma, but she is the best grandmother ever. Mine was a closed adoption. When Grandma Ming said she thought I looked like GG and had similar quirks, I took it as a joke because we liked to spend time together. My adoptive mom looked very much like her side of the family, and so does my adoptive sister. My adoptive father looked Asian. So, my skin color and looks fit right in with him. People said they had one kid for each of them, but most didn't realize I was adopted. They just assumed, because of the way I look, that I was born to the people who raised me. I never knew what to think about that. Sometimes I daydreamed about my adoptive dad really being my birth father. But it didn't make any difference. He was my dad either way.

"But wait—your last name should be Ming, not Ambrose."

"Oh, that. Well, I changed my name a few months before I earned my veterinarian degree. I wanted a generic name, didn't want to be typecast when I opened a practice. I thought Ambrose went well with Anna, Ann, or Annabelle, so I went with it. Then, I found out it is the Greek word for immortal."

"Annabelle!! We've never heard that. Oh, my gosh, any more secrets?"

"I'm sorry, Em. I didn't mean to be secretive. I made the change a long time ago and sort of forgot about it. My adoptive mom had kept her maiden name and the whole name thing seemed impermanent to me. Let's stop talking and dig into this delicious-looking dinner. I need more wine."

"Yes please, me too," Emmaline said. "It's delicious as well."

"You know," Olivia said, "we have had some amazing history lessons come out of Ladies' Night. I have always thought the best way to teach history is through stories."

"I agree, and we are giving our favorite writer information to sink her teeth into and build on. The best part, though, is having best friends. Here's to us." Anna toasted.

"All right, you two, now I am exhausted. Dinner was delicious, the company superb, the information sharing even better, and I must go home. Anna, Ann, Annabelle, you have given me too much to think about and I thank you," yawned Olivia.

"Goodnight, Liv. Come on Emmaline, let's clean up and head home as well."

12
TERROR AT THE SUMMIT

Olivia had left her car at home that morning, so she was tucked inside her down filled coat and cashmere scarf, feeling pleased with herself for having done so. Home was a short walk, less than a mile. Hoping for the rain to hold off. *What a fun evening. I bet Anna's Grandma Ming will love the visit. It might perk her up enough that Anna won't worry about her. Maybe all the woman needs is a little help and friendly conversation.*

The evening revelry, in full swing, meant Umbra River's bars and restaurants were lively and loud. Each establishment had its own personality, depending on the clientele, music choices, and whether meals were served or not. Much like people, each reflected distinct differences and similarities. Light spilled from the windows onto the sidewalk and lamplights illuminated the street. She imagined some might call it romantic.

Nearing the end of the town proper, she lost the light from the storefronts, and the light from the streetlamps gave only a soft glow. A small flashlight pulled from her pocket made up the difference. Thoughts about Jack nagged her. *Who was he? Why was Anna showing signs of doubt? Judging someone before you give them a chance to reveal themselves isn't fair. Although Anna had considerable intuitive powers. She might know more than she was ready to admit.*

The prickle of a familiar memory edged in. Her footsteps and the wind starting to blow high in the trees triggered it. That summer she taught natural science enrichment classes to third and fourth graders on the mountain. Those grade levels were fun, but she always loved getting back into the classroom to teach twelfth grade English.

The park ranger at the gate waved her through, filling her with self-satisfaction. She knew she was one of very few people going up the mountain so early in the morning. Driving up at her own pace, before the bicyclists and hikers arrived, felt exhilarating. She saw coyotes, foxes, rabbits, and deer living their lives. Of course, the trip to the summit took longer for her than most people, but the album loaded with wildlife pictures reminded her of why she took her sweet time. Those days wowing elementary school kids with the magic of the mountain were priceless.

To be chosen as the fourth teacher on a team to teach those classes was a lucky break. Even the prep was fun. Kids on field trips were excited about getting out of the classroom. She never minded that the other three teachers usually showed up much later than she did. They barely preceded the speeding parents, who rolled up the narrow, winding road in their SUVs with speakers pumping out the latest pop music.

The teaching team was dedicated to their craft and the kids. Their diverse curriculum worked perfectly for splitting into four groups, so that they could rotate groups every forty-five minutes. She taught map reading, rock formations and types, along with cardinal and ordinal directions. GPS be damned. Maps, rock samples, compasses, and clipboards were pre-loaded with paper and pencils, and all packed in the trunk. The experience enriched all involved.

Except for that one particular Thursday.

Right after a gorgeous male coyote trotted past her along the road, she parked in the empty lot below the summit lookout. Unusual to have no wind, and it was a beautiful day.

She stuffed everything onto her little pull cart except the large chart holder full of every visual aid necessary for the lessons. That went under one arm. Pulling the cart and shuffling the charts, she bumped up the narrow rock stairs that spiraled around the granite lookout. Drag, pull up, drag, pull up. She was tempted to drop the charts and hold on to the pipe railing but kept navigating the stairs, tugging the cart, eager as she was to get to the top, unload, and take in the 180-degree view.

The door was never locked, but it always stuck, so she knocked it with her hip, nearly falling inside. She glanced around to see why it was so easy to open and looked right into the face of a man she had never seen before. He certainly wasn't the ranger. She noted his rumpled, tattered jeans and stained sweatshirt with a hole under one arm. He was far overdue for a shave and a haircut. Also, a shower. Where had he come from?

Her heart clenched. She was afraid it might stop. He didn't belong there. The gates weren't open to the public for three more hours. Her thoughts raced. No getting around the fact that she was a sitting duck with nowhere to run. If she tried to get back to the car, he would beat her to it. Fighting him was a joke. It might be an hour before any other people arrived. She determined her best recourse was to become an actress. Astounding what a terrified mind can do.

Faking a laugh, she told him he startled her. She mentioned the beautiful day and asked if he was a photographer. She prattled on; he said nothing. Nothing! The silence felt creepy. Her idea was to befriend him, pretend he was only a hiker. Her brain freewheeled. In the silence, an idea: Maybe he was deaf. Sign language! She signed, "My name is Olivia. What's yours?" He giggled. She thought she might vomit. She babbled on. "As you probably guessed, I am a schoolteacher and there are about a hundred and fifty kids—she exaggerated—and their dads on their way. Really moms, but dads sounded somehow tougher, even though she knew what a mama bear does if her cubs are in danger.

Unpacking and still babbling like a brook, she taped charts and maps to the windows. As she held up each map to tape it, she almost expected to be stabbed or choked from behind. The feeling that her heart had its own rhythm section brought on the wish for a nice clean heart attack, a fatal one to save her. No, not the answer. Next decision was to keep up the chatter and start teaching. When she glanced back at him, he appeared completely engrossed in the lessons. His eyes had lost their dullness and looked interested and aware. For a second, she was ready to take credit for her amazing teaching ability. What a joke. When his attention flickered to the wall behind her, she turned and saw the maps sliding off the fogged, damp windows. She froze as she heard him move. Mr. Silence had moved to his backpack. It was big, dark green, and muddy on the bottom. She hadn't noticed it before. What now? He rummaged inside and brought out a roll of duct tape and a red rag. *Here we go*. She thought she was dead.

Without a word, he started tearing off tape, but after a few pieces, he reached behind his back pulled a hunting knife out of his belt. She felt her digestive system turn to jelly and thought about ads she'd seen for adult diapers. Without moving a muscle, she watched him cut lengths of tape with the knife, then slowly stuck the maps back onto the windows, and with care, making sure they were straight. Nearly giddy with relief, she kept up the vivacious teacher act by giving him a lesson in ordinal directions.

The reference material was posted, the clipboards lined up like soldiers along the wide flat rock windowsill, but the compasses were still in the box. She went for broke and asked him to place them out on the table. He did another careful job. She allowed the teacher in her to step in front of her terrified self and look for the child in him who had somehow missed out on school. This mysterious man got a complete field trip of information. He at least appeared captivated. She thrilled to finally hear cars approaching the parking lot.

"They're here!" She chirped, then flew out the door.

People climbed out of the cars. She had only a moment to tell the teachers about her new silent student. With legs like cement and three other teachers flanking, she went back up to the observatory, pulled open the door, but he was gone. His backpack was gone too, but he had left the duct tape for her.

Where was he? No other car was in the lot when she arrived. Had he hiked up and avoided the gatekeeper? It was over three thousand feet in elevation. What was he thinking? Why was he silent? The teachers had made a quick decision to let the parents know, go on with the schedule, and to keep an eye out. To them, he sounded harmless, even though she had told them about the knife and duct tape. She wanted everyone to return to their cars and go.

One teacher drove back down to the ranger station. The ranger refused to leave his post, but promised someone would be called to go up as soon as possible. That meant an hour, no help at all. Sitting geese.

Olivia brought her thoughts back to the present. She was almost home. The temperature dropped as the wind grew in strength. Remembering that guy made her feel a little spooky, so she tried to slough off the feeling by turning on the radio and humming along. *I cannot believe we were that naïve. We should have spun out of there and called the police.*

She remembered that her group began in the summit's observation area, getting the foundation of the lessons before she led them on the 1.5-mile hike around the rim of the mountain. Each child had a parent in tow. It felt secure. The hike showcased rock formations and stellar views. About halfway around, the point of no return, some might say, that prickly feeling of someone watching started up her back. She glanced up at the hillside that boxed in the trail on one side. There he was, quietly observing. He was about thirty feet above the group but only about twenty feet below the lookout, sitting partly behind a large bush with his backpack alongside. He didn't return her wobbly smile as she described the bed of chert, a smooth, waxy-looking, sedimentary rock. She recalled clearly how she kept orating and pointing as though this was the most important rock in the history of all rocks.

Getting the students and parents loaded back into their cars was a deep relief, she remembered that. They might as well have climbed Mount Everest for all the relief she felt when everyone found their way back to their vehicles. The other teachers helped pack up the teaching tools from the observation tower. Everyone left at the same time. As she drove back down the mountain, she had wondered about him as she did now. Had she judged him too harshly? Given more time, maybe he might have revealed himself to be merely a lonely hiker. Could she have helped him garner an education somehow? Partway down the mountain, she had passed a ranger. He was looking over a van parked behind a downed tree. There were rules about parking only in designated parking areas. Most people got ticketed. With a wave, she went on.

Olivia again willed herself back to the present and began a mental grocery list for the café. She tried to get the shopping done on one trip and hoped it might last a few days. She always pictured the aisles of the store and shopped mentally before she got home to start the list. Once inside her cozy, tidy house, she reached for the notepad on the table by her chair and the vivid realization hit her like a brick. She fell into the chair and screamed. She never had given any thought to the van parked behind the fallen tree that day. Now, in her mind's eye, she saw the familiar logo on its side. There it was. The faded, scratched logo with the plumbing company's name and a golden sun above the words. He was older, but it had been him.

13
BAD BOY COUSIN

Straight down through the heart of California, the trip from Umbra River to Garland was now into its fifth hour. Anna and Emmaline had started out at daybreak. Grandma Ming was expecting them for lunch. Anna kept their stops to a minimum, only bathroom breaks, snacks, and gasoline. In the background played Anna's beloved road trip playlist: Journey, Aerosmith, Queen, Twisted Sister, and Prince.

Emmaline reached over to turn the volume down. "Poor Grandma Ming," she said. "I have so many questions. But please poke me if I come on too strong, and please tell me to back off if this is too personal. But do you carry any resentment toward your birth parents? I mean, for not raising you. Do you even know if they were together? Like married?"

Carefully choosing her words, Anna said, "I had the best of childhoods. My adoptive parents did everything just right. I do, however, recognize that being adopted and not knowing the circumstances has shadowed me with feelings of inferiority. Those feelings have driven some of my decisions. But I view those as lessons, too."

They rode in silence for the last five miles of the trip. Main Street in Garland was wide enough to allow nose-in parking, but only six blocks long. Brick buildings and awnings gave the town character.

"What is this town about, Anna?" asked Emmaline.

"I don't know for sure. I remember a railroad station here. As a kid, I'd see passenger and freight trains come through. I think it is closed now. About six thousand people live here. There is a cow on their town logo. What's that tell you?"

The small board and batten ranch style home sat on a corner lot surrounded by lawn with a huge, fenced garden. A cracked flagstone patio abutted a screened porch. Anna felt comforted by the fact that not much had changed since her last visit. Although, the roof looked worn and the eaves on the weather side drooped. The occupants of a large aviary inside the porch chirped, squawked, and flapped, scattering seeds and shed feathers across the floor. A lovely, silent display of blooming orchid plants in several colors preened from the other side.

Anna pulled open the screen door, loving the familiar deep squeak that still sounded to her like an old bullfrog on his last pond lap. She knocked three taps like always. Grandma Ming opened the old knotty pine door and peered through the screen. Her movements tentative, her expression questioning. Both thumbs and pointer fingers worked the hem of her yellow plaid apron. "Grandma, you still have the same apron! Is there candy in one of those huge pockets?"

Her grandmother's face softened. "Anna, it is you! Come here, my girl. How I have missed you."

The screen door flung open, and Anna got pulled in for hugs. "I have missed you too, Gram. Too much time has gone by. This is my friend Emmaline."

Emmaline looked surprised but happy as Grandma Ming drew her in for a hug, too.

"Come in girls, I want to get a look at you."

The scent of something delicious beckoned from the kitchen. "Sit right down. I'm gonna check the beef stew. Anna, honey, grab some drinks for you two. And don't let me forget the rolls in the oven—my timer quit, and I must remember to look at the clock." Grandma Ming acted nervous. Anna wondered if, like many older people, she rarely had guests.

"Gram, let me do that. Shall I set the table? How about you have a seat with Emmaline? She has been dying to meet you. She is a writer and is interested in our family's history. When I mentioned coming to visit you, she practically jumped in the car."

Grandma Ming declared herself Emmaline's grandma, too, and welcomed her questions. When Emmaline asked if she minded being recorded, her slumped shoulders straightened and she spoke more carefully, as if savoring the opportunity to rekindle the old stories. The day vanished into late afternoon, and Anna felt happy to have made the trip. It was worth the time and the drive to hear Grandma Ming's stories and to see her looking relaxed and happy. Plus, her stew was delicious. Just as Anna remembered.

While Grandma Ming visited the washroom, Anna said, "Em, I'm sure you noticed the house needs repair. What do you think about coming back here with me and a crew of some sort to work on fixing it? Grandma Ming will never complain or expect anyone to help, but that roof needs to be replaced, along with many small things."

Without hesitation Emmaline said, "I'm in! She gave me such terrific ideas for my presentation on Umbra River history—which is coming up soon. I love the idea of repaying her. I have a garage full of Trevor's tools, paint, wood samples, and more. Stuff I could never make myself get rid of. We can shop in there for supplies."

The difficulty of saying goodbye, though tempered by the plan to return within three weeks, brought a few tears. Anna made a mental note of the most urgent repairs the house needed. With Grandma Ming's arm around Anna's waist, they walked to the car, promising to return with a small crew."

For the first time all day, Grandma Ming was speechless.

Anna and Emmaline rode in silence. Eventually Anna asked, "We're almost to Sacramento, and it is getting dark. Shall we look for a motel?"

"Nah, if you don't mind, I want to get home. I want a fresh start in the morning to write my notes for the history presentation. It's none of my business, but why aren't your parents helping Grandma Ming? It's just occurring to me that in all the stories, the people who raised you were never mentioned, even though she treats you like a blood relative. Except for the few references of your dad as a young boy. Oh, and the picture of your dad and his bad boy cousin."

"It's okay you ask, Em. I never understood their relationship. Mom always hated it when I spent weekends in Garland, and she never talked about Great-Grandma Ming, other than to call her something derogatory. Many of my parents' big arguments were about Dad's family. Their arguments were so frightening to me that I usually escaped to my treehouse in the backyard. My sister never went to Garland with me, and I didn't think to question it. I have no memory of my mom in Grandma Ming's house. Dad drove me down to Garland, dropped me off, and left after visiting for a few minutes. The minute we arrived, GG took charge of me, and he and I went to fish in the river. Being so young when Great-Grandma died, I don't remember her. None of this ever seemed odd. I was so happy to be with GG I didn't care. I thought he felt the same. My parents and sister mostly spent time with Mom's family and not Dad's."

"It is all so sad. Do you know that I have never met your adoptive family? I know your sister married and moved to Minnesota, but what about your parents?"

"My parents moved east to be closer to my sister. Hoping for grandkids, I suppose. They expected me to follow after graduation. But that's when the cement truck crossed the white line, and they were killed. I spent their last Christmas with them, and I go every other Christmas to see my sister and her husband. Grandma Ming never mentions them. She is my family now. And you and Olivia."

Anna swallowed hard against the ball of tears in her throat. Her past was a mass of knots she mostly ignored, but after a visit to Grandma Ming's, she predictably felt conflicted, like she had done something wrong or that she hadn't done what she should have done or maybe if she squinted hard enough she could almost begin to untangle things, but not quite. She usually dealt with it by cranking up the music and stopping for something involving sugar and ice cream. Today she felt like crying.

"Wait, a minute." Anna said. "What cousin? You said something about my dad and his bad boy cousin."

"Oh, while you were off looking at what repairs were needed, Grandma Ming showed me an old album. There was a picture of two boys, about the same age, who looked like twins. I asked who they were, and she said the boy on the left was your dad as a young boy. She hedged about the other one, and I didn't push it, because I thought maybe they were twins and one died. She mumbled something about it not mattering now, and then said he was her sister's kid. And I quote, 'a more useless human has ever been born. Useless as sneakers for a snake.' She sounded so harsh about it I asked her if she and her sister were close."

"Whoa, Em, you were gutsy to ask."

"Well, listen to this. She said, 'Some relationships have a shelf life.'"

"My family gets more confusing by the minute."

14
UMBRA RIVER HISTORY CELEBRATION

Emmaline and Charlie turned right off Main St. and headed down the trampled dirt path toward the rodeo grounds. The nickering and heavy shuffling of the Clydesdale's huge hoofs sounded from the arena where the team stood by. Emmaline held snugly to Charlie's hand, as each of his steps was followed by a little skip—his body vibrating with excitement.

They had already dropped off Hershey at Besties and walked down the closed-to-traffic Main Street. Vendors were busy setting up booths. History Day was taking shape all over Umbra River. The sun shone as brightly as the smiles of folks bustling about making their preparations. Emmaline beamed inwardly as Charlie pointed out each poster announcing History Day with his mom's poem at the center. "I can hardly believe we're walking right down the middle of the street," he said. Charlie was her life's greatest gift. Her reason for everything.

The parade was scheduled for two p.m. Emmaline planned to give Charlie a preview of the horses and wagon they were to ride on because she knew he likely had forgotten the breathtaking size and potential might of these horses. Afterwards, she would drop Charlie off at Geode, where Olivia and Lucy planned to include him in their preparations. He was to wield the cookie scoop and wrap utensils in napkins. Olivia would make sure it was fun. Emmaline was needed at the Umbra River History Museum where she volunteered on Tuesdays. It wasn't all philanthropy. She regularly picked up ideas for writing. At times, people shared entire stories. Or they unwittingly shared speech patterns, accents, or dress styles. Today she would work a short two-hour shift as a docent. An influx of out-of-towners was expected, and it thrilled her to talk about her town and jot down anything interesting they shared. Her docent shift ended at eleven, which left time to take Charlie on a vendor stroll before they mounted the wagon and joined the parade.

***

Charlie claimed to feel an instant bond with the gigantic horses. Giggling, he said, "They're snuffling the top of my head, Mama." Emmaline had to pry him away to drop him off with Olivia.

With her hand on the door handle to the museum, Emmaline stopped to take in the sounds and aromas of the moment. She loved her part in Umbra River's big celebration. In the distance, she heard the huff and push of the steam engine, along with the clip/clack of wheels rolling over the joints in the rail. The steam engine and two open-air passenger cars had been brought in for the day to offer rides over the old branch line that served the town during its gold fever heyday. A historian served as both conductor and to share stories of the days when the town was thriving as a base for the hundreds of gold seekers. The rhythmic tolling of the steam-driven bell began first, replaced by the mournful moan of the steam whistle. Two longs, a short and a long, the engineer's warning of a crossroad ahead.

Rough-hewn, foot-wide boards formed the museum's porch deck. The railings were "live"—made from actual tree trunks—less than four inches in diameter, the bark long gone. The top rails were made from the same boards as the deck, cut in half lengthwise. Emmaline tried advocating for their replacement with sanded, finished oak that didn't release giant splinters, but the decision makers wanted to maintain authenticity and historical accuracy. So, she created a sign warning about the splintering wood. Two benches and several rustic chairs invited museum visitors to sit and enjoy the display of gold mining machinery placed on and around the deck, revealing their own story as they fell to rust and grime.

Emmaline favorite activity was leading visitors on walking tours around the machinery and explaining their back-in-the-day purposes. Most impressive was a huge, fifteen-foot-long water shooter called a Giant Monitor, which looked like an oversized garden hose attachment, and was used for hydraulic mining. Its powerful stream of water capable of blowing the bejesus out of hillsides and rock outcroppings. Gold is heavier than dirt and as the jet of water dislodged minerals and dirt, the slurry flowed downstream to the sluice boxes. Gold fell to the bottom and the sludge traveled down river. Mounds of these leftovers choked the rivers with sediment, creating a toxic soup that killed the fish, a food resource, Emmaline noted, for the very Chinese miners who were doing the bulk of the labor. The devastation left permanent scars in areas of pristine natural beauty. The story was a difficult but necessary one to tell.

Outside, on the right side of the museum, was a full-sized dredger. Its purpose was to glean gold from rivers and streams by digging out the beds. Beds that had formed over millennia. Dredgers left a permanent calling card—piles of rock where water used to run wild.

Emmaline had a hard time not sharing her critical view of the gold rush. Tunnels built to help drain hydraulic mines still posed a great danger to the community and tourists. Some had been dynamited, but not all. Many remained out in the county, filled with water. She loved to underscore the wickedness and greed that led to such a hazard being left behind. People in town sometimes referred to her as "a lefty," but she didn't care. One of her great fears was Charlie finding his way to one of those pits. Or any kid.

She ended her tours behind the museum, first at the stamp mill, which was put into use in 1835 and stayed in use through the end of the gold rush. It had seen the entire saga unfold and wither. Testimony to its quality of construction, the machine was still in good condition, and she used it as a visual to explain how ore was crushed to extract gold. A young boy, his hair flopped forward almost in his eyes, said, "Miss Emmaline, if ore means rocks, why don't you just say rocks?" *I would have loved to have been a teacher*, she thought.

The final exhibit was a Pelton wheel from about 1900, which sat in the creek behind the museum. Emmaline explained how water from the swift river flowed into the penstock (pipe), which became a jet of water aimed at the turbines (buckets) on the wheel, which made the wheel turn fast. This spun a generator, creating electricity. The faster water flowed through the wheel, the more electricity was created. From the back of the group, a familiar voice said, "There she goes again. Just call a bucket a bucket, for Pete's sake." Then, right in front of Emmaline, an adorable little girl said, "It looks like a Ferris Wheel. We could ride it and get dumped out in the river. It would be so much fun."

Having arrived at the museum, she took in the satisfying aromas of old wood, oil, and dirt. Four windows on each side of the building, as well as open sliding barn doors at the back, let in plenty of light, which was decorated with swirling dust motes. The ceiling was open beamed and dotted with bird nests, including one belonging to a barn owl who had decided to roost and had to be shooed out. Sparrows were one thing, barn owls another. Originally, the building had been a blacksmith shop. The forge, made of local river rock, still took center stage. Tools used for horseshoeing hung from a metal rack suspended from the ceiling. A wooden barrel, its rings barely holding on, stored lengths of metal used for the shoes themselves. Free standing poster boards placed around the room carried photos of Umbra River's history. The photos depicted farming, ranching, gold mining, arrival of the railroad, and the growth of the town. Emmaline felt very strongly that indigenous people for whom the region was once home and who worked in the mines should be better represented. They needed their own museum. Also, the Chinese immigrants who came to work the mines and help build the railroad represented. They, too, deserved their own museum but they at least deserved equal square footage among the existing displays. Emmaline wanted to right these wrongs.

What little time she had left before she needed to pick up Charlie was spent answering questions inside, explaining the photos and tools on display. Near the barn doors at the back stood a refurbished buckboard, which had been used for carrying people and goods was pulled by horses. It had been repainted and the seat recovered by a local historian who kept the upgrades historically accurate. A perfect spot for family photos, with Emmaline serving as the photographer.

***

Right on time, Olivia delivered Charlie to her, ready to go. Emmaline noticed dark circles under her friend's eyes, and her pale face, but she refrained from questioning it. Of the three of them, Olivia was the most capable but also the most reticent. Who did she turn to when she needed an ear if she wasn't turning to her or Anna? Emmaline decided long ago that not everyone needed the same level of assistance with getting through life. Some people were born knowing how to cope. Others leaned on friends and family members. Others cried into their pillows at night. She felt sad realizing that Liv was one of the latter. Olivia smiled and shooed them off as Charlie, practically buzzing with energy, skipped off to check out the street vendors.

She and Charlie sampled every food item they could. She bought many handcrafted items, feeling set for impromptu gift-giving now for decades. Deciding they both needed a little rest before heading for the rodeo grounds, she made a quick stop at Geode to shelve her purchases in her writing room. After the parade Emmaline had planned on attending the rodeo exhibition, featuring steer wrestling, team roping, barrel racing, bronc riding, and a few events for young cowboys and cowgirls such as goat-tying and greased pig chasing. But when she described it, Charlie balked and refused to attend, saying he could feel and hear the fear in the animals. "But not from the Clydesdales," he said "The Clydesdales are happy. They like us."

As they came into view of Geode, "the retired guys", as Olivia called them, were sitting predictably on the deck and called out, "Hey Buddy." Charlie raced up to the table to give out knuckle knocks. They wished him well with his wagon ride in the parade and said they would watch for him. Emmaline was pleased to see male bonding had transpired while she was at the museum. Charlie was part of the gang.

Next, they checked on Hershey and Anna and found them in the play area, with Sparky and three more local dogs tied up for safekeeping. Anna had them doing tricks for treats and was just about to take them outside for a run in a fenced-in section set aside for that reason. Charlie was happy to take the dogs out while Emmaline filled in Anna on the morning's adventures. Soon it was time to head for the wagon and the start of the parade.

A ladder allowed Emmaline and Charlie to reach the height of the wagon seat. Charlie looked for a seat belt and blushed when he realized his mistake. Before they climbed aboard, the horses' handler had both Charlie and Emmaline meet with the horses again. It was pure love for Charlie. He leaned against a huge, warm cheek lowered to his level, stroking the muzzle. The horse's eyes were soft and half-closed, comfortable with this little boy.

With everyone settled in their seat, the driver softly called out, "Hup" and the enormous, sweet-natured team arched their necks and stepped out. Charlie sat between Emmaline and the driver, but that didn't stop him from waving and calling out to everyone he knew, along with those he had never met. Emmaline took in the sights, feelings, and sounds in anticipation of having pages of notes to write. They passed Geode and the crew on the deck whooped and hollered for Charlie. Emmaline had never seen Charlie so engaged and in his element. Her shy little fellow wasn't shy at all. He was thriving with this attention. He was sparkling and happy.

A sizeable crowd gathered at the "accolades" ceremony. The sun had set. Clouds were gathering over the ridgelines, and a light wind was kicking up. Main Street, Umbra River, took on a fairyland aspect, with twinkling lights strung between the lampposts and stores still aglow from the inside. Most vendors had packed up and gone, but a few food vendors stayed and were giving away leftovers. Among other speakers, Emmaline read her poem aloud to the crowd and then proudly accepted a commemorative plaque with much gratitude from the town leaders.

Tired and overloaded with fair food, Emmaline and Charlie picked up Hershey and headed home. As they walked toward their front door, Charlie stopped to look at the dark clouds rolling in. He watched for a time before he turned and heeded Emmaline's call to come in.

15
SOMETIMES STORMS FEEL LIKE TROUBLE

"I don't want to go to Mrs. Jorgenson's today, Mom! You can't make me go. I want to stay with you!" Charlie amped up his volume.

"But Charlie boy, you have a good time there. Isn't there a birthday party coming up soon? I'll bet there will be decorations to make."

"I don't like parties. I don't like field trips. It's raining, there won't be any outdoor time. I feel funny."

"What kind of funny, Charlie? Do you feel sick?" Emmaline reached back to the car seat to feel for a fever. "Maybe History Day and its array of junk food was too much?"

"I dunno. I get this feeling sometimes and it makes me want to stay with you and Hershey."

"Let's see what can be done. I will work at Besties, then I have office time at Geode. Hershey will be playing with Sparky. Neither of these activities would be as fun for you as playing with the kids at school. How about you try it and if you feel worse, have Mrs. Jorgenson call me?" Emmaline ruffled Charlie's hair.

"Okay, Mom. But sometimes storms feel like trouble. I don't like this one."

"All right, Sweetheart. I admire you for thinking about it. Remember, I am right at the other end of a phone call if you need me."

They pulled up at Little River Pre-school, better known as Mrs. Jorgenson's. Charlie quietly unbuckled, grabbed his umbrella, and haltingly made his way to the door. He shook the water off his umbrella and added it to the others in the rainbow-colored stand before stepping inside. Emmaline's heart clutched. He moved like a little man, not a little boy. She worried that his so-called gift was rushing him to maturity. She didn't want that for him. She wanted him to be a little boy for as long as he could.

"Bye sweetie! See you at four!"

Charlie didn't look back or reply.

***

Perhaps it was too much fair food the night before, but Emmaline was barely able to stay awake long enough to make the short drive to Besties. She felt so drowsy she wondered if this was what narcolepsy felt like. Turning up the radio and opening the car windows for fresh air didn't do the trick. Once inside the shop, she was so overcome with the need for sleep that she decided to write for a few minutes, hoping to awaken her synapses. The action of flipping through her file of writing prompts did nothing but mesmerize her further. Finally, she gave in and put her head down on her folded arms.

In a vivid dream, Emmaline floated above Mrs. Jorgenson's. She called to Charlie, but he didn't respond. He played a few games and colored a picture he had drawn of Hershey. When the rest of the kids were having their rest time, he saw the bathroom door was left standing open, hiding the outside door. Mrs. Jorgenson had her head down, working on something. Charlie crept on his tiptoes, carrying his shoes, and slipped outside. Emmaline called and called to her, but Mrs. Jorgenson couldn't hear her.

Through rain and booming thunder, Charlie made his way to the back side of Besties. Emmaline hovered overhead, calling to her son, but he didn't respond. The streets looked vacant, and the stores had no shoppers. Again, she called to him.

She watched as Charlie ran down the alley to the back of Besties and gave Hershey a good boy hug and then opened the gate latch to the dog run. Hershey leaped past him and headed toward the trail into the woods.

Charlie hustled to keep up. Emmaline hovered above them, in full control of this new gift. All of life was in suspended animation except for her, Charlie, and Hershey. She felt herself warm from the inside out with love.

Hershey kept his chocolate brown nose to the ground, snuffling for clues. Every few minutes he stopped, raised his head to read the smells in the air. Charlie waited. At the slightest sound, Hershey cocked his head up and listened. The footbridge across the river appeared up ahead. Charlie had never crossed the bridge without her. She watched as he held his breath, looked at his feet, and ran across, Hershey at his heels. On the far side of the bridge, the path narrowed, grew steep, and the woods darker. Charlie slowed to look around, but the woods were silent except for the rain that reminded his little mind of lawn sprinklers. How did she not know that rain made him think of lawn sprinklers?

A strong breeze started in the tops of the trees, sounding like a car or truck coming toward them. Emmaline had a hard time hovering in place and keeping them in focus. Within minutes, the wind came down to Charlie and Hershey's level, cold, cold wind. She called to him again, telling him he needed to come home. When the wind began to shove the dark, mean looking clouds away, the rain stopped, and sun warmed the woods. Hershey dried off with a huge shake that started with his head, moved down his back, and finished with his tail. Charlie was delighted and tried it himself, but he was still soaked. "Charlie! Charlie" Emmaline called.

Hershey stopped, frozen in place, listening, and sniffing. He slow-trotted to the right. Charlie followed. The trail was crowded with small trees and bushes, difficult to follow. They came out of the bushes to see a river bubbling by. Hershey raised his nose to the air and trotted downstream. Charlie followed, his nose in the air too. Hershey barked as he ran for what looked like an enormous pile of rocks on a side hill up from the river. Bits of black, scary-looking tree trunks and limbs lie around reminding Emmaline of pickup sticks. The area was a scramble of strewn rocks and dirt.

Hershey dug frantically. Small rocks and dirt shot backward like fireworks. Then, voices. "Help, please help us! Is someone there? Help, help, we're stuck." Then two voices screamed "HELP!!"

Emmaline yelled, "Charlie! Charlie! Don't! Don't!"

Charlie scrambled up the little hill. He peeked over a pile of river rock, avoiding the flying dirt to see a wide, deep hole in the ground. The voices came from the bottom, and now the boys were crying. He yelled down to the boys, "Hello! Are you lost or something?"

"We don't know. Help us! We're stuck! There is creepy black water down here, and we can't see anything. We wanna go home." The voices became high pitched, then broke into sobs.

Charlie hollered down, "I'll get my mom and be right back. C'mon, Hershey, we've gotta get Mom."

16
WE HAVE SOMETHING TO TELL YOU

Anna hated rain and wind and particularly mud. The one thing she thought rain was good for was washing off her perpetually filthy car. Most people in town smiled as they passed her familiar blue green, boxy, '89 sedan with windshield wiper swipes through the dinge. Her tidy shop and exacting talents didn't tally with her driving an elderly, dirty car. Pulling up and scraping the curb, Anna saw the water shooting down the gutters and edging toward the top of the sidewalk. Letting out a whoosh of air, she prepared herself for first getting wet, then having a light day at the shop. She had come in later than usual, knowing people would wait for the storm to pass before coming in for pet supplies. Surely no one would be looking to adopt during weather like this. Sparky was on his eternal reprieve. She finally had taken him off the adoption list. "Oh well," she said to Sparky, "You can be my consultant today. You'd better put on your sorting and arranging hat."

With her umbrella up, head down, and Sparky under her left arm, she struggled and sloshed her way around the corner to open the shop. Why in weather like this she didn't park in front of the shop, she didn't know. It wasn't like she was apt to be bustling with customers. As she put Sparky down and the key in the lock, she saw the lights were already on. She glanced down at a dripping Sparky to get his read on the situation. He softly wagged and looked up at her to let her know it was all good. She opened the door and picked up a waft of coffee and iced Danish. Confident that a marauding leash and kibble stealing criminal would not go to that kind of trouble, she squished in with her wet sneakers, leaving puddles on the floor. Sparky pushed his way in with head up, ears cocked, tail thumping a beat. Then he stopped to shake and spray rainwater in perfect fan shape, covering the foyer. Taking a minute to plop her soggy umbrella in the stand, Anna heard voices in the back of the store. Mopping the watershed would have to wait. She was too intrigued to stop and do it now.

One voice was Olivia's. She had her own key to Besties and the one who often brought in coffee and goodies from her café next door. With a mischievous smile, Anna stepped to the back of the store and peeked around into her breakroom-backroom-storage room-office. She never could settle on a name for that small space. At least with the new paint, it was a little more pleasant. Appliances were scattered around the room, a mini fridge, the most important microwave, and a cool box for the fresh dog food she sold. A farmhouse sink she loved was centered against the back of the room. The sink, rarely used for food preparation, was more often a tub for sudsing the four-legged rescues she took in. A warm, soothing bath was often the best sedative for a terrified dog or cat after they had gulped down a good meal. Anna loved to wrap newly bathed dogs in one of her fluffy towels, then softly rub them dry as she let herself receive their story. The most-often used appliances were the mis-matched washer and dryer. One was white and the other olive green. They worked great. Two more easy chairs took up space in the room, along with one caned rocker hosting a seat cushion hand-embroidered with a portrait of Sparky in all his tri-colored glory. Anna knew it was a sort of message that she should keep Sparky, but it took a long time for her to allow her heart to melt around that one. Her Grandma Ming created the masterpiece from a photograph, and it looked exactly like Sparky.

A six-foot oval table took up what little room there was free in the middle of the space, and it had many roles. At different times, a lunch spot, a groomer's table, space for sorting products, and always the desk where she completed her bookkeeping. But no one was in there and the voices she heard were coming from Geode. The door between the shops was wide open, and she found an extremely serious Olivia and Emmaline.

Anna was prepared for a fun reason for this break-in, not so prepared for the worried faces. The vibe felt ominous as a courtroom.

"Anna! We thought you would never get here." Olivia and Emmaline talked on top of each other, so that she couldn't understand either one. Now that she thought about it, when any two of them had something to exclaim, they spoke simultaneously, often using the same words. Neither of them looked ready for anything fun, however. Their faces sagged with sober concern. Anna stammered about the weather, the water, and the gutters, but she realized she was only putting off hearing about what was wrong. If only she could run out and come back another day. Sparky wiggled around Olivia and Emmaline, showing his concern by rubbing against their legs and hoping, she was certain, for a good petting, but getting their pants dripping wet. No one but Anna noticed.

Anna grabbed a towel to rub Sparky dry.

Olivia was first to speak. "Here is your coffee. We have something to tell you." She slid a glance at Emmaline and took a breath. "Two of our boys from town are missing. They haven't been seen since after dinner last night. Sheriff Dobbs is organizing search parties, and we were waiting for you to join us, and for the rain to break. It's Sammy Keller and Michael Spencer, Anna. They are only ten years old, and they have been out there all night. Em's having a hard time with it. She fell asleep at her desk this morning and had a bad dream about it featuring her Charlie. He is only five, and she knows how terrified these parents must be. How are you at dream interpretation?"

"What? Whoa. Whoa. Whoa, whoa! I just walked in the door. I'm soaking wet. What dream? Em, why were you sleeping instead of working? Why aren't you giving me more concrete details? Were you just waiting for me to get here and have all the answers?" She knew why. She just wanted to hear them say it. The energy of her two distraught friends was flying, pulling her in. She needed some calm before this literal storm. Truly, she knew this was personal, close to home, and close to their hearts, each for a different reason.

Sinking into one of the overstuffed chairs, Anna sat stunned, feeling the panic sink in. Questions were bouncing all over the room, silent but all-consuming. This certainly wasn't the way she imagined this day going. Images and thoughts swirled, but she needed calm before she could focus and interpret. Selfish thought, maybe this would end the speculation and rumors about her spiritual beliefs. It exhausted her to be merely tolerated by her fellow Umbra River inhabitants when she knew her ability was real.

Finally, Anna's logical mind took over. "For god's sake, call Dobbs, get instructions, and let's get going. The rain slowed down. Grab raincoats and dogs. Let's Go!!"

The scrambling began for raincoats and hoods, umbrellas remaining behind, freeing hands for phone calls and note taking. Anna grabbed Sparky and his leash, adding a box of dog treats to her backpack. Olivia checked the lock on Geode's front door, leaving the closed sign up. She knew Lucy would be in to open soon and would see her written instructions to keep the free coffee and food going for search teams. A quick phone call to Sheriff Dobbs' deputy gave her a quadrant map for her team to cover and a phone number to use for calling in any findings.

"Paperback Writer," a Beatles tune, filled the air. Emmaline's ring tone, volume high. Anna saw Little River Preschool on the phone's screen. Emmaline drew in a breath and before she answered, said aloud, "Mrs. Jorgenson has never called before."

The woman's loud and frantic voice was audible from across the table. "Is Charlie with you?"

Emmaline fell against the wall. Without explanation, she flew out the door.

The door exploded back open, and Emmaline blew in yelling, "Where is Hershey? Charlie is missing. I need Hershey."

"I'll get him, Olivia said. "He was so agitated this morning, I let him outside in the covered dog run to get his wiggles out."

Anna held Emmaline her by the shoulders, forcing her to focus. "Emmaline, what happened?"

"Mrs. Jorgenson is overwrought and hardly making sense. She said Charlie was supposed to be having a quiet time on his sleeping pallet, although she heard him whispering. The words weren't clear, but she heard him say, "Good boy, let's go." Charlie is so creative, she thought he was working on a story to tell the group after rest time. When she looked back from checking on the other kids, he was gone. Parents are streaming in. Sirens are screaming. Anna, this is exactly what I dreamed! I just need Hershey!"

Olivia's scream echoed through the old building. "Emmaline! Anna!" The two ran to her and saw the gate was open. Hershey was gone.

17
THOSE BOYS COULD BE TRAPPED

Olivia received an SOS text from Lucy. She couldn't keep up with the calls for sandwiches and for searchers taking their breaks at Geode. "If that coffee maker gets knackered, were sunk like a cement ship," Lucy said.

She carried a tray of water glasses and a full pitcher out to the group on the deck. She had no idea who might have wiped the rain off their chairs, not to mention the table. Lucy, she supposed, wondering how she found the time.

"What is with this water?" Albert said. "Didn't we order from the menu?"

"The menu is closed for today, boys. Sorry. We're going to be lucky if we don't start running out of food."

"Say Mike, you still knockin' them knees?" Albert yelled toward a man coming up the street. Mike. One of the deck gang.

Albert was an excellent target for his friends to make fun of. He always wore overalls. In winter, he paired them with sweatshirts, then T-shirts in the summer. His fluffy white mustache reached nearly to his chin and fluttered as he talked. The more forcefully he spoke, the more it puffed. Olivia thought it gave him the look of an emphatic walrus, and once said so, and now and his friends never tired of working that into the conversation.

"Probably be doing it long after your knuckles stop dragging," Mike volleyed. "Got room on your high horse for me?"

"Come on up."

Two new men arrived, and the others shuffled chairs to made room. "Can you join us after lunch, men? We need all the searchers we can get, and you are an old hand at this."

"Just got back from searching three quadrants, looking for those missing boys. One of the women's teams met us on the trail and shared information. No one has seen any sign. Parents are going crazy. I heard one mom had to go to the hospital. Thought she might be having a heart attack," said Chuck.

"That poor family. Both families. Terrifying. We are breaking for lunch, and then we'll go back. But won't you need to change clothes, Chuck? I know you like being the dandy of the group, but you might get dirty or something." Albert looked Chuck up and down, plainly noting his blue-striped, buttoned-down shirt with the sleeves rolled up, pressed Dockers and shined shoes. "Lordy, look at you, clean shaven with a fresh haircut. One would never guess you might be part of a search party."

"Don't get me started on that excellent walrus impression you do." Chuck laughed.

"Meanwhile, while you two are enjoying your wisecracks, Lucy is running her legs off, trying to keep as many folks as possible fed and full of coffee," Olivia said. "And look at that, here she is, right as rain."

"Och, it's only a small little thing I can do, so. Besides, I've got plenty of legs left. I'll tell you something, right enough, if Declan or Fergus, my little chiselers, had scarpered off like this, I would have tanned their hides."

Lucy continued to chatter as she scurried toward them and simultaneously placed plates of food and refilled coffee. Next, she whipped out her order pad and asked Mike what he wished for. When he asked for coffee only, she pulled a clean mug out of her apron pocket and filled it, scooted it over, saying, "Sugar and cream are on the table, luv." Then, over her shoulder, as she passed the next table, "I'll just nip in and grab your order, right enough."

Olivia noticed Mike's smile linger on Lucy. Recently widowed, she assumed he hadn't gotten used to the loss. "Mike, don't you be making googly eyes at Lucy!" Olivia said. "She belongs to all of us.

"Yeah, I see you, Mike. Thinking of keeping her for yourself makes you lower than a bow-legged jockey." Albert's mustache puffed around each word.

With somber eyes, Chuck shifted to Mike. "As a retired lawman, what do you think? Just about the whole town is out searching, has been for hours, and nothing has turned up."

"Have you heard about Emmaline's little guy, Charlie, and his dog? They're missing too," Albert added.

Olivia pulled up a seat. "Emmaline had a vivid dream about it."

"Go on," Albert said.

"She did. She dreamed Charlie skipped preschool and went out hunting for those two boys. He found them in one of the mine shafts. In the dream, at least."

Mike leaned back in his chair. "You know, this county is riddled with abandoned mines and tunnels. Hell, they even dug tunnels boring horizontally into the mountains and shafts going straight down. All supported by timbers that have rotted by now and caved in. Those boys could be trapped."

"Yep," Albert said. "They left behind those deep culls in the riverbed and mine shafts filled with water."

Mike and Albert jumped out of their chairs at the same time, "Let's go. Now!"

***

Albert was out of breath when he reached the Geode deck later that afternoon. "My cell phone is gone, but I have news! Emmaline found Charlie!" Olivia and two customers were the only ones present. She had sent Lucy home to wash up and take a nap.

"Well," Olivia said, "speak!"

"I saw her near a clearing where a helicopter had landed. I was walking solo, having split from the group of searchers to look for my phone. Charlie and Hershey were running ahead of her, so she made it short. But she said her first glimpse of Charlie was him lying next to Hersh in a clearing with a beam of sunlight shining on him like a spotlight! The chopper pilot dropped and landed. Charlie sat up and rubbed his eyes. She was the happiest mom in the universe. She hung out the door until the rotors stopped. By the time she got to him, Charlie was jumping up and down and Hershey was barking and running in circles. Charlie wouldn't stop long enough for her to hug him. He ran down the trail hollering for her to follow. He said there were boys down in a hole. Emmaline was bawling all the way. The entire group ran, including the chopper pilot and co-pilot. What a sight. I heard Charlie tell his mom he saw the boy on the horse again."

"I called out, 'Where are we going? What boy, what horse?' 'Charlie found the lost boys,' Emmaline yelled back. 'Nope. Hershey found 'em,' Charlie corrected. Then the chopper pilot yelled at me, 'You! Guy with the mustache! I radioed the sheriff. You go back and help him tell the search teams. Have the Sheriff bring ropes.'"

Albert caught his breath. "So that's what I've been doing. I came back as quickly as I could. I've got to sit down."

18
HERSHEY AND HIS SIDEKICK CHARLIE

Not one more pair of feet would fit on Geode's deck. All chairs were filled, and people were standing on the sidewalk and into the street to hear what Sheriff Dobbs had to say. He stood in the doorway of the café, a slight step up from the crowd as he scanned. As tall as he was, he didn't need much of a lift. His eyes were sharp and unsettlingly steady and appeared in no hurry to move off until they had taken full measure. Emmaline admitted to herself that she had noticed him, but he was much too old for her. Besides, she was formulating a plan for herself that did not, for the next few years, include Umbra River. She was smart enough to know better than to entangle herself with someone when she planned to get away.

The Sheriff began, "We're all so grateful they found our boys in good condition. A huge thank you to all who searched. Many thanks to Olivia, who kept Geode open to supply the search teams with food, supplies, and information. This little town is full of good people. At five p.m. yesterday, Sammy Keller and Michael Spencer were in an abandoned tunnel that had been dug straight down into solid rock. This was not a mine. It was a vertical tunnel dug to drain the excess water from the mining project. The hard-rock miners used dynamite, picks, and shovels for this mining technique to create debris. Debris put through sluice boxes to separate the gold. Now, when these tunnels went deep enough to reach the water table, they no longer worked as drainage and filled up with water. These were abandoned, creating the perfect trap for unsuspecting boys exploring the woods. Fortunately for Sammy and Michael, they landed on the only shelf we could see above the waterline."

A gentleman shouted out, "How far down were they?"

"About thirty feet. They never could have climbed out. The shelf is about ten feet long and four feet wide. There looked to be a small cave at the back. The boys had no light and were afraid to go in there. But they had room to lie flat or move around a little on the shelf. Sam tasted the water, and it made him nauseous. God knows what that water is contaminated with. So, they had no water or food. It was a critical situation."

Another voice came from the crowd. "I heard there is someone investigating this vertical tunnel. I've been known to spelunk and have climbing and descending gear. Need my help?"

"Thank you." Sherriff Dobbs handed his business card with contact information and motioned for it to be passed through the crowd. "Please call. First thing, we need to find out what is in that water."

A female voice asked, "Are the boys okay?"

"Yes Ma'am. They were hungry, thirsty and in great need of showers but physically all right. Only one broken bone. They are good friends, and I think it helped that they were together. The opening to the tunnel is overgrown and well hidden. Sammy tripped on a downed limb, lost his balance, and stepped over the edge of the jagged shaft before he noticed it was there. He said there were some rocks and roots sticking out and he caught some to let himself down without free-falling. As he grabbed, most came with him, and although it slowed his fall, it also took away handholds for climbing back up. Michael went to work to get Sam back up. There were vines nearby, and he tried tying his shirt, pants, and vines together to get to Sam. Smart idea, but as he leaned over with his makeshift rope, the edge gave way, and he tumbled down. There were a few spots where he could catch and slow his fall. Sam broke his fall by trying to catch him. He wound up with a broken arm and dislocated shoulder. These guys are brave. I'd want them on my team."

"Sherriff Dobbs, what do you know about their mental wellbeing? In the chopper, Charlie mentioned one boy who said they could hear sounds like crying and moaning while they were down there. My son is the one who found them. He rode with Sammy and Michael to the hospital in the helicopter," Emmaline said. "A perfect reward for all three."

"I know nothing about that, Emmaline. I am sure they were so scared they could have heard anything and not known what it was." Dobbs broke eye contact. He was keeping something to himself. It showed in the set of his jaw. "I haven't forgotten the most important person in this rescue. I was saving the best for last. This entire community owes a huge thank you to Emmaline's son, Charlie, and his extraordinary sidekick, Hershey. They are the heroes in this story. I am not sure how an almost five-year-old and his dog pulled off finding two lost boys that so many adults were looking for. When I tried to tell Charlie how proud we all were of him, he waved it off, saying it was Hershey who found them. He is the hero."

Sheriff Dobbs walked off through the crowd to the sound of hoots and hollers of "thank you, Charlie, and Hershey." He looked straight at her, pointed a finger, and mouthed, "You." Surely, he didn't mean her. Immediately Emmaline's ears filled with blood, thumping with her heartbeat. She felt sure she was going to drop to the ground. Still, knees trembling, she accepted congratulations from dozens of people, explaining that the heroic pair were inside, snuggled and sleeping in a beanbag chair at the back of the Geode Bookshop.

As the crowd dwindled, Sheriff Dobbs made his way to where she stood. She feared he had read her thoughts about him. He was handsome. And he had a terrific presence. No wonder he was a police officer. She worried he could see her trembling.

"Emmaline, are you doing okay? This had to be quite a shakeup."

She wasn't certain she could speak. "Yes, um, yes. You do everything you can to keep them safe, and then something like this ... well. I'm sure you know."

"Yes. Yes," he said. "Yes, I do. I understand Charlie sneaked out of the school because his dog needed him. Is that true? How did he know that?"

"Oh, it took me a while to recognize and accept that Charlie has a gift. He is more sensitive than most people and can feel what some animals or people are thinking or feeling. I don't completely understand how it happens, but I have witnessed it several times. I always believe him, now."

"Interesting. We have people who work in law enforcement who have similar abilities. I need to educate myself in this area. Thank you for sharing. Meanwhile, I'm a little worried about you. If you or Charlie need any help working through this frightening experience, we have a wonderful group of counselors. Just say the word."

"Thank you, I will."

19
SHADOW TOWN

Glint of Gold
Rushing toward the glint of gold
Desperate for wealth and easy
Misguided bullies of the placer
Blind to nature's silent pleas

Booming, rolling, rivers tumbled.
Heedless of dangers looming.
Greed will deface their splendor,
No more spellbinding plumes.

Peltons, sluices, monitors
Subdue the river's dance.
Spawning murky pools,
Fish won't have a chance.

Like splash flying off boulders
Humans took up their swords.
"Out of my way, I'm here first."
Blared the self-righteous roar.

Hardened to torture, even death,
Vigilantes in bounty stance.
Fifty bucks per ear, head, scalp.
The culling of natives and emigrants.

Screaming mothers, terrified children
Running, stumbling like the rivers they loved.
Their cries muffled by dredger drone.
As they appeal to The One above.

Emmaline took notice of the five city council members, who had arrived first and were now hunched into a group like a murder of crows. "Oh, my goodness, three of them have their arms tightly folded across their chests." She whispered to Lucy. "I think they read my new poem. Maybe I shouldn't have posted it until after this presentation."

"Bugger them, Emmaline dear. Face 'em dead on," Lucy said.

Darn that Sheriff Dobbs, she thought. What a charmer. She already planned to give a presentation to the community about the area's history. Then he asked her to be brutally honest, thinking it might help people to understand the dangers of the mines and especially children. He aimed to lobby to get the county to put up funds for improved barriers and maybe federal funds for more cleanup, but in the meantime, he hoped a little education would go a long way to prevent any more curious youngsters from disappearing into holes in the ground. Ha! And she was worried he was not thinking along the same lines as she. Giving a presentation was easy. Figuring out men was not.

She reorganized the neat stacks of handouts on the table behind the podium, listening to folks greet each other and the screeching of metal folding chairs being moved to suit. "Lucy, thank you so much for being here with me. Having you on my side gives me confidence."

"Och malarkey, it's you with the talent. I'm riding your coattails. Look what you have put together."

"Aww, Lucy, you are the best. Now, let's look. I have set out the papers listing my research sources, the bulleted list of the prime points of the presentation, and copies of the trouble-making poem and the Clydesdale poem, plus my business card for anyone who wants to get in touch with me. I'd like to shove all this stuff right into the council members' faces. My arms can cross, too." Emmaline still held no faith in her ability to change people's minds. The revenue Umbra River generated from its cozy western image was nothing to balk about, but she believed in faking it until you make it. She at least knew how to act confident. Living in a small town taught you that. You had to go through life ignoring the fact that you knew people were talking behind your back. She also believed there was plenty of tourism dollars in store for a town that decided to tell the truth.

Stepping up to the podium, Emmaline began. "Good evening. I am so happy to be here. What a great crowd. I hope no one was inconvenienced by our having to move the event from the museum to the school auditorium. I'm humbled by your numbers." She felt sweat pooling in her shoes.

"I'll begin, then break for questions and comments. If I stop in the middle, I will lose track of what I'm talking about." She relaxed as soft laughter followed. "First, let me say, this is a wonderful town filled with caring people. My son and I have been fortunate to be part of this community."

Emmaline felt a catch in her throat as she heard a murmur of caring comments rolling through the crowd. "I created a list of reference material I used to assemble the information I will share tonight. That list, along with an overview of this talk and copies of my latest poem, are behind me. In addition, all I will post this information on the museum's website. My hope this evening is to kindle your interest in understanding how the deep darkness of greed and lust for power pushed humans into performing and allowing horrific cruelty here in our county and beyond. I believe knowledge gives us the tools to make better decisions and choices. 'When we know better, we do better.' Thank you, Maya Angelou. Umbra River is one of many towns, rivers and creeks in America that were named for their shadowy history. The very definition of umbra is shadow, and I will tell you tonight why it is so named. I will share what I found through research about the atrocious treatment of humans in our part of California."

"Until 1769, native Americans in California were living independently and sustainably with no sense of ownership or entitlement but one of responsibility for the land they lived on. They weren't prospering, however. In the 1760s, explorers began showing up and finding the rich natural resources of the territory. Spain wanted to own this area of California—not only to exploit its riches but to keep Russia out. Sound familiar?"

"Spain and Mexico began to systematically colonize California with missions, presidios, and pueblos. Presidios were military, missions were religious, and pueblos were agricultural. Each made different promises to the natives in exchange for their labor. These agreements were a cover for servitude. Normal village life, food, and resources were being destroyed by interloping factions. Native men, and some women with children, were forced to join the missions, presidios, and pueblos, thinking it was a way to survive. They built the first mission in 1769. Native Americans were chummed in with promises of work for pay, food, clothing, God's grace, and military protection. The reality was exploitation, servitude, punishment, and disease. The Spanish colonists' objective was to take control of the land by using the cheap labor of Native Americans."

Emmaline heard the groans and gasps, but she kept going, "The Spanish and Mexican explorers and soldiers brought disease along with their brutality and lawlessness. Syphilis was widespread among the soldiers, as well as dysentery, tuberculosis, pneumonia, and typhoid. In 1806, a measles outbreak in the missions killed one half of the adult women, twenty percent of the adult men, every girl child under five, and seventy percent of the infant boys. The Native Americans had no immunity for these diseases and there was very little medicine available. There are stories of workers who were too sick to work being beaten for their laziness. To keep workers in line, they used military force. If a worker escaped, he was hunted, and either killed or dragged back after a solid beating. These actions were excused by couching them as controlling runaways. According to a book called *Rulers and Rebels,* by 1870 at least sixty thousand Native Americans were wiped out because of genocide, disease and the effects of displacement and neglect. Ninety-five percent of native Americans in California were completely wiped out." Emmaline paused to let this sink in.

"The mission system ended by 1836, and then along came the Gold Rush."

"Okay, I promise this won't be one of those memorize the dates history lessons. I'm just setting the foundation. I mention a book, among several sources I found informative. You'll see it on my list of source materials, *Rulers and Rebels*. It is loaded with much more detail."

"Gold was discovered in 1848 in Coloma—near Sacramento. This pulled people in from all over the world in a frenzy of greed. The worst of humanity was unleashed. The 'Indians' were perceived as less-than and expendable. They were murdered, tortured, and run off from the mines. In some of the miners' eyes, these 'savages' were using up resources needed by the miners. Miners thought they were trying to steal the gold. Horrible exploitation occurred, massacres, rapes, murders of women and children for sport. Pervasive was an attitude that fighting with an Indian 'aughta be fun.' Volunteers created forces to wipe out the Indians. With their whiskey courage, they rode out to find someone to shoot. Whooping through the forest, hunting, and shooting without thought—any age, any gender. James Rawls, a historian, writes that some Anglo-American miners banded together to form vigilante groups whose purpose was to "exterminate Indians" because they had become obstacles to the rush for gold. Many communities in Gold Rush California offered bounties for Indian body parts. Heads, scalps, ears. Twenty-five dollars for a male body part and five dollars for the body part of a female child. They killed men, women, and children as they tried to flee. One of these massacres happened at the confluence where Umbra River returns from its split and reconnects with itself. One of the most beautiful places I have ever seen and one of the deadliest, where supposedly thirty-five native people were annihilated. Families, including babies and grandparents, were wiped out. This was happening all over California and the West Coast. This is where the designation Shadow Towns came from, named for the spiritual shadow murder cast over the region."

Emmaline took a sip of water and swallowed against the lump in her throat. "Excuse me, I need a minute." She turned her back to dab her eyes and catch her breath, then turned toward the audience again. "The tribes mostly wanted peace for their families, their lives. They wanted to provide miners with horses, cattle, corn, and other vegetables and to be paid in gold. Many miners boldly took what they wanted without paying. Believe me, everyone, I am not saying every miner was lawless and savagely cruel. Of course not, but after having read about the so-called shadow towns, I dug deeper, which is where I found the origin of the name Umbra River. Translates to Shadow River. To the town counsel, I'm sorry my second poem seemed even more negative than I meant it to be. But I believe in getting to the truth, and we can take pride in the fact we, as a town, have grown beyond the shadow."

"Let's take a break."

Emmaline saw Lucy moving quickly through the crowd toward her. Lucy hooked arms and pulled Emmaline into an adjacent study room. "Och, amazing, you were amazing. Now go on in and take a pew. Just have a breath. Your information ricocheted across the room like an untethered whalebone from a tight corset. If you could have seen the fascinated, horrified, faces. Och, t'was all around the room, along with gasps and whispered comments. I've not seen such a captivated group in a donkey's years. Aye, with your pretty face and beautiful smile, great gobshite, all the while tellin' them like it is. Me heart is bursting."

"Lucy, you are making me cry. Thank you so much for supporting me tonight."

"Take another bottle of water. Drink some of it. Right. Let's go back in."

Emmaline took her place behind the podium. "A minute to get settled, then let's go to questions."

"Emmaline, what about the stories of blankets carrying smallpox?" asked a woman dressed all in pink, even her earrings. Emmaline felt relieved that it was a good question and not someone discounting her information.

"I haven't read much about the east coast Native Americans, but that story I have heard. Supposedly, the British colonists gave the local natives blankets they knew had been used for smallpox victims. This cruelty astounds me." Looking out to the crowd, "Yes, Mr. Brown in the third row. Nice to see you."

"Emmaline, were buffalo really stampeded to their deaths so the Indians would starve? Who did it?"

"I'm not well researched on this, but it is my understanding that the natives stampeded buffalo, then used the meat and hides for their use. There was widespread hunting in the name of Manifest Destiny. People in Europe wanted the hides. I'm not aware of others doing it merely for spite, although maybe they did. If you research and find information, please share."

"But we have all read about Indians murdering white people. Come on," said a grey-haired man wearing a wrinkled T-shirt, jeans, and a purple bandana tied around his head.

"Well, of course they tried to fight back! But they were out-numbered, out-weaponed, tired, and hungry. Keep in mind who was telling the stories. We have to consider how far we can trust these accounts. Their families were being massacred back at their camps, and their food sources were being used up. Their way of life had been decimated. What would you do?"

A female voice from the right called out, "What about the Chinese?"

Emmaline asked, "Do you mean how they were treated during the Gold Rush?"

The woman nodded, and Emmaline continued. "Another sad story of avarice and cruelty. I have mentioned that not all miners committed savage acts. In fact, I have a lovely story about a caring miner and his wife who helped Chinese immigrants. If I run out of time tonight, I will write about it on my website and the museum website. It is wrong to generalize. Yes, Chinese immigrants were seen as interlopers who were grabbing the gold. It became open season for them as well. The worst was the fate of many women. They were taken into what is now called sex slavery. When their usefulness waned by age or disease, they were killed. Chinese wives had to be escorted in fear of being raped. Even young girls were at risk. Chinese men disappeared, were murdered, and tortured. Similar story to the Native Americans. Greed made miners fear and then hate Chinese immigrants because of their potential to grab the gold."

"One more question, then let's call it a night."

A young lady raised her hand to speak, "I am currently a student at U.C. Berkeley and am on a student panel that is looking into the founder of Hastings Law School and his dark past. Do you know anything about it?"

"Thank you for asking. This brings our conversation into contemporary times. You probably know much more than I do, but the overview is that a well-known and well-regarded law school has the name of a wealthy person who possibly funded mass murder. There is ongoing discussion about renaming the school. Serranus Hastings is long dead, but he is supposedly responsible for six thousand native people being murdered by militia groups he sanctioned on behalf of white settlers who wanted the land for their own use. This included Mr. Hastings himself, who owned a vast amount of acreage southeast of here. It was a genocide. There is a news article published by *The New York Times*, October 27, 2021. 'He Unleashed a California Massacre. Should This School be Named for Him?' I'll never forget the disturbing quote from a California cattle rancher in 1860 who said a militia member killed a ten-year-old girl for stubbornness and put crying babies out of their misery. One last bit of horror, a man was standing with a toddler at his feet. The child obviously Native American. When asked, the man said the child was an orphan. Then, when asked how he knew the boy was an orphan, he calmly said it was because he had killed the little boy's parents. Please read up on this yourselves."

"It is time for this wonderful evening to end. I hope many of you will stay in touch through my website and blog. My contact information is on the bookmarks and business cards I left on the table. I will keep writing and will always be the best voice I can for the underdog. As I mentioned, my purpose tonight was to pass on some history and suggest you add to your knowledge. The more we educate ourselves, the less chance of this horror being repeated. Let's keep it that way."

Emmaline picked up her notes and backed away from the podium as an indistinct murmur moved among the crowd. One man stood and began a slow clap. The entire room of people quickly joined him. They were the last to stand, but the council followed suit as soon as the mayor hoisted his large frame to a stand and applauded.

Making her way quickly back to Lucy before anyone could grab her, Emmaline for the second time in as many weeks felt weak in the knees. "Och," Lucy said. "It's a teacher you are, for certain."

Emmaline felt it deep in her gut. The part that completely identified with Lucy's words.

Standing tall among the crowd, Sheriff Dobbs caught her eye and gave a sweet salute.

20
DANGEROUSLY UNSTABLE

Olivia walked toward the café's dining room, careful not to slosh her full mug of Breakfast Blend tea as she stirred in a tablespoon of local honey. She was taking a brief break and spotted her friends Albert, Chuck, and Mike at a table for four. Maybe they could pull her out of this exhaustive slump. She was thoroughly grateful for the boys being found and pulled alive from the deep tunnel shaft. Many good things happened in the last few days, but she couldn't shake the feeling of a shadow still looming. She lived in fear of a migraine, knowing that children going missing was a theme in her life. Oddly enough, she had not had a migraine since her realization about the white van and the man who had likely kidnapped Crystal—and several others. Now she was working on forgiving herself.

"Good morning, you three. Got room for one more?" Olivia smiled.

Two chairs scraped as the gentlemen stood to invite her to join. "You bet, we could use the company of a smart and beautiful woman," Albert crowed.

"How have you been, Liv? I know Geode is always busy these days. You look a little tired," said Mike.

"Yes, I . . ." Olivia stopped as Sheriff Dobbs stepped in, looked over and headed for their table. His expression, grave. Olivia trembled, thinking this was the shadow she felt. This was the news that another child was missing. *It can't be.* She wanted to run but knew her legs would not hold her.

"What are you all doing inside and not on the porch? Weather too chilly?" The sheriff added that he was looking for help, along with a delicious cup of Geode Café coffee.

"Not too cold for me, but Chuck the dandy can't hack it. It *is* colder than a miner's behind. Weird for the time of year. I'll pull up another chair. Get your coffee and join us."

"Tell us what you need," Albert said.

Olivia's table mates, too busy jabbing at each other, hadn't noticed her rapid breathing, stiff spine, and the terror in her eyes.

At the counter, Olivia heard Lucy say, "Och, the sheriff, is it? How about a cuppa?"

Dobbs returned with his coffee and pulled out a chair. "Olivia, nice to see you. Really nice to see you taking a break. I just need a minute or two."

Olivia nodded.

"Albert, Mike, Chuck, have you heard talk about Sammy Keller? He and Michael were the boys who fell down that abandoned tunnel," Sheriff Dobbs asked.

"Yes, I know Sammy. His dad is my good friend, and I know Sam's been having it rough. I should have come to you for help but haven't had the time," Mike said.

"Haven't had the time? Too busy getting that fancy razor cut hairdo," Albert said. "So, Sheriff, what is this about?"

Mike interrupted, "You could use a trim off that walrus face of yours, Albert."

"Come on boys, this is important. Sammy has been having trouble sleeping and eating. His parents are worried and don't know what to do. His nightmares have become so terrifying he's afraid to fall asleep. His folks have been taking turns sleeping in his room. When he finally sleeps, he wakes up shaking and sweating. Yesterday, he was sobbing and told them he saw something horrible in the tunnel. There was an opening to the side of the shelf they landed on, like a small cave. Very little light reached the area, but when the sun was directly overhead, it reflected off a light-colored boulder. Sammy stuck his head in and saw a skeletal foot. He didn't say a word to Michael or anyone else. He was hoping it was a bad dream. His parents called in a counselor, but I need to check the area and see whether there's any truth to it." Olivia thought, *Live with a nightmare and the horror never stops. The panic never stops.*

"So, you are looking for volunteers to get down in that tunnel and shine some light on the cave?" asked Mike. "No need to answer. Sure, I can gather a crew and get out there before sundown today."

"I wouldn't be surprised if you find a skeleton or even more than one," Albert said. "You know, Emmaline has been researching the history of the whole county, especially our area. The information she shared in her presentation the other night is credible and disturbing. Do you know what they named Umbra River for? Umbra means shadow. Like the shadow over the sun during an eclipse. Umbra River is known to academic types as a shadow town, meaning immigrant massacres happened here. Hundreds of Natives and Chinese were exterminated. I always thought someone named it for the shadows of the trees on the water, not the shadow of historical crimes against humanity. Shadow towns are all over this state and several other states. Believe me, the Chamber of Commerce isn't happy about this coming to light."

Dobbs said, "It was my idea for Emmaline to give that talk. Now, spread the word so everybody will shut up. I wanted her to talk about the dangers left over from gold mining. She took a detour, that's all. Talking about shadow towns. I am aware she has stirred everybody up. But everything she said is provable and already published."

"We were there," Albert said.

Olivia had remained silent and began to wobble. Sheriff Dobbs jumped up and caught her as she fell. Lucy was quick with a glass of water and a cool cloth. When the sheriff tried to take her to the hospital, Olivia insisted it was just fatigue and only needed a steady arm to help her get to her back room for a nap. Sheriff Dobbs helped Olivia to her cot in back to lie down, and Lucy promised to keep an eye on her.

***

Within two hours, a crew of six local men had gathered at Geode. Two were amateur spelunkers who spent their free time exploring caves. Olivia had rested, eaten, and was helping Lucy throw sandwiches together and box them up for the searchers. Large flasks of coffee, water, and iced tea sat by the door, ready to go. Olivia insisted on going with the crew to help keep them stay fueled. Geode was in excellent hands with Lucy, and Olivia knew being a part of the solution helped push back the terror. She wanted to help.

Olivia jumped in the work truck carrying Albert and Mike after they loaded coolers of food and drinks in the back. The volunteers all had been to the site of the abandoned tunnel, but none had explored its depths. Each had kids and understood the gravity of Sammy's fear.

Mike got everyone organized, suited up and equipped. Sheriff Dobbs had provided throwaway cameras so no one had to worry about dropping their cell phones into the abyss and so that chain of custody for any photographs could be maintained. Safety lines secured the two men who were going to drop themselves in and then tied off to trees. One man was assigned to each safety rope as the two divers rappelled down the shaft.

The Umbra River was high, its roar extra loud. Olivia couldn't hear over the noise, and likely neither could the crew. She brought this to Mike's attention, and he devised a system of signals for the men going below to use to communicate with those above. Two sharp pulls on the rope meant *GET US OUT OF HERE*. One pull, *all is good, and we've reached the destination.* They tested the system, pulled once, and everyone on top cheered.

When Mike gave instructions to the crew, he explained this search was reconnaissance only. They were not to touch any remains, if there were any. Photographs only. The film cameras were to be forwarded to Sheriff Dobbs once they got back in cell signal range and sent to authorities who would be called in to determine identities if bodies were found.

Olivia was about to pull out the coffee and sandwiches when she heard hollering. The two men in charge of the ropes at the top were yelling and pulling as hard as they could. Two more pullers joined them. Two sets of dual stakes, one foot apart, had been driven into the ground so they could wrap the ropes as they created the slack. Pull, wrap, pull, wrap. Now the hollering was coming from the mine. As they reached the top, the yelling voices became louder and more frantic. They scrambled out screaming frantically for everyone to run—run fast and far. GO GO GO.

She watched as Sheriff Dobbs sprinted to his patrol vehicle.

A bomb squad from a nearby town arrived with sirens blasting and lights flashing in what was to Olivia an astonishingly short period of time. She later heard that Sheriff Dobbs had anticipated the possibility of old dynamite and had arranged for the bomb squad to be waiting at the Sheriff's office for his alert. Being the experts that they were, they instead were waiting at the edge of the forest. She also heard that he had sent out a notice over the federal emergency alert system for citizens of Umbra River to stay away from the area. A patrolman also was assigned to drive the streets using his loudspeaker to warn the public about danger in a certain part of the forest and to stay away.

The amateur spelunkers had found a dozen deteriorating sticks of dynamite in the small cave where Sammy had seen the skeletal foot. A bag that had held the dynamite was in tatters and the sticks had turned grainy and decayed from crystalized mold looking like wisps of hair.

Anyone living in the area of Umbra River knew from the time they were kids that old dynamite was dangerously unstable and sensitive to shock and friction. They had all been told to run for adult help if they ever happened upon it. Olivia had to presume both Mike and Sheriff Dobbs been through this before, based on their level of confidence. She heard Mike tell Albert if anyone had wiggled one stick, had a cell phone vibrate, or lit a cigarette, the dynamite would have blown the mountain and all of them to kingdom come. The detonators were still intact.

The heavy-duty bomb squad van, built on a thirteen- by eight-foot chassis, had a difficult time rumbling through the woods on the path designed for hikers and horses. The van left tree limbs and uprooted bushes in its wake. Olivia yearned to watch them in action, but no one could be close except the bomb squad. One crew member left a mic open, and he relayed information as they proceeded. The same guy walked ahead with a long-handled chainsaw to widen the path for the huge vehicle. The truck carried booms for cameras and featured a rollout ramp to unload a robot to take the place of a human videographer. Once the explosives were spotted by the cameras, the robot would use a long arm to grasp the sticks. Two technicians, fully garbed in anti-bomb suits, were the only ones allowed to stay in the vicinity to run the robot from the truck's control panel. Mike gave verbal directions to the mine and then to the little cave with the corroded dynamite. Olivia listened intently to the reports from the tech with the microphone. She felt in awe of the organizational skills of these people.

Olivia had been smart enough to grab her binoculars from the car and felt a note of feminine pride as she watched the process through them. One of the two techs in the armored truck was a woman who was adding extension after extension to Boomer the robot before the machine was able to reach far enough into the tunnel and make a turn to the left. She kept track of the action on a screen and controlled the robot from the van. As each stick came up out of the shaft, they carefully placed it in one of the highly insulated, thickly walled metal containers used for explosive transport. Once every bit of dynamite found its way to a container, the camera swept the walls and nooks in the mine above the waterline to make sure none were missed.

Then it was time for transport to the designated open area for detonation. A painfully slow process requiring Boomer to move each container out to the field. Fuses with long cords stretched to the detonators, one stick at a time.

Only one fuse was needed. The first explosion was enough to jiggle the next box, then the next until the entire group blew. Olivia jumped at the sound of the explosion ripping through the forest. She was pretty sure it ripped something lose inside of her. The earth quaked like nothing she had never experienced, even living in California. The ground shook with lethal force. Over the microphone came the call "all clear" and those who stayed back jumped in their trucks and headed toward the boom. Olivia left the coffee and sandwiches behind and found a seat in the last truck. Everyone stood silently until Olivia said, "What horror had those young boys been curious and accidentally detonated those decomposing sticks."

21
I HAVE LET DOWN MY GUARD

Anna had a dinner date with Jack. It had been a couple of weeks since their last date and she could hardly believe herself going on a third. Dating. What a quagmire. Still, she looked forward to an evening with adult conversation and getting to know him a little better. As she remained in the dark about what happened with the kids' mother, she intended to bring it up.

The evening came around and Anna dressed in a formfitting emerald, knee length sheath dress with elbow-length sleeves and a cowl neckline. She added a softly knit wrap of taupe, green, and touches of charcoal. Strappy sandals in charcoal leather and a matching handbag rounded out the outfit. She felt well-dressed but not suggestive. For this occasion, she took the time to pull her long black hair into a chignon with a few wisps left to dangle alongside silver drop earrings, framing her face. Her denims and T-shirts were much more comfortable, but an occasional change of routine felt fun. Ready on time, seven p.m. She heard a car door slam at seven-o-one. *On Time. That's good. And in a taxi. Huh.*

"Anna, you are beautiful." Jack's look was sincere, his eyes appreciative.

"Thanks, Jack. You are looking very nice, too." Anna tried to lose her perfunctory tone. He looked like he took some time to put himself together. His slacks nicely pressed, a buttoned-down long sleeve shirt tucked in. He looked good. She noticed that he had worn green as well. *Well, I'll have to think about that later.* "Want a drink, or should we get going?"

"Taxi's waiting, Let's go." Jack held open the door for her and placed his hand at the small of her back as she walked through. He pulled the door closed, took her keys from her hand, and turned the lock.

A beautiful evening. The weather had turned warm, and Jack had made a reservation at the town's nicest restaurant, Jerome's Pool and Brew, an odd name, Anna thought, for a rather fancy place in a very fancy former bank building. He had asked for and received a table on a deck overlooking the Umbra River. After a stormy winter, the water rumbled along, bouncing over boulders and making small waterfalls. Anna heard the changes in sound as the water hit a deep pool just beyond the railing. One, a low *plonk*, a kettle drum sound, and clearly a change from the skittering and gurgling of the shallower part of the river. Background music courtesy the season's rain and spring snowmelt. The restaurant, softly lit with candles and subdued area lights, complimented the deck's illumination, a low glow along the walkway with white Edison lights swagged overhead, creating a romantic, magical atmosphere.

A waiter with a cordial face and menus to offer asked for their drink order. Anna asked for a glass of house wine and Jack ordered club soda with a twist of lime. When the waiter turned away, Jack said, "Anna, I don't drink alcohol. It doesn't agree with me whatsoever." She felt a little baffled, assuming he'd forgotten that he'd told her about the DUI on their first meeting. She nodded and opened her menu.

They talked over the terrifying situation with the lost boys and unstable dynamite. Jack commented that he never wanted to let his kids out of his sight ever again. After some friendly banter, including catching up on Jack's kids and Mama Cat's kittens, Jack said, "I want to know about you. Tell me your story."

Anna looked at her glass of wine as she gathered her thoughts. Where to start? "Well, I was a happy little kid. Is that what you want to know?"

With a directness Anna hadn't heard before, Jack said, "Tell me who you are. What is important to you? You fascinate me. Can you really communicate with animals?"

"Being fascinating is tough to sustain."

Jack tipped his head and looked into her eyes, urging her to share.

Countering with equal directness, Anna began, "Well, I am an adoptee. My adoptive parents died when I was in college, and I have never known my birth parents, nor have I wanted to. My dad always called me pick of the litter," she added with a smile. "They were both killed in a horrific automobile accident, my freshman year, third quarter. I had to make up that quarter. The funds were in the bank, thanks to my folks. They had everything set up for me, almost like they'd had an inkling that they weren't going to be with me forever. Even though they were gone, I wanted to make them proud. I graduated two quarters early, with honors, and my graduation turned out to be one of the saddest days of my life. They weren't there, at least not in person."

"Had they wanted you to be a veterinarian? Did you dream of this since you were a child? Would it disappoint them that you aren't using that degree?"

"Right. I am not using my degree, but I am using my acquired knowledge. Hard earned, I must add." Anna sat up a little straighter and looked right back at Jack. He had already annoyed her. "They were like-minded with my love and interest in animals. They knew I communicated with animals. The day my mom walked in on me talking to my gravely ill cat, she witnessed my gift as even more than an affinity for animals. She heard me telling him I knew he held on because he knew how my heart would break if he left, and he didn't want that. Mom stood there, astounded, as he purred incredibly loudly and rubbed against my leg. I know cats purr, but not him. He was as stoic as a Roman statesman. He had never rubbed against anyone's legs, and if he purred at all, it was barely audible. I held him and told him I loved him but didn't want him to suffer any more. I let him go. He died that night while I slept next to him on the floor." Anna stopped to compose herself and took a sip of her wine. "I may not hang a shingle with 'Doctor' on it. But I care for animals in many other ways. I am enjoying my independence without the trappings of a practice."

"What do you mean by trappings of a practice?"

"I am among the many who dreamed of becoming a veterinarian because I cared about animals. We think we can save them all, or at least make their lives better. Euthanasia about kills us. If a pet owner can't afford treatment for their suffering pet, it's the only option. Vets can't stay in business if they give their services for free—even though frequently, they want to. Veterinary medication is extremely expensive and if clients can't afford pet insurance, they certainly can't afford expensive meds. If you look at a veterinary invoice, we spend much more money on meds and tests than the doctor visit. Clients can be brutal when they are heartbroken. Many new vets are paying off their education debt. Adding up debt, compassion-based fatigue, long hours, it's emotionally draining. Did you know, according to a report that our local TV station brought out in 2021, one in six veterinarians have contemplated suicide? That is two point seven times more likely than the general public. Besties works beautifully for me."

Dinners were served, and Jack ordered more drinks. Their conversation slowed while they ate and enjoyed their steaks. Anna wondered if Jack's thoughts were about the conversation or about how to change course.

"Wow, I suppose that is one of many instances of animal communication." Jack offered, a slight frown line appearing between his brows.

"Oh yes, so many," replied a recovered Anna. "As a child, I didn't know that not everyone heard what a dog thought as it passed by. They're simple thoughts most of the time. They are thoughts that just form. Thoughts such as, 'Walk faster, I'm hungry.' You know, dogs have a heightened sense of smell, and one of my most hilarious eavesdropping moments was as I walked by a sassy little Corgi with her butt swaying side to side. As I passed her, she telepathized the word, 'Stink.' I had been trying out a new perfume, and I guess I had over sprayed it that day."

"Oh, come on, do you hear their voices?" Jack asked skeptically.

"No, as I said, it is words that are impressed on my brain. More like a knowing. Sometimes I hear the words but can't really attribute it to a particular voice. It's hard to explain." Anna didn't need an animal to impress words on her brain at this moment: *Get me out of this conversation!*

"I'm trying to grasp this. How do you know you aren't making it up?" Jack said as he looked out at the water and then turned back to stare—no, glare—directly into her eyes.

"Let it simmer, Jack. Blind faith or blind dismissal, both evidence of a mind not willing to think. I know there is much about me that isn't easy to take in. I hide nothing or apologize for any part of who I am. Feel free to ask for clarifications later on, Mr. Former Lawyer. But now tell me about you. Where is the kids' mother?"

Jack choked on his sip of water. "Getting to the point, are we? I'm not used to that in a woman, but okay. Well, my wife divorced me last year. She has been terrific about sharing custody. The kids have two households with their own rooms in each, duplicated clothes, and school supplies. She even makes it easy for them to bring the cats to her house and then back to mine. I'm not so sure the cats like it, and sometimes I just keep them at my house."

Not used to that in a woman. "Well, what did you do to arouse her ire?"

After several heartbeats, Jack replied, "I collected a third DUI, and now I am disbarred permanently."

"Oh. So that's the reason for the taxi."

"Yes, and why I am a legal consultant now, not a lawyer."

"Disbarred for life? That seems a little harsh."

"Yes, for life."

"But why such a fierce decision? Disbarments change lives!"

"There is more to the story, but I don't want to take up this nice evening talking about my troubles. Help me understand your psychic stuff."

"Psychic stuff, huh? No, you work on your incredulity, educate yourself, and take some time to formulate quality questions. Then I will be happy to respond." Anna's mind rolled like a flip chart at high speed. Something didn't sit right. Pulse quickened, breathing shallowed, her body was telling her to *run*. She needed to pull a bit more background information from ole Jack before she wasted one more minute with him.

"This was nice," she said. "The food tasted good. Hate to leave this beautiful river, but I have an early morning tomorrow and had better get on home." Anna prattled as she gathered her purse and straightened to stand.

Jack sat stunned by the abrupt change. "I thought we might enjoy a walk around the gardens. This is a beautiful bit of real estate here with the woods and the river. All the nature we both appreciate. There is a majestic stand of redwoods I'd like you to see."

"No, thanks, Jack. I'll grab my own taxi. Thank you for dinner." She rushed past the host, asking him to please call an Uber. No need. The same taxi they arrived in already waited at the curb. "Gotta love a one taxi town," she said to the driver.

"Yes," he answered, "and I'm only part time."

Just before she got in, she looked back through the huge picture window. She saw Jack still seated, looking angry, a glass of amber liquid being set in front of him.

***

Anna had the taxi driver take her straight home. She all but threw money at him, then bailed out the door. It took three tries to make her front door key work. Shaking hands caused her to fumble. Before her tossed purse hit the side table, she slid into the computer chair and booted up. Google and newspaper archives might bring this mystery to a close. Starting with reasons for disbarment and ending with the regional newspaper archives. Within thirty minutes, she knew exactly who Jack was, her pulse pounding with fury.

The drive back to the restaurant wasn't far enough to calm her down. She saw him through the window sitting alone at the same table, nursing a glass of self-pity. Confused? How dare he give her that look as she gathered up to leave? She planned to undo that confusion with facts and see how he liked that. When he looked up at her stormy entrance, his face displayed hope. For a nanosecond, she almost felt sorry for him. *What a perfect example he is of how self-absorbed people so easily fool others.* She charged in.

"You son of a bitch! You lying, secretive son of a bitch. Walk away. I never want to see you again." Anna's chest heaved, her eyes sparking with tears, the anger too fierce to let them spill. "How long were you going to let this go on? You must think of me as an easy mark, lapping up attention and good times while you, you smug bastard, were mocking my naivete all along. Go to hell, Jack. I'm going back to my dogs. I can always trust them to be honest and sincere. They never hold back or omit anything."

"I never meant . . ." Jack tried.

"You never meant to tell the truth, did you?"

"Anna, can we take this to the other room? Diners are gawking." Jack moved quickly from the table through a swinging door to the empty extra dining room.

"Don't even talk to me. Go!" Anna had followed but had him backed into a corner and blocked, not realizing no matter how many times she told him to go, he couldn't easily pass her.

Jack smiled, "Anna, I can't go. You're in the way."

"I'm in your way!! Are you kidding me? You have been in the way of my whole life for months. I insanely thought I saw possibility. Long stretches with no communication, I thought you were giving me space, which I much appreciated. Now, you have the audacity to smile at me and attempt humor?" Anna breathed fire. "You irresponsible, self -centered excuse for a man. I don't need this, don't need you. Did you think that since I am forty something and single that I might be desperate enough to forgive and forget the kind of atrocity you are capable of? Were you thinking that you might hide your past forever? The meanest, most untrustworthy, abused dog has more character than you do." Anna's fists clenched, and she spit vitriol through her teeth. "Thank goodness the State Bar Association had the insight to disbar you."

"Ann, please let me . . ." Jack said, his palms in, fingers curled.

"Don't you call me Ann. Look at you! You even point to yourself when you talk. Is there any other human in your world?"

With a lightening quick move, Jack grabbed her by the shoulders and swung her around. "Anna, I am crazy about you. Knowing you, seeing you if only on occasion has made these past months the best I've had since my life went to hell. Please, talk to me," Jack begged.

"All I hear is I, I, I. How dare you. You are the reason Charlie has no father, and my best friend is a widow. For Christ's sake, Jack, his running shoe was stuck in the grill of your car! You were so drunk you didn't even know you hit and mangled a man. Killed him! You didn't stop! You didn't care. Your third DUI. Your life didn't go to hell, you blew it to hell! Then you let our friendship continue without my knowing who the hell you even are."

"How could I know the guy I accidentally killed happened to be your friend's husband? For all I remember, the guy jumped out in front of me! I just can't catch a break. I was even thinking we should marry. I bought a ring."

Jack pulled a velvet box out of his pocket.

Anna was pretty sure she was going to have a stroke on the spot. "Marry you, are you kidding me?" She ducked past Jack's arm as he stood with his hands on his hip and shot toward her car before he collected enough thoughts to give chase. A thunderstorm in strappy sandals, Anna yelled over her shoulder, "You chose to drive drunk. Whose fault is that?" She threw herself in and slammed the door. The old car started, but the engine sounded like a cross between chain saw and weed whacker. The gear caught and gravel flew.

She wanted to drive until she sorted out the soul-sinking feeling of having been so deeply duped. Drama. The word that kept coming to mind was drama. Too much drama lately. The signs had been all around, but she didn't see them. *Em nailed it. It was fun for a minute to have a handsome man interested. But Oh my God, marry him! How oblivious can you be!*

Disbarred! No wonder with three DUIs and a vehicular homicide. Of course, his wife left him. He made more than one stupid mistake. No wonder his ex-wife kept in touch with the AA sponsor. She had her kids to think of. Dear God, how will I tell Em?

Anna said aloud, "How could I have let down my guard?"

22
OH CLAY, WHAT HAVE YOU DONE?

With Bruno Mars pumping out *Uptown Funk*, Olivia's energy soared. She didn't care what the lyrics meant. The beat was flying her high. She boogied through the kitchen, laughing at her silliness as she headed out to her garden to pick roses, dahlias, and deep purple agapanthus for bouquets to punctuate the rooms in her little craftsman bungalow. They would still look good in three days, and the roses would perfume the entire house. She had cleaned and organized the place until it shone like a gold tooth. Jennifer was graduating from college and coming home.

As she clipped the blooms, her hips and shoulders rolling with the music, she tried to recall if she had ever been away from Geode for more than a day. "Ha! Never!" she said aloud to herself. Stopping mid-stride, she popped the dust cloth in the air and belted out with Bruno.

Olivia had already packed her bag and checked the map. If she got on the road by a little after noon, she should have plenty of time to check into the motel, freshen up, and meet Jennifer with her father for dinner by five-thirty. This was such an important day. Her little Jennifer, all grown up and graduating from Southern Oregon University with a double major, earning an MA in English and a BA in Early Childhood Education, along with a multi-subject teaching credential. The ceremony was the next day, Saturday. Monday, Jennifer planned to come home to Umbra River. Olivia felt certain the school district would snap her up for fall term. In the meantime, plans were afoot for her to work during the summer. Lucy adored Jennifer.

Sinatra kept her company on the drive with his low crooning. She thought it best to tame down the music instead letting something too jazzy tempt her to push the speed limit. The sky was clear and blue as blue sky can be only in northern California, trees deep green and carpeted beneath by tufts of ferns, higher up splashes of white dogwood, and no traffic in sight.

She was nearly halfway to Ashland, still on the California side of the border, when she thought about her phone. She did not recall bringing it or the charger. Reaching over to pull her purse closer, she took her eyes off the road for a moment to feel around for the phone. As Sinatra sang about having done it his way, she heard a loud *thunk*. The car juddered and pulled to the right. She wasn't strong enough to control it. She let off the accelerator and the car skidded, thumped to a roll, then stopped perpendicular to the side of the road. The front right dipped into a ditch. Her upper torso straining against the shoulder harness, she waited for her breathing to settle. The phone sat on the passenger seat as though waiting for her to notice. This could have been funny, but it wasn't. "You caused this dammitt!" she said to the phone as she grabbed it, knowing full well it was her fault for taking her eyes off the road. Unlocking the seat belt, she tried to push open the door, which was extra heavy because the car sat at a tilt, requiring all her strength to push it open. It refused to stay that way, so she slid out while the door bumped and bruised her arms. As she stepped away, the door slammed shut with such force the car rocked.

Olivia stood, stretched her back and shoulders, imagining that she'd be sore tomorrow. Not that the soreness could detract from her happiness as she watched Jennifer receiving her degree. Now she needed to get there. The front of the car was a startling mess. The tire was flat. The wheel was at an odd angle to the car, the rim was bent and cracked. It didn't look good. She snapped a picture, Googled towing services in the area, and dialed a number. The dispatcher took one look at her picture and said, "What the hell did you hit?" Olivia explained she wasn't sure. He said not to expect his driver for two hours. She tried two other numbers, but the first one turned out to be the best. Her formerly sunny mood plummeted.

Three thoughts hit her at once. She might miss dinner plans with Jennifer and her dad, Clayton. How disappointing. She hadn't seen him in a long time. At worst, she'd miss the ceremony. She thought about hitchhiking. Thank goodness she had taken the two-lane instead of Interstate 5, or things might have turned tragic.

With no other car in sight in either direction, she decided to walk back and see *what* she had hit, hoping it wasn't an animal. *Oh god, what if I only hurt it and it's not dead?* Within about ten yards, she had her answer. A huge chuck hole, wide enough to fit a whole wheel and deep enough for one to disappear into. *Thank you, California Department of Transportation. Just what is it you do with my tax dollars?* Walking back to her car, it shocked her to see she had missed hitting a five-foot diameter fir tree by about a foot. *My lucky day, I guess.*

Jennifer returned her call quickly. She insisted on coming to pick up Olivia and take her to Ashland. Olivia declined, saying she needed to see to her car, and if all went well, she should make the dinner date.

"Have you heard from Dad?"

"Not yet. But we'll see him at dinner."

With a grin in her voice, Jennifer said, "I wonder if he lost his phone again. Please be careful, Mom."

They disconnected, and Olivia went to look for a good place to read and wait.

Once her heartbeat stopped thumping in her ears, snuffing out the sounds of nature, she settled onto a nest of ferns under the enormous tree she nearly smacked. Birdsong, squawks, and the breeze blowing high in the treetops settled her. The wait was lovely, for a time.

Just as the heroine was about to meet the hero, her e-reader ran out of battery. Next, she saw liquid running from under her car, and then the weather changed. The treetop breeze became stronger, and the formerly clear blue sky was now dotted with clouds that looked like they wanted to clot together into a storm. She had been waiting only an hour, with another hour to go before the tow truck driver was due. Thankfully, she kept a jacket in the trunk, as all good mountain dwellers did, and it felt good to be warmer. The soreness in her back and neck grew worse. Her stomach growled. No houses were visible nearby, and hers was still the only car on this road. *What if some creeper comes by? I will call the police. Maybe I'll get back in the tilting car and lock the doors. Oh goodness, my first day in years I'm away from responsibility, and I am losing my mind.* She curled up with her jacket on and sat on a towel she found in the trunk. The surrounding ferns looked soft and plush, so she put her head down and dozed. The next sound she heard was a truck rumbling up. A tow truck with lights flashing, even though she was still the only one around. Evidently, the driver was thorough.

She knew what he was going to say, might have scripted the comments. Olivia answered. "Yes, I know it is a huge hole in the pavement. Yes, I didn't see it. No, I don't carry orange cones or spray paint, so I am glad you are going to highlight the hole for other drivers." She gave him the identification and insurance information he needed while he chewed his gum like it was keeping his teeth in place.

"So, ma'am, where are you going?"

"Ashland, sir."

"Oh, I don't go to Ashland."

"Is that right? Well."

He continued, "I can take you as far as Yreka, but I don't cross the state line. I can drop you off in Weed, that's closer to Ashland, but there is a good repair shop in Yreka, and you will have better luck renting a car there. It's only thirty or forty miles from there to Ashland."

"What do you think is broken on my car?"

"Everything on the right front, ma'am. Something's leaking, tire is shredded, wheel is broken, maybe the axle—what more do you want?" He smiled. She wanted to smack him.

"All right, get me to Yreka, please."

Olivia would arrive at her motel in her rental car in time to check in, shower, and change. She let Jennifer know she was going to be only thirty minutes late and to save her some appetizers. She was ferociously hungry, but she still had to make the drive from Yreka to Ashland, so she had to settle for a bag of gas station convenience store mixed nuts.

Jennifer texted back that her dad was still AWOL, but she expected him to be shined up and waiting at the restaurant. "The three of us together. I can't wait," she texted.

After driving around town a bit, Olivia finally walked through the gorgeous double oak restaurant doors with its heart stopping stained glass inserts. They looked original to the era of the building, and probably were. Jennifer came flying from the back and grabbed her in a big hug. "Did you bring Dad?" She looked past her mom.

"No Dad, Sweetie. Let's get to the table. I've had a day." Olivia asked the waiter to bring iced tea for Jennifer and coffee for her. She let him know they were waiting for a third party and needed time to order.

"Oh, Jen, I am so excited about tomorrow and so very proud of you. I keep thinking about all you have accomplished. I tip my cup of coffee to you," she smiled. "I don't want you to worry about your dad."

"Mom, I'm panicking. This isn't like him to ignore us at a time like this. I mean, it's a master's degree. But I don't have to walk. Do you think we should go looking for him?"

"He has talked to both of us in the last week, making sure he knew the plan and the details. Am I right?"

"Yes, of course. He asked me where you were staying. He wanted a reservation at the same place. Mom, he was absolute about being here, and he was absolute that I should walk!"

"I know he was. So, let's give him a little more time, and then top of my list is to check with the motel and see if he registered. Does he still have that neighbor he is good friends with? I think his name is Larry?"

"No, Barry. Barry moved to Italy last month. Just up and made a life changing decision. Dad was bummed. He doesn't socialize with too many people."

"Okay, he retired, so we can't check with his workplace. Was he dating anyone?" Jennifer shook her head no. "Of course not, Mom. He still hoped for you to come back."

Ignoring Jennifer's comment, Olivia said, "If he isn't here by the time your ceremony starts, I will call Sheriff Dobbs and ask him to reach out to the police near Dad's house to do a welfare check. Maybe he can check with highway patrol for us, too. But right now, I think it's too soon to worry."

"Let's do it now. Can you call Dobbs from here?" Not waiting for an answer, she added, "I can't go to the ceremony if he isn't there. I just can't. I won't."

"Yes, you will attend your ceremony. Jennifer, you earned this and it's a day you will never experience again. If I don't see him there, I will make sure to video every minute and share it with him when he finds us and grovels for being late. How about you place our orders, and I'll step outside to make the call so you can relax? I'll have whatever you are having. I'm so hungry, anything is fine. Oh, except calamari. Yuck." Olivia was trying to keep things light, but she had a nagging feeling. The day had been too weird. The entire month had been too weird. Something was wrong.

By the time she returned from talking with Sheriff Dobbs and answering his questions, their meals were at the table. "The sheriff is sending one of his off-duty deputies over to your dad's. He will call if he has any information to share. His suggestion was to enjoy this time. Clay is probably fine and had car trouble or something."

"Is he just blowing smoke because it's too soon to report him missing?"

"We talked about that. In California, it is never too soon to report a person missing. There is no waiting period. Law enforcement can ping a cell phone to see how close it is to specific cell towers. Also, if 911 has been called, emergency call centers can pinpoint a phone within a thirty-to-one-hundred-yard radius. I hope he is still in California. I know nothing about how Oregon handles this."

They chatted pointlessly, neither of them able to concentrate. Both had lost their appetites and had to ask for takeout containers. Olivia noticed a mini fridge in the motel room. They might want to nibble later. At the check-in desk, she asked about a single man being registered to stay for two nights. She gave his name and description. The clerk was reluctant, so Olivia told her the story and why they needed to know. Jennifer helped by pinioning the poor girl in place with her seething stare. Yes, he had made a reservation two weeks ago but hadn't registered yet. The clerk glanced back at them as she scurried to a back room.

Olivia's room had two doubles, so it was easy for Jennifer to stay the night. They waited together, pretending to read the paperbacks they had chosen from the lobby library, hoping for the sheriff to call.

Sheriff Dobbs called their motel room at three in the morning. Clayton's house was completely abandoned, even the furniture was gone. The deputy looked through every window. No one lived there. Clay's cell phone last pinged the cell tower near the railroad station in Dunsmuir, which was where he had planned on taking Amtrak to Ashland. His new car would be left at the train station where they planned to pick it up on their way south in the moving truck after the graduation ceremony. Jennifer was excited about following him in the new car.

A grand plan that never transpired.

The deputy found Clay's car in the parking lot of the railway station. A brand-new Miata. Bright canary yellow. The doors were locked, but he had told Jennifer as soon as he bought it that the keycode was her birth date. She gave the sheriff the keycode, and he let her know that an envelope addressed to her was on the front seat, atop two sets of keys. Jennifer reminded Olivia of how excited he was about his new "midlife crisis car," as he called it. He wanted to drive it up to Ashland to show it off but decided to take the train instead.

Olivia had taught both of Sheriff Dobbs' kids, and his late wife had helped in the classroom. She considered him a friend. He paid that off-duty deputy out of his own pocket to drive the envelope and the new car keys to the motel. When Olivia and Jennifer arrived at the motel room, a red light on the phone was blinking. That blink felt louder than a fire alarm. The message told of a note left at the motel desk.

Oh Clay, what have you done?

Angst turned to anger as Jennifer read the letter aloud.

"My Sweet Jennifer,
Please try to understand. I love you more than anyone or anything else in my life. It was not a simple decision to upheave my life, leave you behind, and miss your magnificent day. If you received this letter, you

have found your graduation gift. The car is registered in your name, and I paid for the insurance for the next two years.

I have moved to Italy. The region of Veneto is known for topnotch wine, and Barry and I bought a small winery with a huge vineyard. The owner is dying, and we had to make a quick decision before his heirs became the sellers. I had two days to get here to sign the papers. My realtor hired a crew to empty the house and ship some things to me. There are some boxes I'm having her send to you via your mom.

I am a coward and couldn't tell you this in person. Barry and I will be married in our vineyard in late fall. I know this is a shock, and I wish I knew how to cushion it. I didn't know how. Things have been moving so fast.

Honey, please come to our wedding. I'll send you the plane ticket, and we have a beautiful rustic guest house on the property. Maybe your mom will join in? She won't be too shocked at this. I hope she will be happy for me. This sounds like an excuse, but being a gay man in America is not something I wanted to face. I kept this part of myself quiet for as long as I could. Please forgive everything you need to forgive, especially my cowardice. I wish I had the guts to tell you this face to face. Please be happy for me.

I love you, Dad.

Olivia and Jennifer both stared at the letter as though it had more to say. Neither spoke.

Slowly, Jennifer stood, tossing it to the ground. A cougar's scream filled the room as she stomped on the letter. Stomping and stomping. "Well, there you are, *Dad*, choosing *yourself* first. I thought you were *my daddy*, but you are a whole other person. A person I have never known." Stomp, stomp. "I was your cover! All those hangout trips with Barry! Never just you and me! You said he was lonely. You felt sorry for him. Why didn't you wait one more week or even a few days? No, not you. My graduation wasn't important enough. Well, you can just *pick your grapes*, stomp them into juice, learn to speak Italian—whatever makes you happy *'cause that's what you do, isn't it?"* With one last double-footed stomp, she threw herself on the bed, face down, as Olivia sat quietly, clueless as to what to do next.

An exhausted mother and daughter made it to the graduation ceremony. Olivia watched as Jennifer walked across the stage in her cap and gown and academic hood to accept her diplomas and shake the presenter's hand. *I have never seen anyone so tuned out. She's only making the motions. I hope sadness doesn't come through in the photos. Damn you, Clay.*

The morning brought clearer thinking, and Olivia jumped into action. She turned in her rental car, packed the yellow sportscar with Jennifer's travel bag and what belongings could fit in the tiny space. Olivia's car repairs were to take another week, so they planned for Jennifer to follow Olivia, who would be driving the rented moving truck filled with everything else. They spent most of the day packing and taking care of details around Jennifer leaving her apartment. Using what felt like a second wind, they hit the road. Next stop, Umbra River.

23
TRUTH NEVER GOES AWAY

Two trucks and one car, all loaded to the maximum with building supplies and people traveled south on their way to help Anna's Grandma Ming.

"Grandma, now that everyone is fed, back to work, and the kitchen is gleaming again, let's have a seat on the couch. I have questions," said Anna.

"Great idea sweetheart, I love having your friends here, but there's been no time to sit and talk with my girl."

"I feel the same way and absolutely intend to make these visits more frequent. You are still my family, and I miss you. I have a nice guest room if you want to come north and visit me. You know, Amtrak runs passenger trains from Fresno to Redding. If your neighbor will run you to Fresno, I will pick you up in Redding. I'll even buy the tickets. In fact, I would love to."

"Well, that sounds like a pretty good deal. I'd need to get someone to take care of my birds and plants."

"What about that charming high schooler who has been helping fix the roof? He has good manners and a great sense of humor. He keeps the workers laughing. One roofer complemented him on how capable and quick to learn he is. Maybe a little extra money might help him take a young lady to a prom or something,"

"That's Wanda's boy, Mitch. He is one of the good ones. Gets good grades too. I'll think about this. Today is a dream. These wonderful friends of yours came all the way down here to fix up this old place. How will I ever repay them? Or you?"

"First, did you notice what a great time they are having, Grandma Ming? It's like a party out there. They are probably trying to think of a way to repay you. But I do have an idea. If you come up to stay with me, you might create one of your fabulous dinners and invite them over."

"Oh well, let's do it. Sounds fun. Now, Anna girl, since your last visit here with your friend Emmaline—she's a love, isn't she?—I have done some thinking. Em asked some good questions, and it is time I answered them. Please bring over that photo album. The blue one. Emmaline and I went through it. I'd like you and I to have a look."

Anna noticed Grandma Ming take in a ragged breath and close her eyes for a second. Handing over the album, Anna said, "Here we go. What years do these pictures cover?"

"Let's see, well, mostly when your dad was young. I'm not very organized, so I can't promise the pictures are. How about you turn the pages and ask questions?"

The hour she mentally allotted for this photo conversation scooted by quickly. She knew the workers needed her, but this time with Grandma Ming was priceless. After they got through the many family pictures, she watched the only dad she had ever known progress from an infant to a young man. There never were photos like this around when she was growing up. She turned a page and her breath caught. The photo showed her dad standing with a boy who looked to be his twin. "Grandma, was Dad a twin?"

"That is his cousin, Kai. My sister's boy."

"Wow, they look so much alike and familiar."

"Alike in looks, but not in character. My son was always honest and honorable. Let me tell you, my nephew was worthless. He thought he was a big shot, deserved anything he wanted. My sister raised him that way. Good looks and no depth. All hat, no cattle. They were both handsome and charming, but inside, one was garbage, the other pure gold. Your dad was gold."

"Was? What happened to Kai?"

"Got himself killed, shot by a sniper. He was probably chasing some girl, that was all he was good for. We figured he earned the bullet. He got himself into a problem here at home, and his folks encouraged him to sign with the military. He shipped overseas. Even Great Grandma Ming pushed him out the door, and he was relieved to go. No facing responsibility for that boy."

"Oh, my goodness, what a sad story. Are you and your sister close? Were you able to console her? That poor misguided mother."

"No way. It wasn't her who needed consolation. You know, truth isn't always easy, that's why we hide from it. But truth doesn't do harm. We do harm by refusing to acknowledge it. Truth never goes away. Neither do lies. So, I want to talk with you. I have a truth to tell you."

The story Grandma Ming told knocked the wind out of Anna.

"One autumn day, there was a knock on my sister's door. I was there to help her sort rummage for the church sale. Land sakes, those rummage sales filled the basement meeting room and some of it had to go outside. People came from all over the county just to . . ."

"Please, Grandma, tell me the story."

"Of course, the knock startled us, and my sister looked out of the window before she answered. I glimpsed a teenaged girl looking like she lost her last friend. My sister talked with her for a minute, and I couldn't hear the conversation. The girl came in and both walked toward me and the table where I sat. My sister went mute, and I invited the girl to sit. She did, and her tears flowed. I reached over for a paper towel, and she bawled for a few minutes. When she could talk, she told us she was dating Kai and was pregnant. He was the only boy she had ever been with and thought he was the only one for her. They parted at the end of summer to attend separate colleges and made promises to remain a couple. She came home for Thanksgiving holiday and planned to tell him about the baby. Arriving back home a couple of days before he expected her, she took a walk around town and stopped at their favorite café. Through the glass door, she saw him at a table with her former best friend. At first, she felt excited to see them both, then Kai pulled the best friend close, and they began kissing."

"That poor girl. This was in the 1970s. There wasn't much support for unwed mothers then. I imagine she didn't want Kai now that she knew he was a cheater. What a mess!"

"My sister made it worse. She disbelieved this girl, told her to go away. I think she said something to the effect of 'Go hang this on some other kid. My Kai wouldn't do this. You have the wrong victim here.' I was so ashamed of her."

"Was this a local girl?"

"Either I never knew or have forgotten, although I walked her to the door and asked for her contact information. She gave me a phone number."

"Were you ever in touch with her after that?"

"Oh yes. I went home that day. GG and Great Grandma Ming lived with us then. I told them the story. They were shocked and furious, each in their own way. GG cried and said he knew something like this might happen with Kai. He wanted to find the girl and care for her. Great Grandma silently seethed. Her fury was frightening. Not against the girl, against her daughter, my sister. On top of that, your normally kind Grandpa Ming wanted to shoot Kai."

"But Grandma, what happened to the baby?"

Emmaline burst into the room. "Anna, we need you right now! The roofers need some answers, and the glaziers need direction."

"Wow, this is a lot to take in. I want to hear more of the story, but I better go check in. Need anything before I go?"

"No thank you, Honey. Get out there and crack that whip."

By the time Anna finished trading details with the workers and taking a last look at the house, Umbra River folks were packing up to go home. Several had ridden with her, so she was forced to leave as well. The little farmhouse looked dressed up. New windows and frames, siding replaced where needed, new paint, and an almost completed new roof. The local roofer had scheduled himself to complete the job in the coming week but insisted on being paid up front, and Anna complied. Mitch, the neighbor's boy, had called in his friends who gussied up the yard by pulling weeds, piling accumulated junk to be picked up, and putting yard tools and equipment away in an organized fashion in the shed. Mitch promised to return to bring the vegetable garden back to life and mow the lawn. Anna strolled around the house, taking mental inventory. *What a difference! We will need another trip someday to make over the inside. Painting, organizing a little, and cleaning are all it needs. Maybe some sorting and tossing as well. I can do that with just one or two other people.* She walked back into the house to see her exhausted grandmother doing her best to be gracious.

24
THIEF

Anna worked all day by herself at Besties, the customer count unusually high. Business, always good, had gotten busier in recent weeks. She thought back about Emmaline complaining that she had less time to write while on duty at Besties. Anna had merely laughed, although it surprised her Em admitted to writing while she was on the clock. Also, she apparently hadn't thought about who she was talking to—her employer.

"Well, that's Emmaline. Gotta love her," Anna reflected aloud as she straightened the shelves and replenished stock. She had no boarders this week, all the bookkeeping balanced perfectly, and she wanted nothing but to go home and read a good story. She thought she heard the sound of the door between Geode and Besties opening. The back door had been locked. Everyone who needed access had their own key. She always left a light on in the backroom for the town night-watchman to see through the store on his rounds.

It seemed silly to Anna that the town had a night watchman, as nothing ever happened in Umbra River. Still, prompted by Olivia, she started using the little wall safe in a closet the former owners had put in. She placed the day's income inside of it if she closed after the bank did. The night deposit drop didn't suit her. She knew the deposits were safer in the bank, but sometimes she let them swell in the fireproof wall safe all week. Thinking of closing early, she walked to the cabinet door where she had the combination to the safe disguised as a phone number. The weather, foggy and drizzly. She took a quick look around Geode, looked out the back door and thought, *I don't want to walk to the bank. I'm going home.*

She gathered up Sparky and decided to take the long way home, just because she felt like it. Something about the fog and drizzle made her feel oddly cozy from inside the car. First, she drove up and down the main street. Several shops were closed and those still open had few customers. Umbra River folks were predictable when it came to weather. *Tucked in at home, all comfortable and warm. Of course, people with families go home to start another kind of work.* "We don't have much to do, do we, Spark? Just eat dinner and relax, right?"

Once at home, it didn't take her long to get into sweats and slippers, with Sparky and his full belly nestled in his fluffy pillow bed. Her current read didn't hold her interest, so she paced. Something bothered her, but it hadn't surfaced. Maybe it was still the Jack effect. Briefly it occurred to her that she was experiencing a kind of grief. She still wondered how on earth she was going to tell Emmaline that Jack had been the one to kill her Trevor. Although Trevor had sounded like a case himself after Emmaline revealed the reasons for the gaudy makeup and the false eyelashes in that pink tackle box.

After nibbling on fruit and carrots, Anna decided she didn't need dinner. But that feeling of something wrong stalked her. "Sparky, did I lock the front door of Besties?" Now that she expressed the doubt, the niggling thought became worse. "Why can't I ever be psychic when I need to, Sparky? I better go check. Want to come?" He answered with a groan as he rolled and snuggled deeper into the pillow bed.

"Okay, you stay here, then." Anna kicked off her slippers, slipped on shoes, and pulled her keys out of the bowl by the front door. Concern had taken root as she leaped into the car, impatiently waited while the old jalopy stumbled to turn over, then shot out of the driveway, barely missing a racing yellow sports car coming toward her. *Where did that come from?* She sped up toward town.

Downtown Umbra River was quiet and sleepy. The antique store, Time will Tell, was the only shop awake, with lights on and eager folks sitting in folding chairs listening to a speaker. Anna knew they offered informative presentations about antiques. She meant to go one day. Only two cars were parked out front. *The rest must be in the back.* A few doors up, Besties, all dark. *Oh, maybe that is what I forgot about. The light isn't on in the back.* She drove past, then turned the car around and parked in front. She meant to enter the store quietly, but her car kept running—*kapuck, kapuck*—until it ultimately gasped and stopped. *Well, if there are any intruders, they know they have company now.* Anna headed for the door.

She turned the key in the lock, pushed the door open, and stepped in. The light in the back room flashed on, and she heard a chair scrape. Unsure but working on angry, she marched toward a confrontation. There Emmaline sat at the table with her mouth and the safe door gaping open. "Oh god, Anna, this isn't what you think."

Anna, shocked silent for a few heartbeats, found her voice. Deadly calm, "What is it then? What the hell are you doing?".

"It's not, I can't explain, just know . . ."

"You do not know what I think and have no right to think you know. Stop stuttering and explain why MY safe is open and MY money from that safe is stacked all over MY table. I repeat, what are you doing?"

"It's only a loan. I wanted to tell you but planned to return it before I needed to."

"Two people create a loan, one person taking money is theft. Before you needed to, huh? I thought I knew you. And all this time, I thought you were my friend. I took you to Grandma Mings! I've watched your kid!"

"I didn't mean to lose your trust. I only need it for a short time. It is an emergency. But you won't understand. You don't have a family."

Anna shrieked, "I what? Not having a family makes me a target for a thief? That makes me a moving target for being burgled? A patsy, a chump, a victim—that's what you think of me? Speaking of family, do I need to check with Grandma Ming and tell her to make sure nothing is missing? I trusted you with my grandmother! How could I not have known the real you?"

It struck Anna that this was almost the same conversation she had had with Jack at Jerome's.

Emmaline began to gather the bills and stack them.

"Do not touch my money. Leave it right where it is. I'll need to count it."

Through clenched teeth, Emmaline yelled, "Well, it is your fault. I wanted you to like Jack and to bring a lawyer into our group. He seemed like a nice guy, but you didn't see that. No, he had to measure up to your standards. The poor guy tried."

"So, you need a lawyer. You tried to talk me into a relationship I didn't want because you were looking for a discount lawyer? What? Next, you tried to steal from me. I don't even want to know what you need a lawyer for. Get out, just go. You're fired. Give me the key."

"If you knew what I needed it for, you might drop the high and mighty act. You're the dumb one. Keeping all this money in a flimsy little safe, which everybody knows the combination for. Why isn't it in the bank, huh? What were you thinking?"

"I was thinking I trusted you. Yes, I must be the dumb one. Now get out before I say more. Leave your key on that stack of twenties."

She followed Emmaline to the door and snapped it locked it behind her. With her chest heaving and too furious to cry, Anna counted her money before putting it back in the safe. When she realized she had to change the combination and didn't remember how, she threw the closest twenty-pound bag of dog food across the room, wiping out the formerly organized display of grooming tools.

***

Two days later, after Anna had driven her deposit bag to the bank two days in a row and calmed down enough to recall the procedure for changing the safe combination, she dropped Sparky at home and waited until after Charlie's bedtime to drive to Emmaline's. The longest yet fastest drive of her life. No turning back after the headlights announced her arrival. The engine of her clunker backfired as she pulled up and parked, dramatically announcing her arrival.

She saw Emmaline peeking through her blinds. *Time's up, Cookie*, she thought. *Time to face confrontation.* So began the endless walk to the porch, forcing herself not to stop at the flowers and slowly ogle and sniff as she usually did. Plants had things to say, too, although they didn't exactly transmit words the way animals did. "I'm too wet. I'm too dry. I miss the sun." That was about it. By the time she reached the door, sadness and disappointment had replaced her fury. As she raised her fist to knock, the door opened. "Hi Emmaline."

With a silent sweep of her arm, Emmaline invited her in. No jokes, hugs, or questions. Emmaline sunk into the corner of her wraparound couch and pulled a throw pillow to her chest. Anna chose the straight-backed wooden chair next to the cold fireplace. Hershey scooted up to her and leaned on her leg.

Anna breathed deeply and said, "I accept your resignation."

"But I didn't resign. You threw me out!"

"Technically, yes. But we both know why."

Hershey slinked off when the tenor of their voices raised.

"I know you are mad and disillusioned with me. But you do not know what it is like to be a mom and love a child more than your own life. A good mother does whatever is needed to protect their child."

"Well, fill me in, Mother of the Year. Is it a feeling that allows breaking the law and the heart of someone who thought of you as a best, trusted friend—was there no other way to protect said child? The child who you know full well I love as if he were my own." Anna felt her emotions ramping up and struggled to keep the conversation informative and civil. She took time to breathe in a calming breath. "Also, I have something to tell you."

"Your story will have to wait. You need to know why I needed that money. Still do. All for Charlie. His grandparents, Trevor's parents, are petitioning the court to get visitation rights. They never have shown one iota of interest in him, ever! They joined an ultra-conservative church. One that believes everything I don't. They won't love Charlie. They will try to change him. I checked out their group online. They speak out against LGBTQ people, same-sex marriages, and are politically active about it. They are against abortions and contraception—how unrealistic is that! Of course,

Charlie is too young to understand, but if he hears any talk about this, he will ask questions. One boy in his preschool has two moms and Charlie likes them and has played at their house. He would never understand them as bad in some peoples' eyes. This group's dogma is a staunch belief in being right and everyone else being wrong. Can you imagine what this would do to my sweet Charlie, who loves and hopes and sees beyond the average? Who feels the truth about everyone? He openly shares his ability to see and know things others cannot. This religious group, with their xenophobia, would never understand him.

Anna watched Emmaline, captivated by her vehemence and collection of facts. "How long has this threat been going on?"

"Oh, a while. But it recently heated up. These grandparents have an entire congregation behind them. They never used to even have close friends. How did they ever jump into this?"

"Finding and belonging to a group is intoxicating if you are used to being lonely. Takes away the work of thinking for yourself. Emmaline, you might have come to me instead of stealing from me. You know I'd do anything for Charlie. I agree, he would be so confused, this creative little boy thrown into this mix. A group like this is too constricted by judgment."

"The first thing, if they found out about his psychic gift, would be an exorcism or whatever they do. Snake handling, I don't know. The goal being to change him under the guise of help and certainly with no acceptance. I don't want him exposed to any of this. Why aren't they a sweet couple going to a lovely non-denominational friendly church who cares for the people in need? But even if their belief system aligned with ours, their lifestyle certainly doesn't. Unless they have changed dramatically, there are still drug and alcohol problems. I am frantic, Anna. I don't have the money for a lawyer. Jack was my last hope."

"Let me tell you about Jack."

"Oh, I know you don't like Jack. Whatever."

"Shush, let me talk. Jack turned out not to be who we thought. He hid the fact that he is a monster. He lost his license to practice law because he is an alcoholic with three DUI arrests. One, a hit-and-run fatality. I can't imagine why he isn't in jail. Maybe he has done time and has kept that a secret, too."

"Why do I need to know this, Anna? Is his story—what is it you said—a fairy tale too? Why might someone so out of touch with reality as I am according to you, care about your love life? So, are you saying Jack can't help me, anyway?"

"Oh, for Pete's sake, Emmaline. Grow up and get busy. Call Legal Aid, see about a pro bono lawyer, see if Sheriff Dobbs can help. Make it happen. This is how you protect Charlie. Talk to a trained professional and find out your options."

"But it is all so embarrassing. I don't want anyone in town to know. I don't even know how long I can stay in this town."

Anna blew, "Embarrassing! Is that your worry? How about being embarrassed about the fact that you tried to steal from me, your former friend and employer? How about you worked so hard to talk me into a relationship that is none of your business, just because you saw free legal advice in the works? Is that what you are telling me? Who the hell are you, anyway? How about you make a play for old Jack. You two are apparently meant for each other? Don't invite me to the wedding." She started for the door.

"Wait, Anna."

Anna's heart thumped as she glared at Emmaline. "Damn you, Emmaline, listen to me. Trevor's running shoe was found rammed into the grill of Jack's car. So, no, Jack can't help you. He is a disbarred murderer."

Emmaline lost all the color in her face.

Anna made it to the door in six big strides and turned to face Emmaline once more. "My poor dear Charlie. I hope he knows I love him so much. Hershey too." She slammed the door with such force that it made her cringe to hear how hard the windows shook.

25
NAME'S WALTER

Anna walked from where she parked on the cross street to the front door of Besties. Three weeks had passed since Emmaline's forced resignation. She missed the former Emmaline, the one who wasn't a liar and a thief. Friday ladies' nights were dwindling. They became a little silly, with only her and Olivia. Unless Lucy came. *Get a grip, old girl, you know change is broadening, or something like that.*

She looked up the front step from the sidewalk, startled to see a man with his head leaned back against the door, snoozing. If she unlocked the door and opened it, he'd fall in. Next to draw her attention were the Day-Glo pink high-top sneakers. Then floppy, loose, knee-length shorts with embroidered stars around the hem. Not exactly correct attire considering the chill in the air. A so-called wife beater shirt showed off huge arms covered in tattoos from shoulders to wrists. The design, beautiful, and artistic. Muscle-bound arms didn't quite fit with his skinny legs and the colorful striped socks coming out of the tops of the sneakers. His shirt read *Sempre Fi. Always Faithful* was tattooed in script on the outside of his lower left calf. To whom or what? she wondered. Definitely he was an interesting study. A fully bald head that sort of peaked at the top completed the picture. As she stepped back to take in the full view, he woke up and looked right at her.

"Hi, I'm here to apply for the job you advertised."

Anna could only say. "Aren't you cold?"

"No Ma'am. Name's Walter."

"Walter? No way." She grinned.

"What's wrong with Walter?"

"Come inside, Walter. I'll get us some coffee from next door. Cream, sugar?"

"Black. Could you grab a croissant?"

"Follow me. Have a seat. Back in a minute."

When Anna returned, Walter wasn't where she left him. She heard him moving around in the storage closet.

"Walter, here's breakfast. What the heck are you doing?"

He had the newest rescue puppy tucked in his arm as he rummaged around in the closet.

"This little guy is hungry. I took him out of his kennel, and he won't let me put him down. So, I'm looking for some food. Cute, little guy, aren't ya buddy? How 'bout some kisses, huh? Huh?"

"Well, Walter, see the container on the counter labeled puppy food? What do you think?"

"Got it. Come on, little buddy, we'll feed ya. Yes, we will. Who's a good boy?"

Anna, incredulous and interested at the same time. This guy didn't even pass go. He went straight into being a character. Briefly her thoughts flipped to Jack. But this wasn't Jack. This was *Walter*. The dog apparently liked him too. Thoughts flew. Walter might be great, and she wanted more than anything to hire him on the spot, but she needed to go through the motions. How could anyone feel like a warm fuzzy so instantly? Her heart, brain, and her gut were in alignment, telling her there was no need for caution. She couldn't think of anyone she'd ever met who had such immediate appeal. After the way Jack fooled her—fooled them all, really—she should be cautious, instead, she opened her mouth and out came the words, "As soon as you are confident 'Buddy' is happy and fulfilled, please come sit down, I have some questions."

The interview went well enough. Walter, somewhat reluctant to talk about himself, also acted reluctant to leave. He was a great listener, though.

Anna asked him questions and he not only answered, but also asked her questions, too. Life clearly was not all about him, and yet he was open enough to talk about himself to the extent he should, given he was interviewing for the job. He made consistent eye contact, which she liked, not just in communication, but as if he were searching for meaning instead of thinking about what he was going to say next. If she needed to take care of customers, he played with the dogs or started cleaning kennels. Sparky stayed glued to him, gently wagging the whole time.

She took notes as he talked. Born May 22, 1979. He hated school, found most of it a waste of time, snagging a 4.2 G.P.A. with little effort. He liked diving into subjects that interested him, but public education was just about skimming the surface. He felt almost giddy about going to community college and becoming a little bit of an expert in this thing and that. It made sense. For a while.

"Did you apply for your AA degree?"

"Oh yes. I figured that might be the only degree I'd ever get. I completed the credits in three semesters. Nothing about the work world intrigued me, so I joined the Marines in 2001. Twenty-two years old and hadn't learned a thing. Yet."

"How long, where?"

"Two tours, four years. Afghanistan."

"Doing what?"

"I was the dumb guy who discovered and destroyed IEDs. Improvised Explosive Devices."

Anna immediately thought of the recent discovery of dynamite and the near catastrophe involving the two boys. And Charlie. "Not dumb, Walter, really brave. Why two tours?"

"I love my country. Let's go on to something else."

"Okay, tell me about your family. What kind of people raised a good man like you?"

"Are we still having a job interview? Second thought, don't stop." Walter raised one eyebrow and smiled at her.

"Well, my parents emigrated from the Philippines. They feel fortunate to have dual citizenship and to be in America. Once here, my two sisters and

I were born. We are a big, noisy, cheerful bunch who love music and food. Holidays are a hoot. I have two nephews and two nieces. I am no longer the baby of the family, or so I try to prove to my mom."

Anna laughed aloud, "She sounds like a great mom. You are lucky to have them all. My parents died a few years ago. I will never stop missing them."

"I'm sorry. So, which of them was Chinese?"

"What? Oh, I'll never know. I am an adoptee. But my adoptive dad was Chinese, does that count? I happened to look just like him."

"Brothers or sisters?"

"One sister. She moved to Minnesota with her fabulous husband. I mean it, he really is. We see each on alternate Christmases. They have no kids yet. Back to your job interview. What did you do between Afghanistan and now? What are you interested in doing around here?"

"I jumped jobs, looking for a good fit. Learned a lot about what I want and what I don't want. This little shop is exactly where I want to work. It has everything. Organization, animals, ambiance, friendly proprietor, low key atmosphere and an excellent four-legged greeter. I live simply, need little, and the government appreciates me with a medium-sized check every month."

"Are these checks forever? Why do you get them?"

"Oh, a thing called burn pits. Without warning us enlisted folks, they burned garbage, sewage, plastic, anything, and we breathed in smoke loaded with particulates. Thereby rewarding us for our service with damage to our bodies. I'll quote, 'Among Iraq and Afghanistan veterans, rates of cancer linked to burn pit smoke are on the rise.' Google it, there is a list of about eight or ten cancers to choose from. So, the government pays us ahead of time, just in case. As of now, I have beaten the odds. Let's move on. Give me a list of what needs doing and I'll do it."

"Give me a list of your skills. Hopefully, I'll never need a bomb diffused."

He named off a list of skills, including carpenter and trained dog groomer.

"What? You are a carpenter *and* a trained dog groomer? For real? I need to see a certificate. I can't believe you."

"Well, if you're going to get testy, I'll bring my licenses for both in the morning. Here is a copy of my honorable discharge, driver's license, and referral list. You never asked, but you should. I could be another Ted Bundy for god's sake. What time do I start?"

"Early. 6:30 a.m. I have lots to show you before we open at eight."

26
UNSETTLED FEELING

"Good idea to have our ladies' night here in the café instead of the book side, Anna. It feels so different without Emmaline, but I hope all goes well with her parents. It hurts to have her hide from us. She should be here on her last Ladies' Night to enjoy the toast and our good wishes," Olivia said. "But I understand, I think."

"Och, and here I am. Happy to be included," Lucy said.

"We've been trying to include you for months, Lucy. It's great to have you."

Olivia raised her wineglass. "Let's get it over with. Without sadness, ladies. To Emmaline and our dear Charlie, whenever they make the move to Marin County, may they find exactly what they need."

"I'd like to add Hershey. I'll miss him, and so will Sparky."

"Of course, our beloved Hershey. We wish him the best happy time of his life. Also, Anna, I have said nothing to you yet, but I am so shocked and sorry about Emmaline's betrayal. There was nothing I could say to help explain or fix the situation. I'll surely miss the Em I thought I knew, and I can only imagine your disappointment." Three glasses clinked "Slainte, Cheers, Success."

After a few heartbeats, Olivia said. "Lucy, I have always wanted to ask you, what pulled you to Umbra River? What made you want to emigrate to the U.S.?"

"It was my husband. In Ireland he couldn't find good work. We were always short a few bob. He signed on with the railroad, and we came running. He thought America was a better place to raise our two wee bairn. So, didn't we get ourselves going to make a life over here? But would'ja look where the two of them and their wives live now? Killarney don't you know."

"Geode is so lucky to have you," said Olivia.

"Lucy, what jobs did you have before coming to work at Geode? I was sort of jealous that Liv nabbed you first. Though Besties would waste your culinary abilities."

"I didn't earn a paycheck until me husband left. I just dusted and cooked at home, you know."

"Left you? I'm sorry I didn't know."

"Left me for heaven, you see. He still says hello to me, my husband. Over at the crossing, most folks hear the engine's whistle blow wooo wooo woo woooo. I hear Luu Luu la Luuu." Lucy's laugh filled the room.

"That's our Lucy." Olivia smiled. "Now, here you are, my most trusted partner."

"I'll tell you something. The café wasn't easy at first. Olivia, so smart and patient all along. It took much longer than expected for me to make friends with the machinery. When I started—never told you this — I was terrified of all of it. I feared you'd think I had no wit. The horrible sound of that fancy Espresso contraption came into my dreams as nightmares. It would come alive and try to kill me. Jesus, Mary, and Joseph, I'd wake up trying to run fast as a square rigger under full sail. Then, I had a wee bit of a shock to find out that a convection oven isn't exclusively for confections. Now what? I hadn't a baldy notion what to do with that eejit steamer. On that first opening day, folks burst through the door like a flock of seagulls. I knew I had to be dead-on or out the door. Och, enough about me, ladies. How about you?"

Through the laughter, Olivia said, "In Ireland, did you have school yearbooks, Lucy?"

"A yearbook? Aye, some kids got them, not me. We were poor as church mice. But, by the way, no need to call out for dinner. I have a little something heating up."

"Yes! Lucy food. I'm excited about dinner now," Anna said.

"Olivia, we never got the chance to look at your yearbook. I'd love to see it. Or is it lost in the bowels of the storage room?"

"Not lost. I can go right to it." As she walked to the back of the building and the storeroom, she could hear the wind whipping tree branches, making them slap and scrape in rhythm with her footfalls. She felt a chill and flipped on lights as she went. As she pulled open the storeroom door and fumbled with the light switch, the overhead lightbulb popped. The storeroom went dark. "AHHH," she said aloud, her nerves jangled. Some light was coming in from the other fixtures that helped her feel along the darkened shelf. She grabbed the book, and it slid out of her hand. Light didn't quite reach the floor, so she felt around with her foot until she found it. Walking back into the café, trying to shake off the unsettled feeling, she was relieved to find Lucy and Anna coming toward her.

"We heard you yell out. Are you okay?"

"I felt funny going back there. You can really hear the storm and the lights aren't adequate. Of all things, the lightbulb in the storeroom popped and burned out. But here's the book, right where I left it. I had been looking up the name of one of my English teachers. I might reach out to her, just for fun. Although she would be in her nineties."

Lucy shivered. "I remember that funny feeling. I still am not comfortable going upstairs back there. Gives me the willies."

"Oh, the old boogeyman setup, huh? Okay, dinner and let's get to the book," Anna said.

Lucy jumped, "Ready in a snap. I'll just get to it. Olivia can nab the utensils and Anna, you'll tend bar, won't you?"

Olivia watched Anna reach for the wine that had been breathing on the side table and gather the glasses. They set aside the yearbook as they enjoyed dinner. "Lucy, this Quesadilla Casserole is so delicious. Would the consistency hold up long enough to offer it as an entrée? If you made two trays of it, say, to start, then adjusted the serving size according to the interest. Let's think about it. It could be a Wednesday Special. Or depending on how it goes, a first of the month special. Give me an ingredients list, and I'll have it on hand."

"If it would freeze well, I'd buy an entire tray and share it with Walter!" Anna mumbled through her full mouth.

"Oh, let's talk about Walter," Olivia said.

"Nope, let's not. I'll put the dishes in the dishwasher. Olivia, you look for pages to show us in your yearbook."

Olivia and Lucy continued talking in low voices. The topic was Walter and the fact that he had turned out to be the best decision Anna had ever made. "Maybe she should stop being so secretive. Unnecessary mystery creates unfounded conjecture, you know," Olivia said.

"I think she is afraid to sing his praises and have him lured to a higher paying job."

"Don't think I can't hear you," Anna said. "Okay, I give in. Walter is a miracle."

"Well, tell us more." Olivia winked at Lucy.

"He comes in early every day and gets right to it. I never have to point out what needs to be done. He seems to have a sixth sense and finds chores I haven't yet noticed. Then, before I know it, he takes care of those as well. Now, hold on to your hats! He is a licensed pet groomer. I didn't believe him at first and demanded to see his certification. Of course, he is legit. Walter is honest as a good mirror."

"I see you have set up a grooming station in the front window. Great advertisement."

"Yes, his idea. Also, depending on the temperament of the dog he is grooming, he can raise or lower the new window shade he installed. Some dogs like to watch outside, it keeps them quiet. While others become maniacs when another dog walks by. He has started a contest. He posts before and after pictures of his grooming clients. He tapes them on the window so people walking by can vote for their favorite. Maybe you saw the little table he placed out front with the lidded box, index cards, and a cup full of pencils? I'm not sure where he will go with this, but it has already created interest, and my clientele has grown."

"I've been meaning to follow the paint smell. Is he finishing up the job we started with Em in your back room?"

"Yes, and it looks so 'fresh and cheery.' His words. He is also thinking about building a small rodent area where we can sell hamsters and guinea pigs. I said a big fat no to mice. This all came about because a preschool teacher came in asking for some for her classroom. Evidently, she described them as a perfect way to teach responsibility and kindness. Walter climbed aboard that idea. He is even asking about offering classes maybe taught by local teachers or veterinarians. Frankly, he is making my head swim." Her grin betrayed her complaint.

"You'll need to check your liability insurance, Anna. Load up on folding chairs. You might sweet talk the Geode proprietress into offering some refreshments, or at least lend a coffeemaker. In fact, I would like to attend. I will order some books for Geode to display that would support your topics. I am so excited."

"Slow your roll, Liv. We are just in the thinking-about-it stage. Now, show me that yearbook. It's so thin. Mine is about twice that size. But there probably weren't as many kids enrolled back in those days."

"God, Anna, you are making me sound primeval. You're right, though. There were only about forty-five kids in my graduating class. Small town. Let's see, I'll skip through the faculty. Except, oh my, there is Hook Nose Harriett. If she hadn't been so damn mean, we wouldn't have noticed her nose. Did you know I played on the girls' field hockey team?"

"No, I didn't. I always figured you for being a homecoming queen, not a jock."

Olivia flipped pages, the memories coming almost as fast. "There I was, seventeen years old and not a single idea of what life was about."

"The magic of being young," Lucy said. "If we knew what was coming, would we keep tugging along, making mistakes, and having a great time?"

"Hand me that, Liv, please? Let me look closer at your picture. You look beautiful, the same, but without the defining character markers that life creates. Experience looks good on you. Dress and hair styles were certainly different from now. They were relaxed but no grunge."

"Well, I thank you, but don't look too closely. Ah, my three best girlfriends in the same row of pictures. Obviously, we were alphabetically in sync, at least. They were so much fun. I keep in touch with two of them."

"So, these are your classmates. Ha, similar hairdos. We are all such herd animals. Looks like more girls than boys. How did that work out?" Anna flipped another page. "Wait, who is this? There seems to be a big heart drawn around his picture. O-LIV-I-A, do tell?"

"He is an old friend. Dear friend. I was crazy about him."

Anna stared at the picture for a full minute, then looked up at Olivia. She was no longer smiling. "Look at him. Look at me. Tell me we don't look alike. Who is he?"

"Oh my gosh, you do, don't you? Well, only because he is Asian, right? I bet that happens too often." Olivia stared at the photo, not looking at Anna.

"Not only the same eyes, but look at the shape of our faces, the smiles, and those lines on our foreheads. His hair is blue/black and straight like mine, and we have the exact same coloring. We must be related. Did you know his family?"

"Yes, well, I met his mother."

"I wonder..." Anna looked up into Olivia's stricken face.

"What is it? What's wrong?"

"Oh, I'm just bringing up some memories. Nothing big at all. High school stuff." Olivia felt shaken.

"Did you date this guy? Who drew the heart?"

Lucy dragged herself out of deep thought. "Come now, Anna. Maybe Olivia wants to be alone with her memories for a bit. Any more cute boys to see? Maybe a Fergus or a Declan?"

Ignoring Lucy, Olivia felt the blood drain from her head and said, "Anna, what is your birthdate?"

"April 26, 1976. Why? What does that have to do with this guy in your yearbook?"

Olivia's hand flew to cover her mouth as she whispered, "Oh my god, excuse me." She ran toward the bathroom, Anna and Lucy flanking her like border collies. The bathroom door slammed shut.

"A wee bit of the grippe, have we?"

"Is it the photo? Talk to us."

Olivia flushed the toilet and washed her hands, then flung the door open so hard the handle smacked the wall. "STOP. Please stop and leave me alone." Olivia pushed past the two-person crowd and loped for the back door. Once outside and gulping in the evening air, she thought, *what have I done? Why didn't I see it?*

"Liv, come inside with us. You are trembling. It is freezing out here."

"Yes, get yourselves inside. You'll freeze solid like my Uncle O'Conner. He was determined to show off and refused to . . . Ah, I'll save that story for later." Lucy turned to go in and called back, "You go on, I'll just nip into the kitchen and start things up for morning."

"Bless Lucy, she stoked the fire, and I smell coffee brewing," said Anna. "Please talk to me, Olivia. Explain, please. Explain now. What has happened?"

"I've felt such guilt because I thought I was betraying Jennifer somehow. That boy in the picture was the love of my life. We had been a couple since our sophomore year in high school. I wanted to be with him every minute possible. We talked about our future, so certain we had it planned. We couldn't foresee that we already had everything we wanted."

"What are you saying, Liv?"

"Just let me talk, please. He and I were accepted to different colleges. We made promises to stay together, even though we would be in different states. I thought we were invincible. I was at university, in my favorite class about American expatriate authors. Hemmingway, Dos Passos, Stein, and all the freewheeling fun they had while writing in Paris. I loved it. But the nausea crested to a point I couldn't ignore. I wasn't yet eighteen and the college clinic contacted my parents."

"I'm pretty sure this is a weird dream. I'm going home to sleep on it," Anna picked up her bag and turned toward Besties.

"Och, you'll not be running off. You'll face it dead on. That picture is you in boy form and the dates match. You'd best hear her out." With her cloud of red billowing around her head, Lucy sped back to the relative safety of the kitchen. Olivia laughed. Then she began to cry.

"I gave away my baby girl on April 26, 1976." Lucy trotted over with a glass of water and tissues. After taking a sip and blowing her nose and taking time to settle, Olivia went on. "She was the most beautiful baby who looked just like her father. I begged the nurse not to take her. Three nurses and an orderly were holding me in place. There was an older Asian woman, not dressed as a nurse, standing outside my door. I'll never forget her eyes filled with empathy. I screamed and begged my mother not to let it happen. She kept saying it was for the best."

"It's difficult to understand the social morals and norms of the day. I was too young to know I had choices. My parents couldn't face becoming social pariahs because their daughter was unmarried and pregnant." She saw Anna's face turn to carved stone. "I know, it is hard to believe now, but it was who they were. It was my first year of college, and I was their great hope. They felt my life would derail if I kept the baby. I was so influenced by my need for their approval. When they told me college would be the best years of my life, I believed them and couldn't see beyond. There had been rumors of girls being sent away to a relative or a group home where they would live through their pregnancies hidden from the view of small-town gossips. Their babies to be adopted out. My mother's sister lived close to campus and so they removed me from the dorm and I moved in with her. As it turned out, I hated living in the dorm and my aunt was very good to me. I looked at the move as a chance to take time to think things over. I completed the first two quarters and halfway through the third, I took a withdrawal."

Olivia's voice croaked as more tears slid. "Please listen. I went home for Thanksgiving break. He was coming home too, and we made plans to be together. He didn't know about the baby yet. I wanted to tell him in person. I got home two days earlier than expected. At least, earlier than he expected. I hadn't been to see my parents yet and stopped to grab a coffee at a small cafe where we used to meet. My hand was almost on the doorknob when I looked through the glass panes and saw him. He was sitting at a table with his chair pulled tightly against a second chair. Sitting with him was one of my best friends. The scene didn't register as odd until he pulled her in for a lengthy kiss."

"Wait a minute, Grandma Ming just told me the same story. The same story! What's going on?" Anna said.

"Let me keep going, Anna. I wanted to die. But, at the same time, I was excited about the baby. After driving around for a couple of hours, trying to think, I went to my parents. Of course, they knew about the baby, and knew I hadn't told Kai. They also knew I would never have an abortion, and that I had no plan. They were clear, with a plan of their own. My baby would be born at a hospital near my aunt, the birth, a secret, and the baby given away. I argued, cried, screamed, begged to keep my baby. I loved Kai, and I knew I would love this baby. He would too and would drop my friend like a hot rock. I only hoped to talk to him. Off I went to the next town, over to Kai's parents' house. We had phone books then, and I looked up their address and phone number. I never thought through the fact that I had never met his parents. And he had never met mine."

"Kai's mother opened the door. 'Who are you and what do you want?' I dove in and told her about Kai's and my baby. She was not receptive. She didn't invite me in, but her sister joined us at the door, put an arm around my shoulders and pulled me in. The sister was reasonable, even kind. She tried to start a conversation, but it wasn't to be. Kai's mother kept yelling. She said I was lying, and Kai would never do this. None of this was what I expected. I sobbed my way to the driver's seat and left. I hadn't unpacked at my parent's house, so I drove straight back to my aunt's. She was traveling for the holiday, and I wanted to be alone."

"Shall I open more wine or put on some coffee?" Lucy asked.

"Nothing for me, thank you, Lucy," two voices chimed in.

"When did you finally tell him?"

"I never did. His aunt did. You know, the reasonable woman. For all these years, I have carried the heartbreaking guilt. Depression had a deep hold on me in the last few months of my pregnancy. I didn't care about much of anything. They decided for me, and I just rolled with it. There wasn't an ounce of fight left in me until the minute I saw that sweet face and held my very own baby. I knew what a huge mistake I was making."

"Did you ever hear from Kai? Bugger him, anyway." Lucy was pacing.

"No, I never did. His aunt left a message on the number I left with her. It was my aunt's home phone. She told me he had dis-enrolled in school and joined the military. The coward. I never tried to reach out to him. Because of him, my life changed. My perspective about most things changed. I never trusted and never ever recovered from the loss of my baby."

Anna reached over and put her hand over Olivia's. "I can't imagine what you went through."

"Those last two days before we left for college were magical. We drove out to Pajaro Dunes, near Santa Cruz. I still remember the sound of the surf as it rolled in, then hissed back out. The sunset was so beautiful, with billowing clouds tinted gold and apricot as the sun dipped into the ocean. We laughed about how no steam spouted up as the hot sun fell into the cold ocean. At one point, the beach blanket needed a shake. We stood together, each taking hold of an edge, and snapped it sharply. Too bad, we had put little thought into the direction of the wind. We covered ourselves in sand. Our laughter dissolved into happy kisses. We brushed the sand off ourselves and promised not to talk about our looming separation and to enjoy the timelessness we felt. At sunset, the temperature dropped, and he ran to the car for a second blanket. The ocean always made me nervous. The waves were relentless, always coming at me. Never giving up. The ocean seemed to me like an idling monster waiting to rise and devour. But that night I felt safe because we were together. At sunset, the ocean calmed. The surrounding atmosphere seemed to sparkle and hold an energy that felt like spiritual righteousness. That's the only way I know to describe it. Lying under the blanket, the sky a showcase of stars, we tried to name the constellations. What a joke, we finally admitted to each other. Neither of us knew a fig about stars. Every minute with him was fun. I loved him and believed he loved me. The consequences of that night never occurred to either of us. We promised to stay together, even though we were to be in different states. Foolishly, I thought we were invincible.

Olivia breathed nervously as she picked at her nails and the grandfather clock in the corner ticked loudly. "I am out of words for tonight, and I know this is a big load, Anna, but something has lined up for me here tonight. A possibility I never before imagined. Never thought of for a moment."

No one said a word for a very long time. Olivia felt like she was either going to vomit or have a stroke or a heart attack. Anna. How on earth? How had she not seen? How had all of Umbra River not seen?

"Well, however long those genealogy tests take, this is going to be some wait, won't it, Olivia?" Anna said, as she watched the pendulum on the big, old clock.

27
A STORY THAT NEEDS TO BE TOLD

One more thing in her currently turbulent life needed attention. Anna had to force herself to switch gears and try to handle one thing at a time. Reluctantly, she knocked on the door to Emmaline's small writing sanctuary. She heard, "Come on in," and carefully opened the door. The first thing she noticed was a collection of filled cardboard boxes stacked around, and the second was Emmaline's smile fading.

"Hey, do you have a minute?" Anna asked.

"Only one, I'm busy. I never expected you. What's up?"

"Two things, well, three things. Maybe many things I don't know."

"Have a seat, if it will help you be specific."

"Okay, I'll just start. I am also here to ask for a favor."

"A favor? Is this why you came to talk to me? You needed a favor? I see I am far from unforgettable. It didn't take you long to find my replacement at Besties."

"I goofed. I might have allowed a few heartbeats before I mentioned a favor. Don't forget what happened at Besties. I needed to hire someone. It isn't a one-person endeavor. He is working out very well, by the way. So where do you buy dog food these days?"

"What's the favor?" Emmaline said, dodging the question.

"What are all the boxes? Did Olivia give you the slip?"

"No, she is a loyal friend. I will miss her terribly, but Charlie and I are moving."

"You're taking Charlie?"

"Of course, I'm taking Charlie. He is my son!"

"I know, I know. I'm shocked. It has been hard enough losing you, but Charlie and Hershey, too?"

"You'll survive. Again, what's the favor?"

"I'll be right back." Anna swished out the door. It took a few minutes outside of pacing and processing along the dog run fence before she returned. Emmaline's door stood open, and she strode back in.

"I need you to write something for me. I will pay for your services. It will be business, not a favor."

"Well?"

"I have been asked to go to the spot where Charlie witnessed the boy on the horse and the tunnel where the boys saw the skeletons. We hope that with my sensitivity to the paranormal, I will help release their souls. I feel the reason Charlie saw the boy on his horse is because they are stuck between existences and are looking for help to move on. Well, the boy is, and I am sure the horse will appreciate it too. I need to find out if the souls of the mine tragedy are lingering as well. I am asking to hire you to attend with me and describe the experience in writing for publication."

"Why?"

"It's a story that needs to be told. People must start thinking about spiritual energy and vibrational awareness. Our universe is changing."

"Oh yes, I can be hired to do that."

"One more thing. Charlie needs to be there, too. He can help me and see how he might eventually use his abilities to help souls go to the light. It will help give him power over his power, so to speak."

"I'll have to think about this, talk to him first and see how he feels. I'll text you with his answer."

"In terms of outcome, I hope this can remain between us until it is published. People looking for entertainment might jeopardize the success."

"I understand. Let me know the date and time. I move in ten days. My house is almost all packed, and the realtor is setting it up as a short-term rental. So, the sooner, the better."

"Noted. I'll be in touch." *It's all about you, Emmaline.*

***

Thinking back, Anna had been surprised when Sheriff Dobbs stopped by Besties the week before. Her first thought was, *oh no, what has Walter done?* However, Dobbs had come to talk privately. He had that lawman's sense, always with his ear to the ground, about the citizens of Umbra River. He knew Anna communicated with animals and wondered how far her abilities went. He said after reading Emmaline's article he was thinking it might take a psychic to figure out who those skeletons belonged to. Not only that, but if there was something to this thing about releasing souls, how would anybody go about getting that done. He was always ahead of the pack. She smiled at herself thinking he was as broad minded as he was broad-shouldered. In their meeting, brief but informative, they outlined a plan. Anna agreed to free the earthbound souls if he made two promises. One, it had to remain their secret—leaving the public uninformed for now. Two, Emmaline should be allowed to attend as a writer, and possibly to create a publishable story. The date was set for Thursday, with the time to be determined by Emmaline's schedule. Anna planned to report to the sheriff on her way home from getting the job done. He readily agreed.

Now, as she hurried through the woods to the site, she hoped for the dry weather to hold for the next few hours. With her heart flipping, she worried about failure. If she couldn't help the poor souls, she'd have to resign herself to failure or find someone else capable of doing it.

Ahead, a flash of color. Yellow caution tape around the tree still marked the trail. It felt lonely to be here without Sparky, but he had stayed at Besties with Walter. She followed the trail, planning to get a good look at the site before going back to the caution-taped tree to wait for Emmaline and, hopefully, Charlie.

The quiet felt heavy. No chirps or skitterings, only the sound of the water flowing. As she approached the opening of the tunnel, she centered herself with deep breathing. Breath in for four counts, hold for four and breathe, out for four. In her thoughts, she asked for divine light to surround her for protection and allow her energy to flow. She sat quietly, allowing the peacefulness of the forest to calm her.

She hadn't waited long when the sound of voices in the distance caught her attention. One, a low murmur, and the other, cheerful chatter. *Charlie! Emmaline brought him.* A swirl of emotions caused her to feel out of balance. Distraught over Charlie moving away yet thrilled to have him with her today—though maybe for the last time. When they came into sight, she happily noted they had left Hershey at home. If this was to be goodbye, losing Charlie and Hershey on the same day might destroy her.

Charlie looked up and saw her. His face lit up with a grin and he leapt into a full out gallop before plopping himself into her lap. That did it. Her tears welled and spilled over.

"Auntie Anna, are you crying?"

"Yes, Honey. I will miss you like a right arm. I love you so much. These are love-you tears."

"Oh, but Mom says it won't be forever. We'll stay in the cottage until Mom gets smart enough to teach school. Then we will come back. Won't we, Mom? You promised."

"Yes, I did. I promised." Emmaline looked at Anna.

"Auntie Anna," Charlie said, "show me how to help. Have you seen my friend and his horse? Does he want to go somewhere else? What about the horse?"

"Slow down, Charlie Boy. I will show you instead of telling. Just watch and join in. We will start by breathing together. Do you want to look around a little before we begin?"

Anna saw fear come to Emmaline's eyes and realized her mistake. "One thing, Charlie. See that caution tape by that pile of rocks? Stay away from there. It's a deep shaft in the ground. In fact, let's go look at the river. We will all go."

The river tumbled and roared just beyond a small, shallow pool, rimmed by rock and perfect for a small boy to explore. Anna and Emmaline watched from two nearby boulders, close enough to grab him if he lost his footing. "Look, guys, I almost caught a teeny tiny fish. With my hands!" Charlie hollered over the roar of the river.

Both women gave him a thumbs up. Anna turned to Emmaline. "Want to talk?"

"Will you listen without judgment?"

"I want to hear what you have to say, Emmaline."

"What I have to say is, well, it's no excuse, but I am a mess. As much as I have loved living in Umbra River, I need to go. It's a prison for me, feels like I've pulled in bad mojo from every direction. We are going to Marin County. I reached out to my parents, and they seem honestly happy to have me back in their lives and to be grandparents. We had several phone and Zoom conversations. They are loving, forgiving people. Writing isn't getting me anywhere. The Historical group hates me because I brought to light all the umbra about Umbra River. Charlie's father was murdered here, and I can't follow my dream if I stay."

"And your dream is?"

"I want to earn a teaching credential. High school history. I'm passionate about it, and so my students will be too. Meanwhile, Charlie can experience the city and have good grandparents in his life. Two blocks from my parents' home is an adorable elementary school. My mom sent pictures."

"Charlie said something about living in a cottage. Will there be room for Hershey?"

"Oh yes, when my parents bought the place, a separate smaller house sat toward the back of their property. They first planned to use it as a rental, but never wanted to deal with renters. Honestly, I think they were hoping I might live there some day."

"Hersh?"

"Big, fenced yard. The neighborhood is loaded with dogs and kids. Hershey will love it. Added to all this positive news, I found out my parents had a college fund set up for me. Obviously, they were chock full of wishful thinking."

"You have Charlie's school sorted out, after school care with grandparents, room for Hershey, and money for your education. Wow, look at you."

"A while back, Olivia suggested I reacquaint myself with my folks for Charlie's sake. I started thinking, then the other grandparents unwittingly pushed me that direction."

"Have you applied to any colleges yet?"

"Yes, S.F. State, Sonoma State, Cal Berkeley, Santa Clara, and more. I think I've sent applications to all of them. Somewhere I have a list. You know, I already have my AA degree."

"It sounds like you are on your way. I honestly hope it works out well for you, Em." Anna turned in Charlie's direction. "Charlie, ready to get started?"

28
FRIDAY, NEWS DAY

Sweet Things, across from Besties, kept a newspaper stand in front. The aroma of delicious treats baking made Anna's mouth water. Usually, she stopped here first on her way to work. But today she wanted the day's edition of the local newspaper because it featured local artists. Emmaline's story, scheduled for this week, was due out today. Not sure if she felt terrified or over-the-top excited, she opened it up and scanned. A loud honk brought her up sharply, and a car swerved just in time to miss her. Feeling foolish, she folded the paper, looked both ways, and dashed across the street.

Before her foot landed on the sidewalk, she heard Walter singing Cole Porter's "Let's Fall in Love." In his beautiful baritone. *This man needs to be recorded*, she thought. A woman standing beside her whispered her appreciation as four other people stopped to enjoy the concert.

The music ended, and Walter stepped out to raucous applause. Rather than acting embarrassed, he smiled and belted out one more stanza. His audience, thanking and complimenting him, drifted off. He quickly gave a sales pitch about puppies and an elderly shepherd who needed adoption, each coming with a free bag of food. One lady asked to meet the shepherd.

As Anna walked by, Walter quietly said, "I worried. You are late."

"Not late, Walter. I enjoyed the concert. You are scaring me."

He lifted an eyebrow.

"Well," she said, "is there anything you can't do beautifully?" She kept walking. "Free bag of food, huh?"

Inside the shop stood Olivia, with Lucy trying to peek over her shoulder. Evidently, they had opened the connecting door to Geode, and the café and had been enjoying the concert along with some book browsers. Seeing it wrapped up, they ducked back inside after a quick wave to Anna.

Anna turned her attention back to the newspaper article and the quality of Emmaline's writing. She sat on the stool and spread the newspaper in front of her, found the article, and read it. Emmaline had given a quick review of Charlie's first and second sightings of the ghost boy on the horse. Next, she described Anna's sensitivities and ability to communicate with animals. She drew parallels between Anna and Charlie, showing her understanding and support of both. Emmaline had witnessed several instances of Anna receiving and sending messages with animals during her time working at Besties. She mentioned customers had commented on it as well, then launched into describing the releasing of the souls, which gave Anna a strange feeling, wondering if this was information that shouldn't have been shared publicly. Maybe souls didn't want the world to know they'd been released.

Emmaline had lovingly depicted the scene, however, with no sensationalism. She portrayed the centering meditation and Charlie taking three cleansing breaths, then sitting silently, Anna asking him to close his eyes, relax his body one area at a time, starting with his toes. He was to keep his feet firmly touching the ground and see himself bathed in white light coming from above and traveling through their bodies inside and out. Angels and guides were called in. Then, Anna waited with five-year-old Charlie, who already understood he needed to be silent and reverent. Emmaline wrote that she could tell when Anna and Charlie saw the boy and horse. They became alert. Charlie smiled, and Anna talked quietly with the boy, although Emmaline couldn't see the boy or hear the words. Anna put her arms up, hands splayed, and asked the Universe to take this child home. Anna told the boy not to be afraid and to go toward the light. This light would take him to a safe place with souls who love him and would help him cross over. But this was his decision to make. Charlie elbowed her and asked about the horse. Anna had nodded and made the same request on behalf of the horse. Charlie turned to her to say, "They're gone." Emmaline wrote about the beauty of the scene and the feeling of pure love she felt as she watched Anna and Charlie sitting hip to hip on a log in the forest doing what most of us will never understand or be able to accomplish.

Anna quietly folded the paper and laid it on the counter. Her heart felt full. She was proud of Emmaline and the courage it took to write it. The article was full of voice, description, and facts. Anna's soft gaze was on the sky outside as she daydreamed about Emmaline and how she wasn't a bad person, just a person who needed direction. Blasting her out of her trance, all five dogs currently in residence went crazy, barking like their tails were on fire. Running to the back room, she hollered, "Walter, what's wrong with them?"

"It might be my new ringtone. I didn't think this through."

Before he got to it muted it, another call came in. The distinct sound of rhythmic knocking on a door filled the room, and the dogs were at it again.

"Oh, for God's sake, Walter," Anna hollered over the frantic barking as she turned and scooted to the front of the store where a woman had just arrived, snuggling an adorable springer spaniel puppy. Anna apologized for the noise in the back. The woman explained the dog was a rescue, and that she had just picked him up and needed supplies. She wanted the very best food.

Anna loved helping people with new puppies. She made suggestions about food and supplies, then jokingly asked if the little dog could walk. The woman replied by kissing him on the head and snuggling him closer. Anna threw in a free bag of treats and a sparkly blue leash and watched the sweet pair go out the door.

"What's on the agenda for today, Walter?" Anna asked as he passed by on his way to grab grooming tools and fresh towels for his next appointment. *He never stops surprising me.*

"Three, no wait, four grooming appointments! Two labs, one golden, and a Shih Tzu. They'll take most of the afternoon. I hope you will be here to run the place."

"Where else would I be, Walter?"

Anna was still smiling from the pleasant experience with the woman and her rescue spaniel. She heard the door open and looked up as she clicked the register closed. Two thickset ornery looking men shouldered their way in the door. Behind them they dragged an exhausted looking, scarred, and unneutered male dog. He looked to be part hound with long ears and a buff-colored coat. There was no spark in the dog's eyes, and when he looked up at her, she felt him listlessly plead for help.

The man holding the leash was a swirl of hateful energy. When the dog hesitated to be dragged another few feet, he caught a powerful kick in the ribs by a filthy, steel-toed leather boot. Anna screamed and dropped to the dog. She was met with a kick, catching her on the shoulder. Both dog and Anna sprawled on the floor. Before she could react, a raging torrent of fury stormed in from the back room. In what seemed like seconds, Walter had the creep flipped to the floor with one arm wrenched behind his back and a knee holding down his legs. When the man tried to move, the wrench clamped down tighter. The man's cowardly companion darted out the door and disappeared.

Anna punched in 911 with one hand but kept her free arm around the sorrowful dog. They were both shaking. She thought how grateful she felt that the police were less than a mile away as she heard Walter down on the floor whispering loudly in the man's ear that his ugly neck would be snapped if he moved one inch.

Ten minutes later, young officer Kendrick snapped on the cuffs as he nodded to Walter. The officer reached down to help pull the man to his feet. When Walter leaned in to assist, the would-be bully screamed out like a trapped coyote.

Officer Kendrick recorded Anna's story first, then Walter's. The man in handcuffs tried to say they had jumped him for no reason, that they were trying to steal his dog, but the officer turned him toward the door and gave him an encouraging shove over the threshold. Anna had allowed the bruise already blossoming on her shoulder to be photographed and the look of the dog told its own story.

As he was being guided into the patrol car, the man called over his shoulder to the dog. "Friday!" The terrified dog scooted behind Anna and trembled again. The back door of the patrol car door slammed and before the officer climbed in to drive, Anna heard him call over, "You can house the dog, Anna?"

"With pleasure."

Leaning against the counter with her arms crossed in front of her, Anna watched Walter tilt his head and walk toward her. He slid her into a bear hug and asked, "Are you okay, Wonder Woman?" She replied by hugging him back. How good he felt next to her. He wasn't taking energy. He was giving it. And he had plenty to spare. She said into his shoulder, "You were a wonder yourself, Walter. You handled that situation before I even knew what was happening."

"Don't tell my Mama. She still calls me her little Syota."

"Little sweetheart?"

"You speak Tagalog?"

"Nah, my mom had a friend. You think that chump will try to get this dog back? I can't let him go back to that monster." Anna spoke into Walter's shoulder.

"That bag of garbage will never get near this dog as long as I am alive." Walter backed away and dropped to the floor, crossed his skinny legs, and sat quietly.

"What are you waiting for?"

"For this terrified dog to quit ignoring me." In his smooth baritone, he began quietly to sing.

"Oh, for god's sake, one surprise after another. I'll be right back." Anna pulled open the door to leave. "Keep Sparky away from Friday until we know how damaged he is."

Walter nodded in agreement, then said, "Wait, what day is this?"

"Friday."

29
THE GIFT OF TRUTH

Anna arrived at the railroad depot at two-thirty a.m. The drive over the pass and down to Redding went well. No traffic, few deer. She waited in the dark, concerned about Grandma Ming needing help to gather up and get off the train. But most of all, hoping she loved the adventure enough to make the trip often. Bells clanged as the traffic arms came down, and within moments the signal safety light appeared. The sound of the chugging engine came next.

Grandma Ming's face shone with delight when she turned toward Anna standing on the platform. Her smile meant everything to Anna. She wondered where she would be in life without the love of this woman. Anna grabbed her bags with one arm and hugged her with the other. "Good trip?"

"Couldn't have been better. Comfy seats, nice people. I even met a sweet baby sitting behind me who challenged his mother, but she held firm."

Laughing, Anna offered her crooked arm, which Grandma Ming took, patting it with a tastefully gloved hand.

***

The next morning began at noon for Grandma Ming. While she slept in, Anna used the time to putter around the house and prepare for the dinner and party the next evening. With Ella, Sinatra, Sammy, and Barbra playing in her ear buds, a nod to her grandmother's favorites, she sang along softly as she dusted and organized. Flapping the dust cloth to the rhythm of "Fly Me to the Moon," she felt arms come around her from behind and a sweet familiar voice harmonizing.

"Grandma, good morning!" Pulling out her ear buds, she turned to hug her houseguest. "Did you sleep well? Are you rested?"

"Oh yes, that bed is so comfortable. It supported my old bones and let me sleep for hours. Do you remember singing with me when you were little? We used to belt out the standards, harmonize, and many times, you accompanied us on the drums. Well, wooden spoons and the soup pot, but it's all the same."

"I remember, and I think about it every time I have the urge to sing. Which is often, but only when I am alone. Let's get you something to eat."

Anna cooked up scrambled eggs and set out lemon poppy seed muffins and coffees. Grandma Ming talked nonstop about the wonderfully kind group who drove all the way to her home, then worked all day and far into the evening to fix what needed fixing. "Honey, I am so happy you live in this town with great folks. I don't have to worry about you at all."

"Aw, you know you don't have to worry. I take care of myself very well. Sparky helps. Later I need to go to Besties and check on things. I'd love for you to meet Walter and see the store."

"Yes, let's do it. You can give me a brief tour of your town, too. And let's have coffee in The Geode Cafe, which I have heard so much about. Olivia sounds like a gracious lady, and I want to meet her and the other woman. Lucy."

"Perfect. I also need to order some bakery goods at Sweet Things for the big gathering tomorrow night. Their goodies are fabulous, and they deliver."

"I can be ready in a few minutes. Say when you want to leave. You know, it's as though you and Emmaline lit a cleansing fire, made it a controlled burn, then left me with resources to keep up the improvements. My house not only looks so much better but also the temperature doesn't fluctuate like it used to. That sweet neighbor boy Mitch is taking care of the birds while I am gone. He offered to take care of my yard weekly for what I think is a minimal fee. You bet I'll see to it he never runs out of cookies or hamburgers. Whatever he wants."

"That sounds great, Grandma. He is a nice boy, and so capable. I agree, the people who came to help are capable also, and so willing. They all said they were glad they went, and they loved the day. They're looking forward to your party tomorrow."

"The work weekend spurred Mitch's interest in carpentry. He's grateful to us and mostly to you. He says he will enroll in a local vocational program where he can hone his carpentry skills and hope to sign on afterwards with his contractor uncle. So, I may not lose his help. You launched a life, Anna!"

"Well, you needed help, and you got it. Sounds like everybody wins."

"Okay, then! I'm headed for a shower, and then we go to town." Stopping mid-stride, she turned and said, "Anna, please may I have you all to myself this evening? I have something I want to talk over, and it looks like this is the only time for it."

"Of course! My evening is all yours." The thought crossed Anna's mind: *Maybe she wants to talk about moving up here!*

***

Anna parked in front of Besties so Gram would have a short walk. Friday, who stole the heart of everyone who met him, greeted her first, his tail wagging and eyes bright.

"Who's the whiskey baritone?" Grandma Ming said.

"That's Walter, my right-hand man. He does everything, and I don't know how I coped before he came along."

Grandma Ming looked at Anna, "Porgy and Bess, Gershwin music." Then she hustled toward the back room harmonizing as she belted out, "Summertime—and the living is easy."

Anna stared as her grandmother and Walter walked back toward her, still singing. "Oh my gosh, you two. I haven't even introduced you."

"No need." Walter stopped singing and bowed toward Grandma Ming.

He then turned and led the way to show her the fine points of Besties. Friday following closely beside him, while Anna cleared the till and made out the deposit. She took a quick look at the inventory, made a few notes, and called out, "Going to the bank. Be right back." *Walter keeps on surprising me. Who knew he and Grandma would connect instantly? I must be sure he knows he is welcome to join us tomorrow for dinner.* As she opened the door to leave, she heard Grandma say, "Nice dog, he sure is glued to you."

After her return, she found her grandmother and Walter leaning on the front counter, chattering. "Oh Honey, your store is fantastic. It's so organized, clean, and equipped. I love the paint colors and the large size of the kennels. Those babies need room when they are staying as guests. Wow. Am I proud of you and what you have accomplished—always knew animals would be in your life. Maybe I'll get started on making some soft quilts, washable ones for the kennels. I already measured them."

"Thank you, Grandma. That means so much to have you feel that way. I'd love to add Gram-made quilts to the kennels. So, you and Walter certainly hit it off."

"I'll only say, if I were . . . hmmm . . . thirty-five or so years younger . . ."

"Oh dear, this news might bloat his ego to intolerable," Anna laughed.

"Now, is he the young man who saved you and stood up to that evil dog abuser?"

"Yes, he is the guy. Like I said, I don't know what I did before him." Grandma Ming smiled to herself.

Sitting at a table on the deck of Geode on a beautiful day, enjoying coffee and sharing a turkey on rye created the perfect occasion for several people to meet Anna's grandmother. Olivia came out and joined them. People were friendly and kind, and Anna loved showing off her gram. But the more time passed, the more uncomfortable she became. After a while she felt she couldn't stand it any longer and pushed back her chair and stood. Time to go. *Something passed between Gram and Olivia. I felt it.*

Anna's house was quiet and cool. She noticed Grandma pulling on a sweater and fuzzy slippers. The tea pot sang, and Anna took down two mugs and dropped tea bags in. "Let's get comfortable so we can talk. Wait, you can't sit there. That's Sparky's spot."

"Oh, gosh, how about here, Spark? Okay with you?

Grandma Ming took a moment to settle in. Anna felt fear in her gut. The day and gone from wonderful to off, and she couldn't get clarity.

After a time, Grandma Ming put down her steaming mug and spoke. "Anna, it's time you knew some things. I'm so sorry you have never been told. I'm sorry the telling of this story has landed in my lap."

Anna wasn't sure what to say.

"That picture of the two cousins?"

"Yes, they look exactly alike. Who..."

"I'm trying to tell you." Grandma snapped. She covered her face and bent over. "I'm sorry, Anna girl, this is so hard for me."

"Just say it."

"The cousin on the right, your biological father, Kai. The beautiful boy on the left, your dad, the man who adopted you."

They sat in silence for several more minutes. Anna's body held a storm of emotions. A whirlpool She knew this. *She knew* it. The moment Emmaline mentioned that photo. The moment she saw it. She knew all of it. Identified with it. But she had no language for it. The knowledge had lived in her body all this time, but it had not risen to the level of words. She had felt such heaviness, heaviness like a stone, but she couldn't place its source. Too much had happened. Life had been a train wreck in many regards. *Too much.* She had lodged the knowledge somewhere below the surface and had refused to look at it. She realized that for weeks she had felt out of her body. That was the sensation exactly: *Out of her body.*

At some point the silence became unbearable. "How did this happen? I can't put it together."

"When that distraught pregnant teen came to my sister for help only to be turned away, I kept her phone number, hoping it stayed the same until the baby came. I called her to tell her about my awful nephew and that he had joined the military. I told her to forget him and raise her baby. She sobbed and said her parents were making her give up the baby. Made me sick. Meanwhile, Great Grandma Ming listened to these conversations and took matters into her own hands, so they say."

"What do you mean? What are you telling me?"

"I'll start by explaining Chinese culture at the time. At least as I understood it. Adopted children were considered bad luck. Babies whose mothers couldn't keep them, or were unwed and shamed into not keeping them, were abandoned, or given up for adoption. They believed bad luck stuck with those children through life. Babies were thought to be granted by the will of heaven—and infertility, a sign of heaven's disfavor. The stigma punctuated both sides of the adoption process. Great Grandma Ming did not want you to be thrown into the black market where abandoned babies were sold to who knows who. Also, you were born shortly before the one child per family policy in China, but discussions were starting. People were planning their families, and in this era, male babies were preferred. Female babies were considered second class. Oh my god, can you believe this, Anna? As the nightmare unfolded, Great Grandma Ming became resolute in getting involved. And she did."

"But how . . ."

"Let me keep talking before I chicken out, sweetheart. I'm having a hard time with it because you should have known this since childhood, and I regret not taking matters into my own hands and telling you about it. Your questions should have been answered by the people who raised you, your life cleared of the shadows."

Wiping tears, Grandma Ming continued. "Great Grandma said you belonged in our family, and she planned to see to it you would never be adopted outside the family. Your birth mom gave us the due date and name of the hospital. Your Great Grandmother knew a Chinese nurse's aide who worked there. There are no coincidences, Anna. Many cogs turned the wheel that brought you to our family. The nurse's aide /friend called us the minute your mother checked in. Great Grandma dressed in her best clothes, and GG drove her to the hospital. The car already loaded with a baby seat, full diaper bag, and formula. Of course, I knitted like crazy, all the cotton-ball soft blankets and clothing this special baby needed. She waited for her friend to appear in the picture window overlooking the parking lot to give her a signal that the baby was ready for take-off. Strolling in through the main doors of the hospital, carrying a large carpetbag lined in silk, she said not one person gave her a second glance. Sometimes it helps to be Chinese.

People ignore you. Because she cared about your mom, she went to her room and stood outside for a moment. No way could she speak to her, too many nurses around, so she moved on. As she reached the nursery, her friend smiled and pointed to the only Asian baby in the ten-baby room. The friend/nurse's aide moved among the bassinets, checking the babies. There were no vacancies there. She picked up our baby and loudly said, 'Of course, Grandmother, you may take her to see her grandfather.' Now, remember, forty-six years ago, there were no cameras, scanned I.D. bracelets, or alarms. Great Grandma quietly stepped in, reached out for you, covered you and sauntered out through the almost empty corridor. Stopping for a moment, around a bend in the hallway, to nestle you in the bag she carried. I have to smile when I think of that get-away car careening through the parking lot, speeding to the highway."

"It's incredible she wasn't stopped. No one questioned her? How can you just pick up a baby and walk out?"

"Great Grandma heard someone say, 'It's okay. Nobody cares who has the baby. She's Chinese.' Later, she heard from her friend on the 'inside' an investigation never happened because the baby 'was only' Chinese. It's easier to hate than try to understand. But no matter if you agree or not with another's perspective, there is always more to it than we know. Here, the dislike of non-whites was your ticket to freedom."

"I'm finding it easier to hate right now. That is until I think how lucky it was for me to be raised by members of my own family. So, my father, my adoptive father, the man who raised me is actually my . . . uncle? Or second cousin? But how can I have a driver's license or Social Security number? There must be no birth records. Oh, that's why my adoption is closed."

"Here is the conclusion to the mystery. Your adoptive mom miscarried a few days before you were born. Great Grandma put that puzzle piece together and your mom and dad were thrilled to adopt you. The legal part is beyond my understanding, but a Chinese lawyer who was best pals with GG seemed to be around quite a bit. Honey, it all fell into place. Nothing else matters."

"Wait a minute. That explains something. It wasn't Great Grandma Ming my mom disliked or mistrusted. It was the blood grandmother, Kai's mother. I overheard my parents arguing once. Mom was crying and saying, 'The old witch would love to confuse the girls and make trouble.' Then Dad said, 'GG promises to keep the girls away from her.' I did not know who the old witch was, but I was young enough that I only cared about spending time with the GGs. I never questioned the decision for me to go one direction and my sister to go to the other grandparents. Mom's folks lived close to us, and we saw them often. Now, I'm thinking about my sister the spitfire. Had she gotten wind of this, she would have poked the bear ruthlessly. Wow, how clueless I was. What a tremendous burden for my mom and dad."

"I am going to bed. This information needs to gel and settle, and I am exhausted. You must be too. I love you Grandma. You are smart and brave to have given me this gift of truth."

"Goodnight, Honey. I love you brick loads. See you in the morning."

***

"Come on, Sparky, I don't have time to walk you this morning. How about walking yourself in the backyard?" Anna was in shorts and an old shirt, and Grandma was in a housedress, both hustling to get ready for the night's party. Grandma made two huge pots of her wonderful beef and bean chili, along with pans of cornbread. Anna prepped three charcuterie boards for appetizers, cleaned the vegetables for salad, and prepped the garlic bread.

"I'll walk Sparky. Most of my work is done. Then when we get back, I'll organize the plates, utensils and napkins and make my secret steak marinade," said Grandma Ming.

Anna punched in Walter's number. "Hey, how about manning the grills tonight? I'm sure Grandma will help. You two can team up."

"Sure, that sounds fun. Also, I have a commercial ice machine at home. Shall I bring a couple of coolers full?"

"Oh yes, please. I forgot about ice, and we'll need to cool down the beer. Thank you. But Walter, not many people have a commercial ice machine."

"I know. Aren't you glad you know me?"

"See you tonight, Walter."

As guests arrived, Anna heard her grandmother admonishing them for bringing gifts. She intervened with the first two, then let it slide. It was a fun evening. She watched Grandma and Walter working together at the two grills. Sometimes they sang and sometimes they argued about the state of the steaks. First, they put up all the tables and chairs and Anna placed jars of fresh flowers out as centerpieces. As she laid out the silverware on a table around the corner of the house from the grills, she heard Grandma talking to Walter and blatantly eavesdropped.

"So, tell me about your train trip. Was it a hoot?"

"Well, give me a minute. Let's see I'm trying my best to think of something fun to tell about a seven-hour train trip in the dark. At least two sets of about an hour's worth each of crying, no—screaming—from the baby in the seat behind me, while the frazzled mother tried to settle him was not the worst part of the trip. Maybe the little guy's hips and knees hurt as badly as mine. The millions of stops and starts, 'All Aboard' ticket clipping, and folks stowing their bags might not have been bad either, had it been during the day. I looked forward to an easy trip. People talked it up as a great time. I thought I might sleep the whole way after I found the snack bar, some coffee, and a sandwich. My departure time, seven fifty-eight p.m. and an arrival time in Redding of three-oh-three a.m. might have worked for sleeping. I wanted to sleep but couldn't push my seat back without landing on the baby. No stretching out across two seats—the other seat being occupied and all. My wristwatch glowed eleven-eleven p.m. three hours into the trip and no shut eye yet. They picked up passengers in Davis. I was settling in for a nap after new passengers stomped through and slammed the overhead cabinets. I had rolled my extra sweater into a pillow but just as my eyes drooped to a close, the speaker thundered, 'Next stop Sacramento, Sacramento, next stop Sacramento.' Geez, as if we missed the message the first time. Obviously, it woke up the unhappy baby. But okay, maybe the worst part was sitting on hips that felt like boulders and my vertebrae feeling like they had been welded stiff. I'm not a complainer, but trying to stand up on shaky legs attached to immoveable knees and a stiff back to walk the aisle and hopefully make it to the tiny bathroom on time was treacherous. All the while, the damn train swayed side to side with little surprise jerks now and then to really throw off my wobbly balance. I checked the schedule and thought we had only one more stop between Sacramento and Redding. I let myself relax and slip into a pleasant sleep. Whoops, not so fast, 'CHICO, NEXT STOP CHICO.' I tell you, Walter, it was quite an experience and if you dare tell Anna I said all of this, I'll tell her you are full of nonsense and made it all up."

Grandma Ming the charmer. Anna heard Walter's laughter loud and clear.

30
DNA

Like a tangled witch's knot, Anna's life had tightened to a stop. Her motivation to think or communicate had slumped to nothing because of the envelope sitting unopened on her kitchen table. Her thoughts were on nothing else. Secrets of her lineage were in that envelope. The DNA test results were inside. Her mind changed hourly. Open it up, get it over with, or wait for Olivia. Liv wasn't due home from Jennifer's graduation until Monday. Open and share with someone else first? But whom? Never open it at all? To never know and keep living life as she had been was tempting, though cowardly.

"Hey where are you, anyway?" Walter asked, his tone soft and caring, gentle, even.

"I'm sorry, Walter. What did you say?"

"There is a supply list on the counter. Should I online it or take a supply drive down to Redding and big-box-store it?"

"Oh, thank you. But if you don't mind watching the shop, I'd like to take a day and drive down there to pick up things myself. Tomorrow—yes, tomorrow. Okay with you?"

"Tomorrow! But you will be gone for hours. Aren't Olivia and Jennifer showing up tomorrow?"

"Not until Monday. Anyway, I'll see them later." Anna absently wandered to straighten a shelf that didn't need it.

"Wait a minute. Tomorrow is Sunday. The shop isn't open. What do you mean 'Watch the shop?'"

"Oh, that's right. Maybe you could just watch Sparky and the two weekend boarders? They're older kitties, so they'll be comfortable in the big crate with their food, water, and litter box. Their pillows came with them. They'll hardly know they aren't home."

Walter looked confused. A customer came through the door. The man wanted a brush for his dog, but Walter, visibly relieved by the interruption, ushered him around the store like he was in the market to take over the mortgage.

***

Happy to be on the road and out of the emotional clutches of Umbra River, Anna slowed down, turned off the radio, and nestled into her cocoon of isolation. One way, the trip took an hour, so she planned to make a day of it. She might get a haircut or a pedicure while she was in town. There was a Chinese day spa that was open on Sundays. Maybe she'd find one of her relatives there. "Sorry," she spoke aloud to the universe if nothing else. She shouldn't be making jokes about the situation, even to herself. She reminded herself that energy is energy, good or bad, and the universe doesn't understand good or bad, only energy, which is why Grandma Ming and GG taught her never to talk badly about anyone. "You give away power," GG always said.

Whiskeytown Lake appeared on her right and drew her in. On a whim, she pulled over, swung a U-turn, and headed back to the campground entrance. *Oh, the beautiful blue water*. Wading in the cool, crystal water, she barely remembered parking and getting out of the car. A paddle boarder drifted a few yards away and a small pontoon boat carried a laughing group out toward mid-lake as ski boats zoomed by. Several fishing boats poked into the shallows, their quiet trolling motors pushing peaceful anglers toward their prey. For a few minutes, Anna let go of the thoughts thudding in her head. A picnic table and bench right near the edge of the water beckoned her to sit. The coolness would enliven her feet while her head stayed in the clouds.

What if the test shows I am Olivia's daughter? How much had Mom and Dad known? Her adoptive *mom and dad. Why did Olivia give me up and not Jennifer? Jennifer got to have her all her life. What was so special about Jennifer? What is she going to think about all of this, and does she even know? I need to work at not being jealous of Jennifer, who did nothing but come into the world at the right time. I really need to know the truth.*

With conviction coming from having essentially decided to open the envelope, Anna stood, grabbed her shoes, and headed for the car. The clock on the dash indicated she had been at the lake for two hours. Evidently, she had needed the time. She planned to come out with it, simply ask these questions, and let the chips fall.

As she waited at the stop sign for the traffic to clear, a car raced past in front of her, going west, toward home. The car wasn't familiar, but she swore it was Olivia who was driving. *I must be seeing things.* Olivia wasn't due home until the next day, so clearly she was imagining things. Anna turned right onto the two-lane and headed east into Redding.

***

Once back in Umbra River, Anna drove straight to Besties. She nabbed a parking spot right in front and breezed in with her newly trimmed and styled hair shining and her nails—all twenty—lacquered in lusty, deep red. She felt liberated.

Walter, ready to leave, stared. "What happened to you?"

"I made some decisions," she said over her shoulder as she carried the first package into the back room. "I'm going to open that envelope and see what my history is. Then face it head on. I'll ask every question in my head and take the answers as best I can."

Walter still stared as she emerged from the back. "What envelope. What history? Am I supposed to follow this?"

"Oh crud, Walter. I never explained. Come to my house for tea and I will. I'm too road weary and everything weary but also a little jazzed. I need sweatpants, a hot cup of tea, the sofa, and my feet up."

"Yeah, sure. I was just going to lock up and take Sparky home with me. He and Friday have been playing all day. I just fed the two boarders and cleaned up their litter box. They're sweet girls. I held them for a bit while their little motors ran. I'll bring in the supplies. By the way, I just gotta say, you look beautiful," he prattled, still staring.

"Pshaw. But thank you. Now, let's get moving." She turned away quickly before she flat giggled out loud. She felt giddy as a schoolgirl. Did she have a crush on Walter? No. She was mixing emotions. *Remember Jack.* She mustn't forget that people aren't always what they seem.

***

By turning the car radio off, Anna created the quiet space she needed to let herself feel without distraction. The trajectory of her life was riding on the opening of one envelope. Finally, after all this time and torment, she knew what she wanted. Olivia must be her birth mother. She loved Olivia. It was less than a two-mile drive from Besties to home, but it felt endless. The possibility of disappointment made her body cold and empty. The what ifs were interminable.

Walter, with both dogs, followed closely behind. He and Anna had never visited each other's homes.

Anna's driveway was wide enough for only one car and paved with dark grey stamped concrete. She watched him park behind her car, step out, and take in the sight of her contemporary glass and rock home with windows large enough to see through from the front porch to the full glass wall looking over the backyard. She felt proud as she watched him take in the angular roof line, sloped to the right with the trapezoid window near the peak. The outer walls, in varying shades of grey stucco, were complemented by a river rock wainscoting about four feet high. The front door and porch pillars anchored the design. They were clear red oak, and she thought to herself, *magnificent.* Black metal framed the windows. She never tired of the sight of her house as she turned the corner and pulled into her driveway. Walter apparently liked it, too. He turned from walking across the carefully groomed lawn with its rock-rimmed flower border along the porch and gave her two thumbs up.

Pulling herself together, Anna said, "Come on in. I'll put fresh water down for the dogs. Will you please grab that cooler and bring it in? Gee, Sparky, you haven't seen me all day, and you rode with Walter and Friday."

Walter brought in the cooler, hefted it on her counter, and looked around. "Your home is amazing. Are these baskets Hoopa? Wow, where did you get this collection of arrowheads? This is beautiful."

"The baskets are Coastal Miwok. I bought them from a lovely woman in Sonoma County who wove them herself. Some of her family still use them for catching fish. It's a pride thing. The arrowheads are from my hiking days."

"Are you an artist? These paintings are magnificent—the faces so real they are *sur*real. You can see the scars on this man's face. Pride and resolve in the eyes. The detail of the horse, incredible. Love the way his forelock and top of his mane are brushed so they're matching."

"Yep, all those points are why I chose it. Nope, I don't paint—just curate beautiful objects with heart." Anna swept her hand around. "Please make yourself at home. Look around. It won't take long, not a big house. Just tall and airy."

Anna watched as Walter looked quickly at the tidy, simply furnished home. He gravitated back to the collection of Native American art. She coughed, getting his attention, and he came over to her, sitting at her kitchen table with her unopened envelope, staring at it as though it stared back.

"I apologize for gushing. I had no idea what kind of home you lived in. It suits you, all sleek and bold outside—intelligent and thoughtful inside."

"I had it built a few years ago. The architect understood me and was so talented. Inheritance money bought it."

"Okay Anna, tell me the story." Walter pointed to the envelope.

She began with a deep breath. "Irrefutable bits of data came to my attention."

"Come on now, just tell me. Don't make me grab a dictionary."

"I want you to know it's real, so you won't barrage me with 'who says' type questions. I have plenty of backup information. Enough to tell me I needed to find out for sure. These are the results of my DNA test. I was adopted as an infant, and this might tell me who I am."

"Is this a great idea, or ripping open an enormous box of problems, Pandora?"

"No questions, Walter. I mean it."

"One, why did you want me here, and two, do you need a knife to open it?"

"No, thank you." Anna pealed back the flap, like an old lady saving the gift wrap. "I think I wanted a witness. I didn't want to be alone with whatever I found out, and you were convenient." The look on Walter's face told her that wasn't the answer he wanted. "I'm kidding, Walter! I wanted you to see the place. It sort of felt right that you be here."

Anna finally ripped open the envelope. After a few moments, she pulled her eyes from the paper and looked up. "Olivia is my birth mother."

***

Over a cup of tea, she shared the story of her origins with Walter.

"Well, you can sit here and drink tea all night, or you can drive over and tell Olivia. She probably deserves to hear it right away, don't you think?"

Without a word, Anna picked up her car keys, walked to the door, then remembered Walter had parked in her way. Back to the kitchen, she plunked down her keys and grabbed his. Behind her, Walter called out, "No worries. Sure, take my car. I'll just stay here with the dogs."

During the drive to Olivia's house, she tried to think about what was coming, but her mind was blank. Wait! Olivia wasn't due home until Monday. It was still only Sunday. But she pulled in the driveway to see an unfamiliar car behind a moving van and a cute little yellow Miata. She felt completely confused, but she'd come this far, so she might as well see what the heck was going on. The doorbell chimed and when Olivia, still in her daytime clothes, opened the door, Anna pushed past her and said, "Hi Mom. May I call you Mom?" Olivia stared at her for what seemed to be an endless amount of time, taking in, Anna supposed, her new haircut and nails as much as anything else. With still no words, she reached for Anna and drew her in.

"But wait. How are you here? Where's your car? Who's is the yellow car?"

Olivia filled her in. Jennifer's father and his boyfriend and the move to Italy. The accident. The tow truck. Jennifer's anger. The awful feeling of sitting alone during the graduation ceremony, knowing how awful Jennifer was feeling, the mottling of years of work by life-changing emotions.

"So that was you!"

"What?"

"I went to Redding to shop and have some alone time. I saw you, but the car was unfamiliar, so I let it go."

The next hours were a happy time. A time for a mother and daughter to understand their feelings were real, their long-time connection more than a guess. Anna couldn't keep her eyes off Olivia, who held her hands, patted her face, hugged her, and patted her back. The DNA test report sat on the table, its paperweight a geode with clear crystals sparkling in the lamplight.

"Anna, how I wish your adoptive parents were still living. They would be happy for us, I bet. And I'd love to thank them for raising you so well. I have so much to say to you, to explain why I am me. So, where is Sparky?" Olivia rambled.

"I left him at home with Walter and Friday. I forgot about all of them. I better call."

"Whoa, whoa, whoa. Walter is at your house? Your *employee*?"

"Olivia, you may be my mother, but you can't start acting like it! He's . . . Look, I like Walter. I think he likes me. It may be, I don't know, something one day, but not yet. I'm still nursing the Jack wound."

Within seconds, Walter answered his phone. He told her everything was fine, the dogs fed, walked and asleep. He found a blanket and was dozing on her couch. She should take her time, and if she didn't have to do so, no need to wake him. He could let himself out in the morning if she was okay with that arrangement or he could take her car home and take the dogs with him, but it was late, and he was groggy. Of course, she told him to stay. She didn't want Walter crashing and burning as a thank you for being there for her. Anna hung up and stared for a moment. Walter sleeping over at her house? This day was too much. These past months had been too much.

"I'm not going to say a word about Walter staying over at your house."

"Good. Thank you. Olivia, have you talked this over with Jennifer yet?"

"No.

"She will be home soon. She had to go pick up a few things. Please wait so we can talk to her together. She knows they forced me to give up a baby when I was young. Though you both need to hear the entire story."

"I'm not sure it is a good idea. You two might want to talk about this mother to daughter and I don't want to be in the way. I really don't know Jennifer that well and she is going to need all your attention right now."

"Anna, we are family. She is your half-sister. I love you both. Much of your life was lived without me and I hate having so much regret. I'm so sorry I wasn't strong enough, or smart enough – whatever it was- to have fought my parents harder. Hell, I should have taken you from that hospital and made a run for it. How could I have been so tamed and trained?"

"But I think . . ."

"No, I'm doing the thinking this time. I want you here with Jennifer. Both of my ladies talking it out, whatever that entails. And I love your hair. And your nails."

As if on cue, Jennifer's key snicked open the lock. Anna watched her face closely and saw pleasant surprise. "Hey guys. Am I missing a party? Whose car is that?"

"Walter's," Anna said.

"Who is Walter?"

Olivia greeted Jennifer with a hug. Jennifer's face grew shadowed with concern as Olivia asked her to get comfortable and to join them.

"Now, you two, please stay put while I fix you something to eat and put on coffee. I have so much to say and explain that I'll burst if I don't say it. I need to clarify a few things. I need you both to know at the same time." Her third quick U-turn from the kitchen prompted Jennifer to say, "Mom, stop. We don't need food or coffee. We need you to stop flapping like a chicken."

"Yes, okay, you're right." Olivia took a seat mid-couch and sat for a moment without speaking. Anna and Jennifer, each on opposing overstuffed armchairs, waited while she gathered her thoughts.

Anna gave Olivia the nod to start and held her breath, waiting for Jennifer's response. When Olivia finished telling Jennifer about the DNA results, Jennifer let out an overjoyed shriek and fairly flew across the room. She grabbed Anna in a fierce hug.

"You are my sister! I have a real live sister! I always had this feeling, even though you were older than me, I always had this feeling that we were more than passing friends."

Olivia's wistful smile made Anna want to melt. "I never dreamed that this would be the response from either of you. I expected you to hate me. It is important to me that you both understand how horrifying it is to give up a baby. You can't imagine the sorrow. Adoption is grief. Period. For birth moms, it's the painful loss of the opportunity to parent and nurture the child they bore. Science has pretty well proven that feelings of grief and pain activate the same area of the brain. Grief is physical and mental pain, and it does not require a death.

"Anna, when your birthday comes around every year, I am consumed with grief. I guess it's a form of PTSD. I experience the day I let you go all over again. My body feels empty, and I feel bereft. The day always concludes with an overwhelming migraine headache. Trust me, I have read a lot about grief and living with chronic grief. Sigmond Freud was the first to recognize anniversary reactions. He also wrote that physical and psychological problems can be part of it, migraine included. That mind–body connection. Listen to this! Recently, I read we mothers can carry a small number of the babies' cells in our bodies for decades, causing changes in our DNA."

"Mom, really?" Jennifer asked with an eye roll.

"Google it, Jen. It's called fetal microchimerism."

"I bet she can spell it too," Anna stage whispered.

"Many women never overcome the loss. I know I never have. The feelings are fierce. They hang on all our lives. Added to the emptiness, is a copious amount of fear. Are the adoptive parents going to love her well enough? Will she be abused? Will they tell her she was chosen and special, or will this child be filled with hatred, assuming I didn't love her? Will she have a favorite stuffed bear? Then, of course, how will they handle her biracialism? The not knowing is so painful.

"Compounding all of this is the family's reaction. Also, that of some nurses. I was told to 'put it all behind you' and to 'move on with your life' and 'oh, you'll get over it, you'll forget it after you have another baby.' I could not put pain like that aside, so I buried it, or tried to. With work. With a busy life. Imagine the fury and resentment I felt toward all those people, family and otherwise, who could not find a way to rescue me. They refused to understand what giving away my baby was doing to me. I felt powerless and betrayed. Weakened already by Kai's cheating. The unfairness never left me and colored so many relationships. No wonder our bodies react. I was a pending implosion. I think of my headaches as relief valves. It's a wonder I didn't have an early stroke or heart attack."

Anna remained silent, as did Jennifer, soaking in every word. After a short breather, Olivia began again, "Anna, I loved you instantly. From the moment you were born. You looked straight in my eyes and your little face became seared into my memory. You were the image of your father. I have dreamed about you. Pictured you at each stage of your life, consistently renewing my heartache. Jennifer, when you were born, and I was so in love, I felt afraid. Since I gave up a baby, maybe I didn't deserve you, or maybe something would be wrong with you. My karma for not being strong enough to stand up to everyone and keep Anna. I was so afraid of losing you too, somehow. Then, oh god, when that kidnapper took Crystal right in our own town and from her front yard, I couldn't believe it. I've told you about the grocery store scene when that monster was this close to you." She held up her fingers, inches apart. "You can see why my reaction was borderline psychotic. That's why I held on to you so tightly as you grew and denied you the level of independence you should have had.

"I'll stop my story in a minute, but I want you both to know I loved your fathers. When I realized Kai didn't feel the same, I felt worthless and loaded with shame. He wasn't a bad person, merely a product of his rearing with a huge dose of narcissism. I loved the person I thought he was. Jennifer, I will always love Clayton. He is a kind and loving man. We lived a life together.

Without living together. He has always been a willing and consistent part of your life. Jennifer, you have to forgive him, he loves you so much. Let's be happy for him now, and you must remain part of his life. He deserves it. Had I not been loaded with feelings of worthlessness and shame, I might have been more aware of who he truly is years ago. He was good to me but never in love with me. You he adored from your first heartbeat. He has been a good father, as good as he possibly could."

Anna caught Jennifer's smile, "Whoa, looks like we have story sharing to do after we have digested what we have heard. But no more tonight. I am exhausted. Except there is one more thing. Anna, how did you wind up in Umbra River?"

"It's simple, really. My parents were gone, my sister moved away, and I was looking for a new start. I earned my degree and knew I didn't want to be a practicing vet. I wanted to work with and around animals. I started searching online for storefronts and found several in several states. Immediately, I felt drawn to Umbra River, for rather obvious reasons now, and the rest became history, as they say."

"Adding to the synchronicity, I was the person who suggested online advertising to the former owner of the store. This was not random. Obviously, you were drawn here," Olivia said.

Anna yawned. "Either I'm sleeping here, or I need to go now. I can barely keep my eyes open. Too much for one day. Goodnight, Mom and sister!" She kissed first Olivia then Jennifer on the cheek. A man asleep on my couch, and I need to go home and thank him for dog sitting. Besides, my brain is a twirling hula hoop." After hugs all around, Anna walked to the front door.

"Me too. Goodnight, I'm going to pass out now, but when I see you again, you are going to tell me about Walter," Jennifer said.

31
GOODBYE CHARLIE

Today was Charlie's party day at school. No more preschool. He was a big deal kindergartner. Yet he wasn't excited, Emmaline could tell. She had pulled out the Halloween box and found his favorite superhero costume. She cried a little when he put his costume on. Hands on his hips, legs spread, chin up over one shoulder, he said, "Look at me, Mom. I can do anything!" He spread his arms and ran full speed around the house, his cape flowing behind. "C'mon Hershey, be my super dog." When Hershey didn't follow, Charlie plopped down. "MOM! Hershey needs a super dog cape."

"It's almost time to go to school, Charlie. Hershey will have to be fine without a cape. He is staying here anyway."

"But Mom, can't he come in to see everybody, just for a minute?" Emmaline took a big breath and turned away.

"So, Mom, what's in these boxes?"

"They're full of our stuff, Charlie Boy. We are leaving for Grandma and Grandpa's in the morning. Maybe I wasn't clear. Remember the cottage I told you about and the school you can walk to?"

"You mean we are going there forever? What about Auntie Anna and Sparky? Hold on, you mean Olivia and everybody? Mom, you promised. It's a visit, not forever." Charlie pulled off his superhero cape and ran to Hershey. "I am staying right here with Hersh. You can go if you want to."

"Yes, I did promise, and we will come back, but I need to finish school first. You are starting kindergarten, and I will be a third-year college student. We are moving into the cottage I mentioned until I graduate. Hershey is coming too, of course. It will be our big adventure."

"I hafta go to Geode and Besties now. I hafta to see 'em. I don't care if I miss the party."

Emmaline took a deep breath, then stared out the window. "Mom, this'll work. You go to your school. I'll stay here with Auntie Anna. Hersh can stay here too, with Sparky. Just don't stay a long time."

He saw his mom put down her car keys, sit on the edge of the couch, and hold her head in her hands. "Mom, what's wrong? You're crying? Don't you want to go, either?"

"Charlie, sit down."

She watched Charlie's face as he listened to her explain again the changes that were coming to their lives. Nothing felt the same between them on the drive to school, but when they walked into his classroom, and Charlie saw all the kids in their superhero costumes, he appeared to forget to be mad about going away. The kids were busy building things and drawing, but they jumped up when they saw him and hollered, "He's here! Now can we start?"

Charlie said he felt great after pizza, cupcakes, ice cream, a dancing game, and a movie when his mom came to pick him up. The day was over, and they waved a quick goodbye to the class and went out the door. She took his hand, and he tried to shake her off. "I'm in kindergarten now, Mom. Don't hold my hand."

"We are going to cross the street, Charlie. I always hold your hand when we cross."

"What about when I'm fifty, and my hand is bigger than yours, huh?"

"Charlie, this is going to be hard, but we are walking to Besties and Geode to say goodbye. For now. Think you can handle it? You can put your superhero cape back on if you need to."

"I wish Hersh was here." They walked toward Besties.

Anna was with a customer when they walked in, but she took the time to wink at Charlie. Emmaline walked him to the back, straight to Sparky. While Charlie explained their plans to him, Spark hunched down with his nose between his paws. His eyes locked on Charlie's. When the customer left, Anna came to the back, and Emmaline explained why they came. Anna went to her knees and pulled him in for a long hug. She let go, saying, "I love you, Charlie Boy. Never ever forget that." Then she turned and ran to the bathroom. Emmaline led Charlie through the inside door to Geode.

"Mom, I don't think I can say bye to Olivia. Can we just go?"

"No, but let's be fast."

They walked through the bookshop, and Olivia was right on the other side. Charlie ran to her, and he was the first to spill tears. Olivia told him he didn't need to talk, that his hugs told her everything. She said, "I'll be right here at Geode when you come for visits and when you come home for good. Meanwhile, Jennifer will move to her own place and the guest room will be yours and your mom's whenever you need it. Please be sure to bring Hershey." He finally pulled away and Emmaline stepped in to hug Olivia as Charlie scurried backwards toward the door.

"Wait, Charlie!" Olivia reached over to the counter and grabbed a bag of goodies. She hastily stepped to him and handed off the bag. "These are for your long drive tomorrow. Inside there are some dog cookies too. Now, you better go, sweetheart. I am about to cry buckets."

32
NANA LUCY

Olivia felt it like a hoof to the chest. Lucy announced she was moving back to Ireland. Her thoughts spinning—why were her thoughts a perpetual tumult lately? Would the upheavals never stop? —she tried to work out a plan. Emmaline, Charlie, and now Lucy. Not only was she losing dear friends, but also employees she relied on daily. Geode would not be the same. Many customers came just because of their love for Lucy, not to mention the fact that she was entertaining. Might they not return if Lucy wasn't there? Who was going to organize and replenish the bookstore with Emmaline gone?

Thankfully, Jennifer was home and not yet employed. *She might pitch in.*

Part of Olivia felt thrilled for Lucy. She was to be Nana to twin baby boys. Like she said, she had plenty of practice raising boys. Since her husband passed away, she's had no close family. Although Olivia thought of Lucy as family, all the while she knew there was nothing like the people you raise or help raise.

After Lucy's announcement, Olivia asked her to stay two extra weeks. In return, she'd pay double her current salary. One caveat was that she leave copies of her recipes at Geode. Olivia suggested the two of them take one day, head for Redding, and shop for baby items. What a fun day for both. Olivia planned to ship whatever treasures they found. Lucy told her she was excited about the day and had a request of her own. She needed help packing.

***

Moving day arrived, and Olivia watched Lucy and Jennifer as they organized and packed, admiring the efficiency of both women, and trying to push away thoughts of how much she'd miss Lucy. Each box was clearly labeled and given a code number indicating which room in the new house it belonged. Lucy planned to have them shipped the day after she left, hoping to get to Ireland first and have a few days to ready her new home before she unpacked. "Lucy, your skills with organization are outstanding. This move is a choreographed performance."

"Aye, right enough. I only wish Ireland was closer so I could visit at will. We all know I can't miss out on the new little chiselers. But I'll be giving you a bell now and then. Isn't that what a phone is for?"

"We will all look forward to your calls, Lucy. And pictures too."

"Jennifer, thank you for creating such an upbeat playlist. It's lovely to have it in the background. We might wind up in a pile of tears otherwise. You did a great job," said Olivia.

"Och, yes, better a craic than a dirge. I'm settling my mind that way. Did I mention I leased my house? No sense severing the ties, you see."

"You never said, Lucy. This gives me hope!"

"Lucy, I'm looking for a place. What are you asking monthly?"

"Wouldn't I love that, Jennifer. But I think I have it spoken for. I'll put you next in the queue."

"Whoever she is will be lucky to live in this cottage. The cozy warmth, the garden, and the proximity to town is perfect. I would love to live here myself if I didn't love my house," Olivia said. She daydreamed as she carefully wrapped figurines in tissue paper and placed them in a padded shipping box. "These boxes are going to take good care of your precious collection."

"I couldn't part with them, so I'll put them in storage until I'm ready to have them sent to me. Will you trot to the shipper tomorrow and make sure they are doing their job? I don't want them to mix up the shippers with the storers."

"Of course, I will. You might think about coming back permanently eventually, though, Lucy. Mike is a good man, and you might be breaking his heart a little."

"Ah, get yourself along. There are many fish in the sea, and Mr. Mike will snag one someday."

"Maybe, but she won't be Lucy."

Flipping the subject, Lucy said, "You mentioned a woman moving in here, well don't ya know, it is a man. He will be by this afternoon to decide what furniture he can use, and which will go into storage."

"Oh good," Jennifer said. "We can meet him and give him a once over."

"You already know him. It's our good Sheriff Dobbs. Did you know his father is English, but his mother was O'Flannery? I'll leave my shamrock pillows."

Olivia and Jennifer came out of their shocked silence and laughed about Lucy's pillows. They continued packing and humming along with the music until the Temptations' "Ain't too Proud to Beg" started with its signature percussion intro. The beat of the cymbals kicked the ladies into gear. Jennifer bumped Olivia, hip to hip, and Lucy's lilting laugh filled the entire space. By the time the song ended, they were howling with laughter. First Olivia, then Jennifer plunked down on the soft couch. Lucy sat on the arm. In a moment, her laughter turned to sobs.

"Aw Luce," Olivia said, as she reached to hand her a tissue.

"I just want to be cut in half so I can leave and stay at the same time," Lucy said through her tears.

Olivia respectfully waited for her to sort herself out, then noticed Lucy straighten her shoulders and take a deep breath.

Without warning, she jumped to her feet. "Enough of this earwigging. Let's finish up around here."

A few items in the kitchen were the last to pack. Olivia felt like moving slowly to stretch out this last day with their dear friend. Sheriff Dobbs planned to drive Lucy to the Redding airport in the morning, where she'd take a short flight to San Francisco International Airport to catch the flight to Ireland.

"Lucy, have you described your new home for Jennifer?"

"Och, no, I have not. Well, Jennifer, my son, Declan, built a small cottage on the large lot behind his house. He intended it to be an income producer. Then, he found out being a landlord was hogwash. They built the house of stone and wood, and it has a nice big fireplace in the living room. The ceilings have open beams, and they painted the walls in shades of green. Of course! It is lovely. There are shutters. I think they are charcoal—maybe black—it's hard to tell in the pictures. But the best is, he painted the front door deep red just for me. It's to shoo off evil, don't you see. Also, he has prepared a garden area to plant whatever I want. When you park in front and walk to the door, you'll walk on a stone walkway with dichondra growing where grout joints usually are, and a flower border follows along on each side. Like a picture, I say. Now, don't you ever forget, I have a guest room. I'm having my bedsteads shipped over, but it's too dear to ship the mattresses. Declan is shopping for those and will have them delivered. So please, don't let it be donkey's years before you come over."

"It sounds dreamy, Lucy. I promise to drag Mom out of Geode and Anna away from Walter and bring them over. We'll make a plan," Jennifer said.

"Lucy, what more can we do? Are the bathrooms packed up? The garage? I see the house is down to bare bones." The music had stopped an hour before and only two medium-sized boxes sat empty.

"Oh, the good sheriff does not want much of the produce from the garden. How about you take one of those boxes and kindly pick the fruit and vegetables to use at Geode? Dobbs already said he'll be happy for you to use the garden."

Olivia marveled at this woman's generosity. "It will be like keeping some of you here since we have your recipes and now produce. I will enjoy every minute of harvesting."

"What time is it? Oh, I see it's almost three. My new lessee will be here about five. Why don't you dear ones scarper off, and I'll enjoy a short rest.

He will pick me up early in the morning to head for Redding. I won't be able to sleep much tonight. So."

"We know you need rest, Lucy. How about coming to Geode later for some dinner?"

"Can't. My stomach is clinched like a fist. Thank you so very much for helping me and being my dear friends. I'll probably cry again now, so run on."

Olivia and Jennifer walked back to Geode in silence. For Olivia, the loss felt too heavy. "I wonder what customers thought about Geode being closed on a weekday?"

"Mom, I think the whole town knows where we were and what was going on. Lucy turned several people away who wanted to help today."

As they crossed to the other side of the street, the somber sound of a northbound freight signaled the crossing. Two longs, a short, and a long. Olivia remembered how Lucy heard her husband's voice in those sounds: *Luuu luuu la luuu.*

33
AN UNESCORTED ADVENTURE

The Umbra River tumbled and flew like a herd of wild mustangs. Although the temperature was ninety degrees, mist dampened the heat as water bashed boulders along the way. Such a beautiful day for her to let her thoughts run free. Olivia almost never ventured to the river alone, although it felt right this day.

Taking a seat on the flattest of the huge rocks, she let her legs dangle over the water. She was high and dry and felt brave in her precarious position. She had never learned to swim, more observer than swimmer.

Life was changing. Sweeping changes, and the thought of coping was overwhelming. She realized coping with change wasn't all that different from coping with loss. She thought of a part in a James Michener novel where he wrote about nomads leaving behind their sick and elderly when they no longer could keep up with the tribe. Olivia felt like she was being left behind, even though she wasn't sick and didn't think of herself as old.

Geode for sale? Not a chance. For a moment the thought had entered her mind, but she immediately realized she was merely trying to throw out the baby with the bathwater. The café and bookshop were where people came together for good food, coffee, books, and friendships. Geode mattered to the town, and it was her joy. But Lucy moving back to Ireland had definitely put a wrench in things, and Olivia couldn't imagine running

Geode without her. With Emmaline gone, she had no choice but to shutter the bookshop, since she had no one to manage it.

Anna looked so happy as Walter held her hand and they shared their plans. Her beloved Anna finally found and now soon to be lost again as she and Walter started a new life together. How could this be? What was the lesson in all of this? Anna and Jennifer instantly had become sisters to each other, and to her mind, it was too soon to separate them.

Leaning over her knees, she took in the water's beauty, the shades of color starting with deep green variegating to light emerald with hints of blue low lights. White froth formed and bubbled at the rocks and the river's edge before being set free to blend back into the flow. *Should this lifetime end? Have I played it out? Am I ready? Is Anna accurate? Do we truly reincarnate to get it right next time?* The water churned recklessly as she watched a log, about ten feet long, being bounced and thrown as if it were a toothpick. Turning to splinters and splits and before long, nature would take its course. Hail to the strongest.

Olivia raised her head to scan the treetops and cloud formations. She felt tired of herself. Groveling in self-pity had worn thin, and she noticed a sensation of waking up. Thinking back on a conversation with Lucy, centered on Olivia's feeling glum and having no future, bless Lucy, she would have none of it. She told Olivia that Anna and Walter were young and had a right to make their own mistakes. Why shouldn't they motor bike off into the sunset and see where it goes? Lucy added, "Great gobshite, weren't you brave to open Geode? Many people had never seen a geode, let alone understood what they represent and what the café and bookstore planned to offer." Olivia remembered saying that she had made too many mistakes and wanted to protect her daughters from making them. Lucy's reply was perfect: "Well, did you make them twice?"

The log disappeared, along with a few more. Her granite seat grew unforgiving and intolerable. She slowly rolled to a crawl, then stood and climbed to solid ground. Looking back at the river, she saw its beauty rather than its treachery. *This is not the day for feeling sorry for myself. Lucy is right again. Glum looks good on nobody.*

Walking home through the woods, she straightened so that her shoulder blades moved toward each other, tipping her head so her neck loosened, Olivia resolved to face her life "dead on." Lucy's words again. *Besides, I don't want to live my mistakes over just to make them right. I love Geode and will make it all work. Bookstore, too. Somehow. I'll have to trust the right person will come along, just like Lucy once did, just like Emmaline, and just like Walter for Besties.*

Walking into Geode felt like coming home. The exercise and the river had done her good. She wanted to talk to Lucy, so she checked on time zones and decided it was okay to call.

"Aye, Olivia. Everything all right?"

"Hey, Luce. You have been on my mind all morning. I took a long walk to the river to think things over. I think my head is back on straight. Would you like to hear my thoughts?"

"Right so."

"To start, you know Anna and Walter have a months-long adventure planned."

"Well, look at that. They are a good couple. I don't think they know it yet. But I expect they'll come back married."

"I'm not sure how it will go. They bought huge motorcycles with side cars for the dogs. Not much room for luggage but sleeping bags and a small tent. Walter mentioned researching places to stay on the way where Friday and Sparky would be welcome. Lucy, they do not know where they are going! Only that they are heading east because 'everybody heads north or south.'"

"I know you will fret and dither. But what fun for them. When they come back with their stories, what fun for you."

"Yes, you are right again. Meanwhile, I won't sell Geode. I've decided. You know I thought about it, but it is my life, and I'll run it. Thank you for leaving copies of your recipes. I'll ask Jennifer to do whatever people do to bring in resumes and put the need for a janitor at the top of the list. I'll offer reduced rent on a room upstairs, and politely ask the ghost to move on."

"Bugger her. Don't be too polite. She nearly scared me to death."

"Oh Lucy, I am sorry. That was a horrible fright. But, back to my plans, I need someone to serve and bus tables. The bookshop will temporarily close until I find someone to fill in there. Jennifer has jumped in to keep Besties going while her sister is traveling. I hope she can do it all. What I'm having a really hard time with is missing Hershey, Sparky, and Friday. Do you think I should get a dog? What do you think?"

"Och, I think that was some walk you took."

***

A month had passed since Lucy left. Olivia began her day at six in the morning at Geode, starting the soup and baking muffins and scones for the morning coffee crowd. She looked over the café and felt pleased with the new janitor Jennifer had found. The kitchen sparkled and the dining room shined. His name was Andres Lara. He had emigrated from Honduras, and Jennifer found him on one of the online professional sites where people posted jobs and their resumes. He was bilingual, definitely a benefit, and was trained in restaurant service. He was looking for a place to land. Every single one of his references was glowing, with comments about how much people enjoyed him as a friend and employee, and about how dependable and capable he was. Olivia liked him instantly. She had barely finished the interview when he offered to help cover the lunch crowd, serving and bussing, for no pay, just so she could see how it felt to her. He told her he liked Geode and the room upstairs that came cheap with the job. He was so excited and positive, she offered him the job that afternoon. He accepted on the spot – even before his room was ready. He asked Olivia if he could borrow some tools to begin the remodel himself. He was a carpenter. How could she refuse? They made an agreement that he'd have a three-month probationary period and that if it worked out, in exchange for the renovations he would enjoy rent-free living for the first year, should he decide to stay on that long.

Olivia enjoyed hearing the table saw and hammer making progress upstairs. The sound of productivity. How fortunate that he had experience with carpentry, which gave him something in common with Walter, if Walter and Anna ever returned.

One evening, after closing time, she climbed the stairs to look the room over. Clearly pleased to see her, Andres took the opportunity to show off his work. She helped paint the baseboards spread across two sawhorses while he finished painting the last wall. He had chosen the largest of the rooms, which featured a five-by-eight window overlooking the area behind the building. From there, if he wasn't downstairs working, he could see the colorful mountain sunsets. With new drywall on all four walls and the ceiling, and the outside wall insulated, the room smelled fresh and felt much cozier and warmer. He told her he felt they should keep the original oak floor, as it was in good shape, only needed to be polished. With Olivia's approval, he chose pieces of furniture from other rooms and lined them up in the hall. Amazon delivered a mattress to replace the inflatable one he had been sleeping on. The bathroom was useable, but he said he wanted to upgrade it after his room was finished. They went over the receipts for materials, and she promised to run back up with a check, or cash if he preferred. When he suggested he redo all the rooms eventually, so she might add more renters, she cancelled the idea of rent payments ever resuming. *How am I so lucky to have hired this hardworking, personable man?*

Light footsteps trotted up the stairs. Jennifer poked her head in the door, her blonde hair cascading over one shoulder as she leaned, "Wow, this is looking great, Andres. You even fast talked my mom into painting. Bravo."

Olivia enjoyed the easy banter between the two as she finished painting. "Well, kids, I need to go home. This has been a long day."

"I'll be there in a few minutes. Some numbers are not adding up in Bestie's account books. Maybe I'll bring them home to work on."

Olivia had driven to work and was relieved her tired legs didn't need to walk home. She closed the blinds and locked up Geode, then sat in her car for a few minutes. Jennifer and Anna had done a great job planning for the temporary changes at Besties. Jennifer's new teaching job would not become full time until the next year, and she jumped at the chance to take over Besties while Anna was gone. Jennifer planned to take care of the bookkeeping, inventory, and ordering. She taught three days a week and planned to run the shop on Saturday, Tuesday, and Thursday. Besties closed on Sundays. Before she left, Anna and Walter interviewed then hired a young man who was also working part time across the street at Sweet Things to run the store on Monday, Wednesday, and Friday. They sent out emails to customers explaining the temporary changes, promising great things when they returned. Right away, Jennifer designed two classes. One by a dog trainer and the other by the veterinarian she contracted with to look over incoming strays. He would talk about pet diseases, medications, food, breed characteristics, and more. Exactly what Walter had dreamed of.

With a laugh, Olivia thought, *well, the public will have to do without grooming and Walter's spontaneous vocal concerts for a few months.*

She had yet to hire a full-time bookshop person, although two ladies from town had volunteered to come in during the after-school hours so kids still could use it for homework and research.

It made Olivia happy to see Anna's and Walter's relationship grow. What a surprise when Walter announced they had bought motorcycles, rented out his house, and planned to cross the United States. Olivia was used to knowing Anna's every move. Grandma Ming had planned to come upstate regularly to visit the "wonderful people of Umbra River" and to check on Anna's house. Anna said she thought it gave Grandma Ming a sense of purpose she lacked at home.

When Anna and Walter shared their open-ended plan with Olivia. She knew better than to ask too many questions, so she wished them well and bought them travel mugs.

The previous Wednesday, when Anna and Walter revved their engines in front of Geode's deck, Olivia feared she might shed tears in front of them. She reached deep into her common sense and reminded herself they were having the adventure of a lifetime. She loved them both. They'd be back in a few months. With syncopated revving and woofs from Sparky and Friday in their sidecars, off they went.

She heard Anna say, "Bye Mom! Watch for my texts!"

Mom. Two grown women now called her mom.

In the mail that day was a hand drawn picture from Charlie showing Emmaline, Hershey, and him standing in their new front yard. He had drawn smiles on each, including Hershey. It occurred to her that in truth she had three daughters. Emmaline felt every bit as much like family as Jennifer and Anna did, not to mention Charlie.

Hard work kept her busy and tired. She felt lonely in the evenings. But when sadness sneaked in, she turned her perspective on its heel and reminded herself that this was her time to fly solo and find out who she is and what she wants from life from here on in. All will work out, she told herself. *It is my time for an unescorted adventure.*

Slipping the pan of muffins into the oven, she turned back to the soup. Coffee was brewing and the aroma alone woke up her senses. Thank goodness Lucy had shared her recipes. How she missed that little redhead with the big attitude. At eight o'clock, Olivia flipped the closed sign to open, turned on all the lights and made a last tour around the dining room before going outside to wipe off the tables and chairs on the deck and raise the umbrellas.

Customers came along, and Olivia scooted inside to be ready to take and fill orders. Business was brisk, and the deck was filling up. Soon, about four of the tables inside were taken and the pleasing sound of conversation punctuated with laughter helped lighten her mood. She looked forward to hiring more help for the summer and tourist season. Working both behind the counter and acting as server was starting to wear on her. The first signs that she was truly aging, she supposed. The inevitable.

Olivia rang up a customer's order and snapped closed the cash register drawer. The front door whooshed open, and a tall man walked in. Rather than turn to fill the last order, she stared briefly. His hair and a well-trimmed mustache were highlighted in silver. An easy smile and eyes, sparking with intelligence and humor, begged her attention. She smiled at him without speaking. He ordered coffee and a scone. "And how is *your* day going?" he asked.

ACKNOWLEDGMENTS

From the first jotted ideas to the thrilling launch of an actual book with a beautiful cover, it takes the support of a select crew to get a book out into the world. These people are crucial to the quality of the outcome. I am so grateful to Black Rose Writing for seeing the quality and promise in *Geode* and supporting my efforts by publishing it.

Infinite gratitude goes to Paula Coomer, my gifted teacher, writing coach, and editor. She never wavered in her enthusiasm for *Geode*, or in the belief in my ability to write it.

Thank you to my family. My daughters Gina and Christie, who can pull out a word or phrase to fit the perfect piece to one of my puzzles. Also, for their patience during my periodic, though frantic quests for Internet and social media assistance. My husband Dave for answering all questions about railroad and automobile mechanics.

In addition, a huge shout out to Sarah Yosick, Carol Reed, Jessica Baer, and Andrea McBride. These gifted professionals supplied me with factual background to enrich my story. They were so kind and willing to allow me to tap into their expert knowledge. Any inaccuracies are solely on me.

A special thank you to those beta readers, Shirley Miller Kamada and Phil Cuevas, who bravely read early drafts and still cheered me on. Their time and efforts were so welcomed and appreciated. Lastly, I want to give thanks to those many lovely people who never failed to inquire with enthusiasm about the progress of *Geode*. Your encouragement buoyed my progress.

I hope I have remembered to mention everyone who directly had a hand in keeping me going. If not, please know I appreciate all of you.

SELECTED RESOURCES

Shoup, Laurence H. (2010). *Rulers and Rebels*, iUniverse, Inc. Bloomington, N.Y.

Gulick, Bill (1981). *Chief Joseph Country, Land of the Nez Perce*, The Caxton Printers, Ltd,
    Caldwell, Idaho.

Bennion, Ben and Rohde Jerry (2008). *Traveling the Trinity Highway*, Mountain Home Books,
    Trinity County, California

Scott Historical Museum, 15-2 Airport Rd, Trinity Center, CA 96091

ABOUT THE AUTHOR

Photo courtesy of Morgan Jenkins Photography

Corliss Corazza is a retired educator and writing tutor. She loves being outdoors and has an affinity for all animals. When time permits, she dabbles in piano and photography. Corliss is also passionate about VW bugs. Always red. She resides in the San Francisco Bay area with her husband Dave, Goldendoodle Sophia, who accompanies her when gardening, and twin orange tabbies. *Geode* is her second book and first novel.

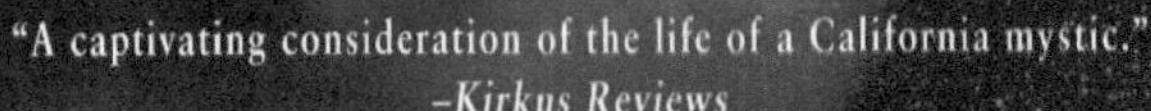

"A captivating consideration of the life of a California mystic."
–Kirkus Reviews
CORLISS CORAZZA
CUT OPEN THE SKY
THE STORY OF CONNIE CASTRO JACKSON
A well-known psychic, much loved for her poignant, hilarious stories,
and her perspective on life and the world of the unseen.

NOTE FROM CORLISS CORAZZA

Word-of-mouth is crucial for any author to succeed. If you enjoyed *Geode*, please leave a review online—anywhere you are able. Even if it's just a sentence or two. It would make all the difference and would be very much appreciated.

Thank you.
Corliss Corazza

We hope you enjoyed reading this title from:

www.blackrosewriting.com

Subscribe to our mailing list – *The Rosevine* – and receive **FREE** books, daily
deals, and stay current with news about upcoming
releases and our hottest authors.
Scan the QR code below to sign up.

Already a subscriber? Please accept a sincere thank you for being a fan of
Black Rose Writing authors.

View other Black Rose Writing titles at
www.blackrosewriting.com/books and use promo code
PRINT to receive a **20% discount** when purchasing.